WHEELS OF PERIL

Churchill and Pemberley Mystery Book 5

EMILY ORGAN

Wheels of Peril

Emily Organ

❧

Chapter 1

"Is that a cake tin I spy on your desk, Miss Pemberley?"

"Yes, Mrs Churchill," replied her secretary proudly. "I decided to bake us one."

"What a lovely idea. May I see it?"

Doris Pemberley prised open the lid and Annabel Churchill stepped over to peer inside. A rich, fruity odour wafted up into her nose.

"It smells interesting," she commented, "and looks must unusual." A flat, moist, brown cake hugged the bottom of the tin. "May I ask what flavour it is?"

"Prune."

"Prune?"

"I'll cut us a slice each," said Pemberley excitedly as she got up to fetch a knife.

"Not too much for me," replied Churchill. "I've only just had breakfast."

Pemberley paused. "That doesn't usually deter you from partaking in cake, Mrs Churchill."

"I'm not deterred from it; I just had rather a lot of toast this morning."

"I see."

Pemberley appeared so downcast when she returned with the knife that Churchill decided to appease her.

"Oh, go on then. A normal-sized slice for me, please."

A smile spread across her assistant's face. "Right you are, Mrs Churchill!"

The cake was damp, heavy and so sweet Churchill had to make a concerted effort to stop her lips from puckering.

"What do you think?" asked Pemberley.

"Interesting."

"You don't like it?"

"I'm sure I shall grow accustomed to the taste. I've never eaten prune cake before. Is it cooked?"

"Of course it's cooked!"

"Good, good. I didn't intend to offend, Pembers. It just looks a little different from the usual sort of cake."

The combination of toast and heavy prune cake began to sit uncomfortably in Churchill's stomach.

"I think I need a little air," she said.

"It's the cake, isn't it?"

"Absolutely nothing to do with the cake; it was the breakfast. I blame the toast, personally. I'll be right as rain again once I've stepped outside for a little amble up and down the high street."

"I'll come with you," said Pemberley.

As she went to wash the knife, Churchill dropped the rest of her cake onto the floor for Oswald the dog to devour. She wiped her fingers on her tweed skirt and retrieved her handbag from her desk as Pemberley re-entered the room.

"Right then!" said Churchill brightly. "Let's get going."

"Why is there cake all over the floor?" asked Pemberley,

surveying the mess.

Churchill glanced down and was dismayed to see that Oswald hadn't eaten a single bite.

"Oh, I accidentally dropped a little bit."

"And didn't pick it up?"

"I was planning to tidy it when we got back. I really do need that air, you see. Quite urgently."

"You were hoping Oswald would eat it, weren't you?"

"No! Not at all. I know he's not supposed to have cake."

"Even he's not eating it," said Pemberley sadly. "What's wrong with my prune cake?"

"Nothing's wrong with it, Pembers. Now, let's get outside. Everything will feel much better after a breath or two of fresh air."

"What a lovely morning," enthused Churchill, attempting to lift her secretary's subdued mood once they were outside. "I do like mornings on the high street, don't you? Everyone setting up for the day, colourful shop signs and awnings, and fresh produce laid out just so. I enjoy the sense of anticipation as we all wonder what the day will bring… and then there's the sunshine!" She gestured up at the blue sky above their heads. "Everything feels better in the sunshine, don't you think? And talking of this lovely weather we're having, I'm planning a long stroll in the countryside this weekend. I'd like to get to know the high-ways and byways of Compton Poppleford a little better. Perhaps you and Oswald would like to join me, Pembers."

Pemberley gave a conciliatory nod. "That does sound rather nice." Then she jumped. "Is that a horse charging toward us?"

Churchill peered ahead to see a large skewbald

carthorse bounding in their direction, its hooves clattering over the cobblestones.

"Crikey! I do believe it is."

The two ladies stopped as they watched people leap out of the animal's path. The occasional brave soul stepped forward in an attempt to grab its harness, but a fearsome shake of its head was enough to put each of them off.

"It looks as though it's broken free from somewhere," said Pemberley.

"It's certainly not going about its usual business, that's for sure. And there's no sign of its rider, either."

"It wouldn't have one; it's a cart horse. It has no saddle and look at the size of its feet. I wouldn't want to get trampled beneath those!"

"Neither would I. I haven't had much to do with horses in recent years, but I was quite an accomplished rider when I had my little pony, Mindy."

The horse managed to pull itself away from another person who had tried to catch it and was cantering ever nearer.

"Get out of the way, Mrs Churchill!" yelled Pemberley, grabbing hold of Oswald. "It's about to trample us!"

Churchill stood her ground, however, feeling rather sorry for the frightened horse. "They tend not to trample people unless they've truly lost their mind," she said. "I think I can catch it."

"Oh, don't! You saw the greengrocer try just then. It flung him off like a fly!"

The horse was only a few yards ahead of them now, its nostrils flared.

"There, there, horsey," said Churchill, still standing her ground. "There, there. Auntie Churchy will look after you. Gosh, aren't horses big, Pembers?"

The horse slowed to a walk, tossed its head and adopted a nervous zigzag.

"There, there," said Churchill again, edging slightly closer. "It's broken away from a carriage of some sort, hasn't it? It's got nice long reins to grab onto. Come on, then, little horsey. Let's be catching you."

Churchill approached the animal, reaching out a hand in an attempt to grasp the reins.

The horse stopped and stared at her with its large, unblinking brown eyes.

"Look, Pembers, it's listening to me! Now all I have to do is reach forward and..."

The horse skipped to one side, then took off past Churchill and proceeded down the high street.

"Oh, I didn't expect it to do that! Oh dear, poor thing. I hope someone catches it soon."

The two ladies watched as a small man in a smart suit stepped into the path of the horse.

"Goodness, that's exceptionally brave."

The horse stopped and allowed the man to grab hold of its reins. Once it was still, a few other people walked cautiously over and held onto it.

"What a clever gentleman," said Churchill. "I don't recognise him. Do you know him, Pembers?"

"No, I've never seen him before."

"Interesting. I thought it would be as simple as catching my little Mindy, but there was something particularly large about that horse, wasn't there? I wonder whom it belongs to and why it proved so difficult to keep it tethered to its cart."

"Well, you saw the size of it, Mrs Churchill. I don't know much about horses but I suspect that if that one decides it doesn't want to be attached to its cart, there isn't a great deal anyone can do about it."

Chapter 2

"I REALLY DO APPRECIATE BEING ABLE TO TAKE THESE lovely walks, Pembers," said Churchill as the two ladies and Oswald strolled along a pretty little lane that wound its way down a hill. The banks rising high on either side of them bloomed with an array of wildflowers. The sun shone brightly, and each tree they passed beneath offered a pleasant, dappled shade. "Quite a steep lane, isn't it? I'm glad we're walking down it."

"That's Grindledown Hill for you," replied Pemberley. "It is a bit steep."

"Stop a moment to listen. Isn't it wonderful? Utter peace. Nothing more than the distant baaing of sheep and tweeting of birds. Goodness, would you listen to those sparrows in the hedge! Such noisy little things, yet they sound so happy, don't you think? Much as I miss the delights of London, I really do feel quite at home in the countryside now. I used to consider Richmond Park as good a piece of countryside as any. How wrong I was! Look at those delightful rolling hills ahead of us. They just go on and on, don't they? I really don't think there can be anywhere more beautiful than the English countryside in summer."

"It's downright miserable in winter," replied Pemberley. "Grindledown Hill is impassable when it snows."

"But rather fun going down it, wouldn't you say? I'm tempted to buy a sledge this winter for that very purpose."

"I wouldn't, Mrs Churchill. For one thing, the lane is very windy and you'd need to be an expert at steering a sledge to make it down."

"How do you steer a sledge?"

"Precisely. And secondly, the duck pond is at the end of the hill, so you'd almost certainly end up in that. I really don't like winter. It was the season my lady of international travel used to seek out the pleasures of St Tropez or San Marino."

"As anyone of considerable means might well do. Detective Chief Inspector Churchill and I used to enjoy our little visits to Weston-super-Mare when we needed a change of scene." Churchill sniffed the air. "There's only one little problem with the countryside. It can get slightly whiffy sometimes, can't it? Some days I have to pinch my nose because Farmer Drumhead's farm smells so much. I don't know what he does in there to create such a stink."

"I think it's less to do with Farmer Drumhead and more to do with his cows."

"I realise that. I didn't think the farmer was personally responsible for the odour; I'd be terribly worried if that were the case. Could you imagine someone smelling like that? The shops on the high street wouldn't let you in, and neither would the public houses. Can you hear something, Pembers?"

The two ladies stopped to listen.

"I can hear a gentle humming noise," Churchill continued. "What on earth could it be?"

"I heard a voice then, too."

"A voice and a humming noise?"

"Several voices. And they're getting louder."

"Where are they coming from?"

"I think they're behind us."

The two ladies turned to look up the winding lane they had just walked down.

"If this track weren't so bendy, we'd be able to see them, Pembers. And the hedges are so high, too. Perhaps it's someone in the neighbouring field."

The humming noise seemed to abate a little as the two ladies continued on their way. Churchill was just about to comment on the prettiness of a purple wildflower when a sudden burst of laughter startled her.

"What on earth?"

The two ladies spun around as the humming noise developed into a loud whir. Shouts and laughter accompanied it, and suddenly, from around the bend, several people moving at great speed appeared on bicycles.

"Make way!" the bicyclist at the front called out, ringing her bell vigorously.

In that brief moment, Churchill saw that the bicyclist was a mature lady with grey curls swept back from her face. She wore a blue jacket and matching bicycling breeches. Several other ladies followed closely behind.

"Move!" the lady called out again as she came closer.

"Do you mind?" retorted Churchill. "We're on a peaceful—" Seeing that the bicyclists had no intention of applying their brakes, Churchill swallowed the rest of the sentence.

More bells rang out and she stepped back into the hedgerow to let them pass. Oswald stood transfixed in the centre of the lane, watching the bicycles hurtling toward him.

"Oswald!" Pemberley cried out, stooping over to grab him. She had only just picked the little dog up and flung herself into the hedge opposite Churchill by the time the bicycles came shooting past in a blur of spinning spokes, glinting steel and blue breeches.

"Well I never!" gasped Churchill as she watched them zip down the hill. She smoothed her lacquered hair, which had been disturbed in the bicyclists' wake. "The gall of it. What hooligans, Pembers. Absolute hooligans!" She shook her fist at the group of bicycling women, all of whom had now vanished from sight. "Did you see that? They were prepared to mow us down! Not a care in the world about who lay in their path!"

"They almost killed Oswald!" sobbed Pemberley, clasping the dog tightly to her chest.

"Do you think there are any more of them?" asked Churchill, cautiously peering up the hill.

"I'm hoping that's the lot."

"We need to report them! They shouldn't be allowed to get away with behaviour like that. Did you recognise any of them?"

"I think the one at the front was Mildred Cobnut. I've heard she heads up the Compton Poppleford Ladies' Bicycling Club."

"So that's who they were! Did you recognise any of the others?"

"No. They all flashed by in a bit of a blur."

"They certainly did. The rudeness of it all! Bombing down a quiet country lane with no thought for who could be just around the bend. It's disrespectful and highly dangerous!"

Chapter 3

As Churchill and Pemberley approached the small white police station at the bottom of the high street, they saw brown-whiskered Inspector Mappin outside listening to buck-toothed Mrs Harris.

"Farmer Jagford tells me they speed through his farm most days," Mrs Harris said. "Apparently, they wind up the dogs and send the chickens scattering in all directions."

"Pardon me for listening in, Mrs Harris," ventured Churchill, "but are you talking about Mrs Cobnut and her bicycling gang by any chance?"

"Yes! That's who I'm talking about all right. I simply cannot understand how they're allowed to get away with it. If they were young lads they'd have been rounded up by now and had their ears boxed."

Churchill and Pemberley nodded in agreement.

"But because they're ladies of a certain age, everyone assumes they're harmless," continued Mrs Harris. "They woke my daughter's baby up the other evening. On three occasions! Each time she managed to get him off to sleep they whizzed past her cottage, a-whooping and a-hollering.

They frightened me so much when they shot past me the other day, I dropped my shopping basket and everything fell out. Then one of the bicycles ran over my loaf! Clean over it, they went, and we had to eat the bread even though it was completely squashed in the middle."

"Did you eat the bit where the tyre went over it?" asked Pemberley.

"Certainly not! We had to give that bit to the pigs. What a waste of good bread, though. It was very disappointing, and there was no apology or anything."

"Something has to be done, Inspector Mappin," said Churchill. "These bicycling ladies are terrorising chickens and running over loaves of bread. It's not right!"

"You're not the first to complain, Mrs Harris," responded the inspector, "and I suspect you won't be the last. I've already had a word with Mrs Cobnut about the whole affair and she's agreed to stick to the speed limit when bicycling through built-up areas."

"And what speed limit might that be?" asked Churchill. "The speed of sound?"

"I should hope not. That would be enormously fast, wouldn't it?"

"I was joking, Inspector. I simply meant that I don't believe she'll be sticking to any speed limit whatsoever. They're a danger, all of them, and sooner or later there's going to be a terrible accident. How awful it would be if an innocent person happened to be involved. People should be free to walk around Compton Poppleford without fear of being mown down by crazed bicyclists!"

The inspector consulted his notebook. "I've had four other complaints from people, one of them from Mr Cobnut."

"Mrs Cobnut's husband?" queried Churchill.

"Yes. He's very annoyed by his wife's new-found hobby.

Apparently, she's out of the house for great lengths of time these days, and on one occasion he even had to make his own supper!"

"Goodness, poor man," said Mrs Harris.

"Yes, I must say that I felt some sympathy for him," said the inspector. "They've just lost their housekeeper, Miss Plimsoll, you know."

"How careless," commented Churchill.

"It can be a terrible bind having to do things for yourself when you've been used to having someone else do them for you," he added.

"Surely you can't go getting yourself involved in Mr Cobnut's complaint," said Churchill. "That's more of a domestic issue."

"You're right, Mrs Churchill, and I told the gentleman precisely that."

"It's a shame Mr Cobnut seems so powerless to stop his wife behaving like a menace," said Mrs Harris.

"The poor fellow is completely powerless," said the inspector. "I think he's hoping this is a passing fancy of hers, and that she'll soon forget all about it and return to her duties in the fold, as it were."

"Perhaps she's bored with her duties in the fold," suggested Pemberley. "Perhaps that's the very reason she began flying about the countryside on her bicycle. In fact, maybe that's the reason why all these ladies are doing such a thing. They're bored with tending to their menfolk and would rather be out and about seeking their thrills on two wheels."

"Are you defending them, Miss Pemberley?" asked Churchill.

"No, I'm just trying to see things from another point of view. It's something I like to do from time to time."

"They must be neglecting their domestic duties, that's

for sure," said Inspector Mappin. "Who's tending to the house while they're off gallivanting on their bicycles?"

"No one, by the sound of things," said Mrs Harris. "The social order is falling apart."

"I shall have another chat with Mrs Cobnut later," said Inspector Mappin, checking his watch. "I'm on my way to greet a new resident in the village who's just moved into Marigold Cottage."

"That's not something you routinely do, is it, Inspector?" enquired Churchill.

"No, it's not. But this new resident is of particular interest to me. He's none other than Monsieur Legrand."

"*The* Monsieur Legrand?" replied Pemberley in an excitable voice.

"The very same."

"Did you hear that, Mrs Churchill?" continued Pemberley. "Monsieur Legrand is here in Compton Poppleford! Can you believe it?"

"It sounds perfectly believable to me," replied Churchill, "but that's probably because I have no idea who the man is."

"He's the renowned Swiss detective!"

"What's he renowned for?"

"For solving lots of cases," enthused Pemberley. "The Naples Heist, for example."

"And the Cologne Kidnapping," added Inspector Mappin.

"The Murderer of Marseille was the one I'd heard of," said Mrs Harris.

"You've heard of him too, have you, Mrs Harris?" asked Churchill. "Then why have I never heard of him?"

"He caught the Murderer of Marseille with nothing more than a broken locket hinge to go on," said Mrs Harris. "Isn't he marvellous?"

"Quite marvellous," agreed Pemberley.

"Rather miraculous, by the sound of things," said Churchill. "So what's he doing in little old Compton Poppleford?"

"He doesn't want a big fuss to be made about it," said Inspector Mappin. "Apparently, he was looking for a peaceful place to do some quiet work on his memoir."

Churchill laughed. "A fat lot of peace he'll get with the Compton Poppleford Ladies' Bicycling Club tearing about the place."

"He's already proving himself quite useful," continued the inspector. "He managed to catch Farmer Glossop's runaway horse the other day."

"Oh, that was him, was it? Very good."

"He's clearly a man of many talents," added Mrs Harris.

"Well, if he's as adept as everyone says he is," said Churchill, "perhaps you should ask him to do something about that pesky bicycling gang, Inspector."

"Good idea," agreed Mrs Harris. "Something certainly needs to be done about them."

Chapter 4

CHURCHILL POPPED INTO THE HABERDASHERY SHOP THE following morning to buy some new buttons for her cardigan.

"Oh, good morning, Mrs Churchill!" chimed the haberdasher. She had artificially red hair and wore a floral tea dress.

"Good morning, Mrs Thonnings."

"You'll never guess who's just been in here."

"I suppose you'd better tell me, in that case."

"It was that foreign gentleman. That expert detective everyone's talking about."

"Oh, him. Monsieur Legrand, you mean."

"Yes, that's the one!"

"Why would an expert detective be visiting your haberdashery shop?"

"He needed some thread to mend one of his suits."

"He does that himself?"

"Yes, it surprised me, too. He's quite adept at needlework, or so he told me. He likes his repairs done just so; therefore, he likes to do them himself."

"He sounds rather particular."

"Oh yes, I think he is. But why not, eh, Mrs Churchill? He needed to make a repair to one of his jackets and brought the thing in so he could match it perfectly to the threads I had in stock. It's a very fine jacket indeed. I noticed the label was from a Parisian tailor."

"How wonderful."

"You should have seen the way he examined the spools of thread, Mrs Churchill."

"Interesting, was it?"

"Fascinating. You can see why he's such an accomplished detective. He clearly has a marvellous eye for detail."

"That's what we detectives need, Mrs Thonnings. It's a requirement of the job, you see."

"I realise that, but you can tell from his bearing that he's a cut above the rest. Masterful, he is."

"Good for him. Do you have any shell buttons in a lilac shade?"

"Oh yes, just over here." Mrs Thonnings led Churchill over to the relevant shelf. "It's said that wherever Monsieur Legrand goes there ends up being a murder, and then he goes ahead and solves it."

"That doesn't bode terribly well."

"Apparently, he's only after the quiet life these days so he can write his memoir, yet the murders keep happening and he has to keep solving them."

"Well, I don't like to speak ill of the police, having been married to Detective Chief Inspector Churchill for so many years, but if they were better at their jobs they wouldn't need this Legrand chap solving their cases for them. Thank you, Mrs Thonnings, these buttons look perfect. I'll take six."

. . .

"No chocolate eclairs left this mornin', Mrs Churchill," said Mr Simpkin the baker.

"But it's only ten o'clock! How many did you bake?"

"Usual amount, but someone's already been in and bought 'em all up. I'll bake some more this evenin'."

"But that's no good for now, is it?"

"Not so good for now, no. Can't complain, though… I'd rather be sellin' 'em than 'avin' 'em sittin' round goin' stale. I'll tell you who's bought 'em. It were that Swiss detective everyone's talkin' about."

"Oh, him."

"Nice chap. Caught the Cologne Murderer or summat, weren't it?"

"Something like that."

"Them famous ones looks down on the rest of us sometimes, but not 'im. Modest, 'e is."

"Good."

"I ain't never met no one famous before. 'E looked smaller than I thought 'e'd be."

"Famous people are often smaller than you might expect. I've noticed that."

"Met a lotta famous people, 'ave you, Mrs Churchill?"

"A few, but I don't like to drop names." She surveyed the baked goods and sighed. "I suppose I'll have to make do with a few custard tarts instead."

"Righ' you are, Mrs Churchill."

Churchill walked into the office with the new buttons for her cardigan and the bag of custard tarts. "Good morning, Pembers. No chocolate eclairs today, I'm afraid. The expert detective bought them all. I do hope he doesn't get chocolate and cream smeared all over his expensive Parisian suit. That would be a real travesty."

"Never mind about the eclairs, Mrs Churchill. We've still got plenty of prune cake left. I'll cut us both a slice."

"Oh, well I did get us some custard tarts."

"Let's save those for later. We can enjoy a bit of prune cake first."

Pemberley made the tea and served Churchill a thick slice of cake.

"Thank you, Pembers, I shall eat that up in a moment. I must say, there appears to be a great deal of fuss being made about this Monsieur Legrand."

"Oh, it's only because so little ever happens in Compton Poppleford."

"Quite the contrary, Pembers. A great deal happens here."

"Maybe it's because he's a foreigner, then. We're not used to foreigners in these parts."

"I can certainly agree with that. But do you really think anyone will be interested in reading his memoir?"

"Oh, they will. His last volume of memoirs sold exceptionally well."

"He's already written some?"

"Yes, and I'm planning to visit the library to see if I can borrow a copy. I'd be very interested to find out how he solved the Naples Heist. I'm sure we could learn a thing or two from him, Mrs Churchill."

"Do you really think so?"

"The Cologne Kidnapping was a very famous case, and I'd like to know how he worked out who the kidnapper was. Such an insight into Monsieur Legrand's exceptional mind would be marvellous."

"With all due respect to the man, he was only doing his job, wasn't he? I'm sure the cases he worked on just happened to be famous for other reasons."

"But he solved them after so many other people had

failed!"

"Through his own brilliance or with a bit of luck, do you think?"

"I like to think it was brilliance. The investigation into the Murderer of Marseille case twisted and turned so much it was turned into a play."

"Goodness! Other people's misfortunes being turned into entertainment, eh? If you ask me, Monsieur Legrand has cashed in on it a little. I can't imagine how he has anything left to write for his second volume of memoirs."

"I'm sure there'll be something gripping. He's led a long and interesting life."

"Haven't we all? Only we're not all big-headed enough to go writing about it."

"I've noticed your attitude toward the detective seems to be rather cool, Mrs Churchill, but you haven't even met him yet."

"If my attitude is cool it's because I'm struggling to understand why everyone should be making such a fuss about him. He's only a detective, after all. He's no different from us, Pembers!"

"Is it because you'd like someone to make a big fuss about you instead?"

"Goodness me, no. That's the sort of behaviour one might expect to see in a schoolyard. It would be quite immature! No, I simply fail to understand why the man should be so revered when all he's done since arriving in the village is catch a horse and buy up all the chocolate eclairs."

Footsteps on the stairs leading up to the office brought an end to the conversation. After a knock at the door, Churchill welcomed in a lean, shambling man wearing shabby clothes.

"Pyeman's the name," he announced, removing the

cloth cap from his head and sitting down. "And it's about me goat."

"Your goat?"

"Yep."

"Does the goat have a name?"

"Ramsay."

"I see. I'll just locate my pen and notepad so I can write this down." Churchill got herself together and began to take notes. "What seems to be the problem with Ramsay?"

"He's missin'."

"Oh dear. Stolen?"

"He could've been, but I reckon it's more likely he's escaped."

"I see. And how have you come to that conclusion?"

"He's eaten his way through a fence."

"He ate the fence?"

"Not all of it; just a bit. Enough so he could get out. He's a clever goat, he is."

"I see. Has he ever done anything like this before?"

"Never."

"And where have you looked for him so far?"

"Where ain't I looked for him?"

"I don't know, Mr Pyeman. I asked you the question in the hope that you might furnish me with an informative reply. I get the gist from the question you just fired back at me that you've looked everywhere for him you could think of."

"That I have."

"I see. And when did you last see him?"

"Two days ago. Evenin', it were. Just before I retired for the night."

"And where was he then?"

"Out the back."

"In a yard or a field?"

"A bit o' both really."

"A yard *and* a field?"

"Yep."

"This land belongs to you, does it?"

"It surely does."

"So he was out in a patch of land belonging to you, which could be described as both a yard and a field."

"Yep."

"How large is this patch?"

"About half an acre."

"And how large is that?"

He shrugged. "Like I said, half an acre."

"I'm afraid I'm not very good at picturing acres. Would it be bigger than a tennis court?"

He gave a shrug. "Dunno. Depends on the size o' the tennis court."

"Was he in this yard-field on his own?"

"Nope. I got three other goats besides him."

"And you still have the others?"

"Yep, it's only Ramsay what's missin'."

"They weren't tempted to follow him once he'd eaten his way through the fence?"

"They ain't as clever as him, you see."

"Right. So you retired for the night with four goats in the yard-field, and when you woke in the morning you could only see three."

"Two."

"Just two? So another is missing as well?"

"No, he were just behind the trough."

"So there were three?"

"Yep, but I only saw two till the other one come out from behind the trough."

"Right. So three remained in the yard-field." Churchill

wiped her brow. "Taking down these particulars is tiring me out a little, I don't know why. Now, what does Ramsay look like?"

"He's brown."

"Just brown? Any other colour?"

"Nope, just brown."

"Horns?"

"One."

"Just one horn? Is it a big horn?"

"What d'you mean?"

"Well, is it one of those large, curled ones that loops around itself?" Churchill twirled a finger at the side of her head to demonstrate. "Or just a little pointy one like the devil has?"

"The devil? Cor blimey, Mrs Churchill!" Mr Pyeman made the sign of the cross.

"I do apologise, Mr Pyeman, I had no wish to offend. Now, which is it?"

"Which is what?"

"Which type of horn is it?"

"Oh, it's curved a little."

"I see. And is it on the right or the left?"

"Erm…" He closed his eyes, as if trying to picture the goat. "As I look at him it's on me… right." He opened his eyes again. "On the right."

"His right or your right?"

"Eh? The right, I said."

"When you're looking at the goat or when the goat's looking at you?"

"I ain't got no idea what you're talking about, Mrs Churchill."

"I'm beginning to wonder the same thing myself. I suppose it matters very little, really. There can't be many brown, one-horned goats on the run." Churchill made a few more notes. "And supposing we were to happen upon him, how should we tempt him over to us in order to apprehend him?"

"He likes food."

"Good. So we can tempt him over to us with some food, can we?"

"Yep, that'll do it. Then call on me and I'll come fetch him."

"Supposing we find him and then come to tell you where we've found him. Won't he move around in the meantime?"

"He might. Or he might not. There's no telling wi' goats."

"You say this is the first time he's escaped. Do you have any idea where he might have gone? Is there another place he knows well, or somewhere he's likely to be attracted to? A field of carrots perhaps?"

"Already checked the field of carrots, I did, but he ain't there."

"I see. But he could be there now, couldn't he?"

"He could be, yep. But if we left now and went down the field o' carrots to fetch him he'd proberly of moved on again and ain't there no more."

"Yes, that's rather tricky, isn't it?"

"It is, Mrs Churchill, and that's why I've come to you."

"Thank you, Mr Pyeman... I think. Do you have any experience of locating goats, Miss Pemberley?"

Churchill's trusty secretary shook her head.

"I see. Very well, then, it'll be an interesting challenge. We do have a third member in our detective agency, and that's our helpful hound, Oswald. I'm sure he'll help us round Ramsay up."

"That little dog there?" He looked down at Oswald sceptically. "Ramsay'd eat him for breakfast."

Chapter 5

"The cucumber and grated horseradish sandwiches are particularly good today. Wouldn't you agree, Pembers?"

The two ladies were seated in the tea rooms beside a paned window overlooking the high street. Other customers dined quietly around them at little white tables covered with lace doilies.

"They're very nice," agreed Pemberley, "although I must admit I've been picking out the horseradish."

"But that's the best bit! Gives them a bit of a kick. I tell you what, I've been thinking about that Legrand fellow. Perhaps we should pay him a visit."

"I thought you were harbouring rather a cool attitude toward him, Mrs Churchill?"

"I am, but perhaps it could be warmed by an introduction; a meeting of detective minds, so to speak. We should think of something to take him."

"I could bake a cake."

"Maybe some elderflower wine would be nice. I saw a nice-looking one at the grocery store the other day."

"Mrs Gollywood makes that elderflower wine."

"What's wrong with that?"

"I don't think she makes it quite as it's supposed to be."

"Well, that shouldn't matter if we're taking it over as a gift."

"He might not like it."

"If he doesn't like it, he can give it to his neighbour."

"I think his neighbour *is* Mrs Gollywood. Inspector Mappin said he's in Marigold Cottage, which is the one next door to hers."

"So he did. It would be rather embarrassing if he gifted Mrs Gollywood her own wine, wouldn't it? That's convinced me that we should give him some, Pembers. Wouldn't it be amusing to watch him trying to palm it off on her?"

"How would we be able to see that? Hide in a hedge close by, you mean?"

"It's quite a fun thought, isn't it? Only, knowing our luck he'll like it and guzzle it down instead."

"I'd like to visit him, anyway. I do enjoy meeting people with brilliant minds."

"I can't imagine that his mind is any more brilliant than yours or mine, Pembers. We could claim to have solved dozens of cases if we'd spent years working as detectives like he has. We don't have a bad tally. Not bad at all. I wonder if anyone's mentioned us to him. It would be quite something if the great detective had been told all about little old us, wouldn't it? Perhaps he's planning to pay us a visit and bring us some elderflower wine!"

"I certainly don't want any of Mrs Gollywood's elderflower wine."

"Is it really that bad? I find it rather hard to believe. I'm tempted to try some myself just to find out."

"I wouldn't if I were you; it's too risky. What if it puts you out of action?"

"You're right. I wouldn't want to be put out of action. That would completely ruin things, wouldn't it? Oh, look out, Pembers. Here comes trouble!"

A windswept lady in a blue canvas shirt and matching breeches was dismounting from her bicycle on the other side of the window. Her grey curls were swept back from a sun-tanned, sharp-featured face, and she had keen, no-nonsense eyes. As she leaned her bicycle against the window she was joined by a group of female accomplices, who also dismounted and left their bicycles beside the window.

Churchill and Pemberley watched as the gang swaggered into the tea rooms, chattering loudly and sending the bell above the door into frenetic chimes. Several customers turned to look at them, annoyed that their peaceful cups of tea had been interrupted.

The windswept woman placed her hands on her hips, surveyed the room, then pointed at a table.

"Here will do, won't it, girls?" She proceeded to drag two tables together, the legs scraping noisily on the floor. Chairs were pulled into position and the women fell into them, laughing and chatting all the while.

"The Compton Poppleford Ladies' Bicycling Club," muttered Pemberley under her breath.

"Yes, I thought as much," replied Churchill.

"That's Mildred Cobnut," added Pemberley, nodding in the direction of the windswept woman.

"The one who rudely shouted at us to get out of the way as they sped down Grindledown Hill?"

Pemberley gave a nod.

Churchill surveyed the rest of the group. "Good grief, I don't believe it! Is that Mrs Thonnings with them?"

Sure enough, the red-haired haberdasher was sitting among the group.

"I didn't realise she enjoyed bicycling," said Pemberley.

"I can't believe she would have anything to do with those awful women. They're a menace!"

"Tea for seven!" hollered Mildred Cobnut across the tea rooms as a waitress placed a pot of tea in front of a customer who was almost entirely hidden behind a newspaper. "And sandwiches. Four cheese, two ham and two egg and cress!"

"That makes eight," said Churchill wryly.

"I'm sorry?" Mildred twisted round in her chair to face Churchill, who felt embarrassed that she had been overheard. "Did you say something?"

"I noticed you'd ordered eight sandwiches but only seven teas."

"May I ask what concern it is of yours?"

"I was merely wondering whether you were ordering for seven people or eight."

"I really can't see why it matters to you."

"Normally it wouldn't at all, but seeing as everyone here in the tea rooms has to listen to you placing your order I would argue that it matters to all of us."

"Do you expect us to sit in silence?"

"No, but you could wait for the waitress to approach the table and place your order at a more reasonable volume. That way the rest of us wouldn't have to have our conversations interrupted."

Mildred Cobnut's hardened glare riled Churchill. The detective decided there was no moment like the present to mention the group leader's recent behaviour.

"While we're on the topic of impositions," she continued, "you and your bicycling friends very nearly mowed

Miss Pemberley and me down on Grindledown Hill the other day."

"Ah, yes," replied Mildred Cobnut with a hint of recognition. "The two old ladies who were standing right in our way."

"And dog!" added Pemberley.

"Yes, our dear Oswald would have met with certain death under the wheels of your bicycle if it hadn't been for Miss Pemberley's quick thinking. She managed to rescue him just in time."

"Your dog was never in any danger. We'd have swerved around him, no problem."

"It didn't look like you intended to swerve around him. We were in genuine fear for our lives!"

Mildred Cobnut threw her head back and laughed. "From a group of ladies on bicycles? I doubt that very much."

Churchill wagged a finger in her direction. "You clearly have no idea how dangerous bicycles can be!"

"I'm aware that they can be quite dangerous when ridden at speed, but we weren't riding at speed. We were merely pootling."

"It didn't look like pootling to me."

"That's because you were walking so slowly! You should join us, you know. Get used to the feeling of wind blowing through your hair. It's utter freedom! Wouldn't you agree, Mrs Pikely?"

"Oh yes," replied a lady with fair curls and freckled skin. "It's such a healthy pursuit."

"Not when you're running people over, it's not," retorted Churchill.

"But we haven't run anyone over," said Mrs Cobnut with another laugh.

"Not yet you haven't, but it'll only be a matter of time."

"Oh, nonsense!" replied Mrs Cobnut, turning away. "Thank you for the tea," she added as the waitress brought a tray over to the table.

The owner of the tea rooms, a small, thin lady with frazzled hair, made an appearance. "Could we please stop the bickering, ladies?" she requested. "My customers have the right to enjoy their tea in peace."

"Well said," replied Churchill. "It was a very peaceful place before this bicycling crowd barged in. I'm surprised you let them in here, I really am."

"She doesn't want to miss out on our custom," replied Mrs Cobnut. "We're here most days, aren't we, Betty?"

The frazzle-haired woman nodded and Churchill sighed.

"Let's forget about all that for now," whispered Pemberley to Churchill. "I don't like arguments."

"How can I just forget about it?" hissed Churchill in reply. "Those women are a menace, and especially that Mildred Cobnut. She thinks she can do and say whatever she likes without the slightest regard for anyone else. And no apology at all for almost killing us the other day! It's shocking, it really is. And I'm sorely disappointed with Mrs Thonnings."

Although the Compton Poppleford Ladies' Bicycling Club members were noisy, their visit to the tea rooms turned out to be a brief one.

"Right then, girls. No time to hang about," announced Mrs Cobnut. "We have to get all the way over to Thriddleton Wallop this afternoon."

"It's quite hilly out that way," said Mrs Pikely.

"Of course it is, but that's all part of the fun, isn't it?

29

Don't forget that whenever you go up you also get to come down again!"

"That's the exciting part," enthused a lady with a large nose.

"How many points will you award yourselves for each pedestrian you hit?" asked Churchill.

"Don't, Mrs Churchill!" hissed Pemberley. "Just leave it be."

"Do you have a problem with our group?" asked Mrs Cobnut, rising out of her chair to face Churchill with her hands on her hips.

"You know I do," replied Churchill, also standing to her feet. "I've already explained what the problem is, so I'm surprised you even had to ask me."

Mrs Cobnut took two steps toward Churchill, thrust out her bosom and lifted her chin. "Your problem is that you're too big to ride a bicycle!"

Churchill took a step closer herself to demonstrate that she wasn't the slightest bit intimidated. "I can ride a bicycle perfectly well, thank you very much." As soon as she had spoken, she prayed that neither Miss Pemberley nor Mrs Thonnings would mention her previous bicycling mishaps.

"In my opinion, you could do with getting yourself back on one and taking some much-needed exercise!"

"Your opinion counts for nothing here, Mrs Cobnut."

"And yours does, does it?"

"Now, now," said the frazzle-haired proprietor, emerging from behind the counter. "That's quite enough, ladies, I've already asked you once. Please leave the premises so my other customers can enjoy their food in peace."

"We were just on our way out, Betty," replied Mrs Cobnut. "In fact, we'd already be gone if this sour-faced old trout hadn't detained us."

"Better a sour-faced old trout than a jug-headed lugworm!" retorted Churchill.

"Ladies, please!" the owner appealed.

Mrs Cobnut glared at Churchill before turning to face the ladies of the bicycling club and giving them a nod that suggested they should follow her out of the door. They began filing out of the tea rooms with Mrs Thonnings bringing up the rear.

"Psst, Mrs Thonnings!" hissed Churchill. "What on earth are you doing with this motley crew?"

The red-haired lady's eyes darted between the door and Churchill. "I just wanted to go for the occasional bicycle ride, that's all. I've been interested ever since Mrs Esmerelda Kitchen came to the village and gave a recital from her book, entitled *Scenic Bicycling Routes for Dorset Ladies*."

"But have you seen how that Cobnut woman behaves? She's shocking! I'm afraid you're falling in with the wrong crowd."

"Oh, please don't worry about me, Mrs Churchill. I'm fine. I try to stay out of all the arguments. I must go or they'll have bicycled off to Thriddleton Wallop without me."

Churchill shook her head sadly as Mrs Thonnings scurried out through the door.

Chapter 6

"A ONE-HORNED GOAT NAMED RAMSAY," MUSED CHURCHILL as the two ladies circled the duck pond. "I wonder where he can be. I'm trying to think like a goat, Pembers."

"What does it feel like?"

"I'm not sure; I haven't fully managed it yet. I'm trying to work out what a goat would be thinking if he'd escaped from his field. He'd be looking for shelter, wouldn't he?"

"I think he'd be more interested in food. Perhaps he'd look for shelter at night-time, but goats aren't exactly the shy, retiring type. I think he'd be quite happy in the great outdoors so long as there was a plentiful supply of food."

"Which there should be, because goats eat anything, don't they?"

"Yes they do. And that suggests that he doesn't even need to have strayed too far from his home."

"That's a good point, Pembers. If Ramsay isn't particularly fussed about shelter, at least not during the daytime, and all he needs is food, you'd think he'd be fairly easy to find." Churchill surveyed the duck pond. "He probably comes down here for a drink from time to time."

"He's not here at the moment," replied Pemberley.

"Not unless he's hiding inside the duck house on that little island in the middle of the pond."

"He wouldn't fit in there. Besides, how would he get to it? Goats can't swim... Or can they?"

"It was a little joke of mine, Pembers."

"But can goats swim? I should know the answer to that. I'm beginning to think they can, on second thoughts. Zebras can swim across rivers, can't they?"

"Zebras are not a close relation to goats."

"But they have four legs. I remember Mr Atkins telling me how zebras and elephants swim in the Zambezi. Oh!" Pemberley pulled a handkerchief from her sleeve and dabbed at her eyes as she thought of her former employer and the sticky end he had come to in that very river. "And it turns out crocodiles do, too." She gave a low sob.

"Now, now, Pembers. He wouldn't want you to upset yourself over his untimely demise. Let's console ourselves with the thought that there can be no chance of any crocodiles making an appearance in the Compton Poppleford duck pond."

Pemberley dried her eyes. "I feel quite sure now that goats can swim."

"Good, well that's something to bear in mind while we're looking for Ramsay. Although we can hardly go wandering about aimlessly looking for him, can we? I think we need to ask around for any sightings of him. That's likely to be more fruitful. I'll place a notice in the *Compton Poppleford Gazette* asking people to telephone us when they see him. Now, where's Oswald off to?" Churchill watched as the scruffy little dog scampered off ahead of them. "There's a man reading a newspaper on that bench over there. Oh, call him back, Pembers, he's about to bother the poor chap."

Pemberley gave a shrill whistle. Oswald stopped, looked back at his owner, then decided to ignore her, launching himself straight at the man with the newspaper.

"Oh dear," said Churchill. "He's probably got sandwiches with him."

As the two ladies hurried after Oswald the man on the bench lowered his newspaper. He wore a panama hat, a smart pinstriped suit and had an extremely neat, wide moustache.

"Is that him, Pembers?" whispered Churchill. "The famous detective?"

Seeing the ladies approaching, the man folded up his newspaper, rested it on top of the folded overcoat on the bench next to him, stood up and gave a short bow in their direction.

"Gosh, how polite," said Churchill.

Then he bent down to greet Oswald. The little dog lay on his back and let the man tickle his tummy.

"Oh dear, I do apologise," said Churchill as they reached the bench. "It's Monsieur Legrand, isn't it? I'm Mrs Churchill, the owner of Churchill's Detective Agency."

"It's a pleasure to meet you, Mrs Churchill," he replied with a heavy accent, which Churchill could only assume was Swiss. "And your companion here is Miss Pemberley, I believe?"

"Yes," replied Churchill. "You've heard of us, then?" She gave a flattered smile.

"I most certainly have."

"And this here is Oswald. Please don't feel you must oblige him, Monsieur. He's terribly demanding when it comes to attracting the attention of everyone he meets."

"I am more than happy to oblige, Mrs Churchill. He is a most delightful dog."

"How are you finding life here in Compton Poppleford?"

"It's a very pleasant place, I think."

"I hear you chose this spot to spend some time writing your memoir."

"Ah yes, that's the plan. But I cannot say I have made much progress yet. Each day I sit at the typewriter and write a few words, but then something distracts me through the window."

"Oh, I know that feeling, Monsieur Legrand. I can never sit still for very long either. You'll find the village isn't quite as silent and sleepy as you may have hoped."

"I am well aware that appearances can be deceptive, Mrs Churchill. No matter how calm and peaceful a place may seem, there is always something stirring."

"Well yes, very true indeed. It's a shame really, isn't it? It would be better if we could all just muddle along in peace without anything untoward happening."

"Ah, but then you would not have a business, would you, Mrs Churchill?"

"No, that's quite true."

"The mere existence of your detective agency suggests that, at any given time, there is always something that must need resolving. Be it big or small, there is always something, non?"

"Non. I mean, *oui*, Monsieur Legrand. I hope for everyone's sake, though, that nothing untoward occurs during your stay with us."

He spread his hands and gave a shrug. "It is human nature, Mrs Churchill. People are not capable of living in harmony."

"I suppose you're right. How long are you planning on staying with us?"

"I have paid the rent for three months, and I hope that

by the end of this time I will have made good progress with my memoir."

"I don't suppose having to tickle the tummy of a pesky little dog is likely to help much, is it?"

"It's a welcome distraction, Mrs Churchill. He looks like the sort of dog who knows a few tricks."

"If only! He doesn't know any."

"Roll over!" commanded Monsieur Legrand.

To Churchill's amazement, the little dog rolled over onto his back and then onto his tummy again.

"Good grief!" she exclaimed. "Did you see that, Miss Pemberley?"

"I certainly did."

"Has he ever done that before?"

"Not when I've asked him to."

"Now, sit," commanded Monsieur Legrand, "and give me your paw."

Oswald sat up and lifted his left paw. Monsieur Legrand bent down to shake it.

"Now the other paw," he instructed.

Oswald placed his left paw on the ground and lifted his right.

"Very good. Now both paws." He made a gentle gesture with his hands.

Oswald lifted both paws off the ground and sat in a begging position, his tongue hanging out of his mouth in delight.

"What a clever little dog!" enthused Churchill with a clap. "Oh, he's so clever, isn't he, Miss Pemberley?"

"He's a genius!" his owner replied, her eyes moist behind the lenses of her spectacles.

"Now, stand," commanded Monsieur Legrand.

Once again, the dog did as he was told.

"And up!"

Oswald raised himself onto his hind legs.

"And twirl!" announced the detective, slowly spinning his hand above the dog's head.

To Churchill's total astonishment, the little dog made a complete rotation while balancing on his hind legs. All the while he followed the detective's hand like a cobra following the end of a snake charmer's pipe.

"And down. Very good! What a clever boy. Lie down."

Oswald happily lay on the ground and the detective patted him on the head.

"How did you do all that?" Churchill asked him.

"What, exactly?"

"Make our dog do tricks like that."

"I have not made him do anything. He did it all by himself."

Churchill and Pemberley bid Monsieur Legrand good day and walked on. Once they were out of sight they stopped and shared an incredulous look.

"How on earth did he do that, Pembers? It was bordering on witchcraft!"

"It was certainly magical."

"How did Oswald know all those tricks?"

"I didn't teach him any of them."

"Remind me where you got him from again."

"Farmer Drumhead, but I can't imagine him taking the time to teach Oswald any tricks."

"Perhaps it was one of the Drumhead children." Churchill bent down toward Oswald. "Paw."

The little dog looked up at her happily but made no attempt to move his paw.

"Give me your paw, Oswald." Churchill held out her hand to him but he just sniffed it. "You're supposed to give me your paw. Paw. *Paw.* Try the other paw, then. This paw." She pointed at his left leg. "Raise this paw, Oswald! Raise your paw for Auntie Churchy! Oh, darn it, Pembers!" She stood up straight again. "This dog won't do a single thing I ask him to do."

"Roll over!" commanded Pemberley.

Oswald remained where he was, looking at his mistress cheerfully with his tongue hanging out of his mouth.

"How is it that Monsieur Legrand has the magic touch and we don't, Pembers? What are we doing wrong?"

Chapter 7

"IT WAS VERY INTERESTING TO MEET THE FAMOUS detective yesterday," said Pemberley as the two ladies enjoyed a plate of ginger snap biscuits in their office the following morning.

"Interesting, do you think? He's certainly a funny little man."

"He seemed slightly eccentric, but he's obviously an observer. Observers are often rather eccentric, aren't they?"

"An observer of what?"

"Of people. Of their subtle mannerisms and gestures. And he'll be rather adept at listening too, no doubt."

"Listening? That's hardly a tricky skill to master."

"But he combines his observational skills with listening before drawing his conclusions. Like all great detectives, he must also possess a great understanding of human nature."

"Gained through a little life experience, I suspect. That's not so difficult either when you've lived to a certain point. By the time you reach my age you've seen it all."

"Have you really seen it all, Mrs Churchill?"

"When it comes to human nature, yes."

"I don't relish the idea of having seen it all. I like to think there will always be something new to experience."

"I've had enough of new experiences myself." Churchill helped herself to another ginger snap. "They're too tiring. I can use my experience to understand human nature instead, and to listen and observe... and things like that."

"Ah, but it's not just that, Mrs Churchill."

"There's more?"

"Yes. His other skill is noticing what he *doesn't* hear or see."

"And how does he manage that?"

"With immense skill. If someone is lying, for example, they'll go to great lengths not to do or say certain things. And that's where the detective's skill really comes into its own because he can deduce, from their actions, what they really mean. People give all sorts of hidden clues when they're lying."

"You don't need to explain all this to me, Pembers. One of the first skills we learn as humans is to spot a liar! It's hardly a new area of expertise."

"There's no doubting that many of us can spot a liar, but he seems able to effectively combine many vital skills into one super skill. And that one super skill is being an expert sleuth."

"You appear to think very highly of our new detective friend, Pembers. What's brought on all this admiration of his fine qualities? You've only just met the chap."

"I spent some time yesterday evening thinking about what it is that makes a great detective."

"What a delightful way to spend your evening. I fear you may be talking Monsieur Legrand up a little, though.

If you ask me, the chap is nothing more than a harbinger of doom."

"What do you mean?"

"It's quite obvious, really. You're aware that there are some bitter and twisted people out there who like to think they could pull off the perfect murder, are you not?"

"Are there really people like that?" Pemberley shuddered.

"Of course there are. And if there happened to be one here in the village right at this moment, he or she might decide to put Monsieur Legrand to the test!"

"Then his presence would be a good thing, wouldn't it?" replied Pemberley. "If someone decided to commit a murder while one of the most accomplished detectives in Europe was staying in our village, I'd say that would be particularly useful timing."

"But you do understand why Monsieur Legrand's presence could be dangerous, don't you? He might awaken the wolf, encouraging someone with murderous intent to emerge from the shadows."

"Oh no! All this talk has made me feel terribly afraid, Mrs Churchill. I don't want him awakening any wolves! Can't we send Monsieur Legrand away before anything untoward occurs? How about South Bungerly? They haven't had a murder there in a long time."

"I'm not sure how we'd manage that, given how established he seems here. I didn't mean to scare you, Pembers. There's probably nothing in what I said; it was just a thought that crossed my mind. Nothing more than a fleeting thought."

They were interrupted by a thunder of footsteps on the stairs, then the office door was flung open and Mrs Thonnings practically fell into the room. She was out of breath and her red hair tumbled into her eyes.

"Mrs Cobnut!" she exclaimed. "She's had a terrible accident!"

"Oh dear," said Churchill. "Is she all right?"

"No, she's dead!"

Churchill rose to her feet. "Really? Oh gosh, how awful! What sort of accident?"

"She came off her bicycle."

Churchill shook her head and tutted as she helped Mrs Thonnings into a chair. "Well, that is a terrible shame indeed. Inevitable, some might say, but still terrible."

"Why was it inevitable?" asked Mrs Thonnings.

"Given the manner in which she whizzed around on that machine it was only going to end one way."

"She simply enjoyed a spot of bicycling, Mrs Churchill!"

"Yes, she certainly did. A little too much, perhaps. They do say that a little too much of what one enjoys can be bad for one."

"I can't see how it was inevitable at all," protested Mrs Thonnings. "She encouraged every lady in the village to get on her bicycle and enjoy the great outdoors; to get a bit of fresh air and exercise. Joining the Compton Poppleford Ladies' Bicycling Club was one of the best things I've ever done!"

"Well, when you put it like that, she did do rather a marvellous thing. But she could have done it with a little more consideration for others. Expecting them to leap out of her way whenever she went speeding along the road was a bit much!"

"She still didn't deserve to die," said Mrs Thonnings with a sob.

"You're quite right, Mrs Thonnings, of course she didn't. Driving that machine around the way she did put her at a greater risk of meeting an untimely end, but she certainly didn't deserve it. She simply needed to slow down a little."

"She liked to feel the wind in her hair."

"Yes, that was quite evident."

"She enjoyed the freedom."

"Don't we all?"

"I'll miss her."

"I'm sure you will, Mrs Thonnings."

"I shall never ride a bicycle again."

"Surely there's no need for such a drastic decision."

"But I won't! I'm too scared to; they're dangerous things."

"They're only dangerous when ridden dangerously."

"Or if someone else does something dangerous while you're riding one," added Pemberley, handing Mrs Thonnings a cup of tea.

"Exactly," agreed Churchill. "I suppose there is a slight degree of danger about bicycles, which is why I prefer the old two feet, to be quite honest with you. But there's no doubt that many people like them, and they help one transport oneself from A to B in a timely manner without having to endure a temperamental horse or a complicated, noisy motor car. What a sad day it is for Mrs Cobnut, though."

"Poor Mildred," wailed Mrs Thonnings. "The village will never be the same without her."

Chapter 8

"I KNOW WHAT'LL MAKE US FEEL A BIT BETTER," SAID Pemberley. "I'll cut us all a slice of my prune cake."

"Have we finished the ginger snaps?" asked Churchill.

"I'm afraid so. Prune cake to the rescue!"

"What's all that shouting about outside?"

"Sounds like the paper boy," said Mrs Thonnings.

Churchill left her side and walked over to the window that overlooked the high street. "So it is," she said, observing the noisy young lad with a bundle of newspapers under his arm. "Looks like the *Compton Poppleford Gazette* has rushed out a second edition to include this morning's tragedy. I'll go and fetch us a copy."

A few minutes later, the three ladies gathered around Churchill's desk to read the cover story.

A Terrible Bicycle Incident: Murder Suspected!

By Smithy Miggins

. . .

Compton Poppleford has been thrown into a state of shock this morning by the horrific news that a popular local woman has died. Mrs Mildred Cobnut lost control of her bicycle on Grindledown Hill and suffered fatal injuries when her machine careered into a field.

Following an interview with Inspector Mappin this morning, the Gazette can exclusively reveal that Mrs Cobnut's death is being treated as a murder.

Inspector Mappin said: "An examination of Mrs Cobnut's bicycle revealed that the cables connected to the brakes were purposefully cut with a sharp implement."

It was initially believed that Mrs Cobnut had lost control of her bicycle due to an error of judgement. However, the bicycle was examined by Inspector Mappin as a precaution, and it's just as well he did so, for the keen-eyed inspector discovered that the brake cables had been neatly cut. As Mrs Cobnut had been seen by many to be safely riding her bicycle as recently as yesterday, it can only be assumed that the brake cables were vandalised during the night. It's believed that Mrs Cobnut's bicycle was kept inside a shed within the grounds of her home, Haggerton Cottage, on Grindledown Hill. Police are making extensive enquiries in the area to discover whether anyone saw anything suspicious last night.

Mrs Cobnut's husband, retired bookkeeper Barny Cobnut, told the police his wife had noticed some damage to the shed when she fetched her bicycle for her morning ride, and reported that an upturned urn was found beneath a broken window.

Having determined that nothing had been stolen from the shed, Mrs Cobnut assumed the damage had been inflicted as part of a failed burglary and told her husband she would inform Inspector Mappin once she arrived in the village. She mounted her bicycle at eight o'clock for her customary morning ride, which wound steeply down Grindledown Hill until the lane reached the duck pond.

Inspector Mappin told our reporter: "While negotiating the first bend by Sloping Field, Mrs Cobnut would have attempted to apply the brakes so she could safely negotiate the road ahead. However, it appears the brakes failed due to a deliberate cutting of the cables that ran from the handlebars to the brake housing on the front and rear wheels.

"Mrs Cobnut was undoubtedly travelling down Grindledown Hill at a good speed, as she was unable to steer her bicycle around the bend without applying her bicycle brakes. Sadly, it appears that her velocity was sufficient to project her bicycle through the hedge at the top of Sloping Field. From this point onwards, the uneven ground would have disturbed the trajectory of the bicycle and unseated Mrs Cobnut, causing both to tumble quite dramatically down the steep field."

Sloping Field belongs to Farmer Drumhead, and it was one of his farmhands who discovered Mrs Cobnut in the field at a quarter past eight this morning. Doctor Bratchett was summoned and, upon examination of Mrs Cobnut's body, confirmed that she had suffered swift and fatal injuries.

Inspector Mappin added: "There can be no doubt that someone intentionally vandalised Mrs Cobnut's bicycle so that it would be rendered unsafe in the course of its normal, everyday usage. By rendering it unsafe, the person or persons intended to inflict significant harm upon Mrs Cobnut. The culprit would have known that she lived on a steep hill and must therefore have anticipated that the injury to her person would be substantial if she bicycled down the hill without the use of her brakes. There is no doubt in my mind that the culprit intended to cause Mrs Cobnut significant harm, and possibly even her tragic demise. For this extremely serious reason I have no choice but to treat this as a murder case."

The residents of Compton Poppleford are hopeful that the culprit will be caught swiftly, given that Mrs Cobnut's death happens to have coincided with the recent arrival of a Swiss detective of international renown, Monsieur Pascal Legrand. Although the great man is busy writing his memoir and claims to have retired from detective work, *there is hope among many in the village that he will lend his expertise to this tragic case.*

Inspector Mappin said: "I have no idea who could possibly have wished to murder such a delightful lady as Mildred Cobnut. The discovery of the cut brake cables has left an entire community shocked, saddened and sickened. We shall leave no stone unturned in our investigations and will soon expose whoever was behind this terrible act."

The inspector is urging all bicycle owners to thoroughly check their machines before mounting them, noting specifically that the brake mechanism is in proper working order. Bicyclists are also being advised to remain particularly vigilant about where their bicycles are stored, and to be on the lookout for anyone carrying cable cutters. The set used in this gruesome incident have not yet been found, and the inspector has asked that residents keep an eye out for a pair of cutters which may have been discarded in a hedge, stream, well or somewhere similar.

He added that he didn't wish to make people afraid that their bicycles would also be targeted, but he could neither confirm nor deny whether he thought the attack on Mrs Cobnut's bicycle was an isolated incident. Inspector Mappin urged anyone with information to contact him immediately, but also stated there was no need for panic and that he was confident the culprit would be apprehended before long.

Mrs Mildred Cobnut had been a resident of Compton Poppleford for more than forty years. She and Mr Barny Cobnut bought Haggerton Cottage shortly after they were married in 1890. The couple had no children but instead threw themselves into village life. Mrs Cobnut's most recent appointment was that of chairperson of the Compton Poppleford Ladies' Bicycling Club. The ladies of the aforementioned club have already laid out lovely floral wreaths in Sloping Field this morning.

"Murder?!" said an astonished Mrs Thonnings. "Someone cut her brakes? How awful! Who would do such a thing?"

"Someone who didn't want to see her bicycling around the village any more," replied Pemberley.

"That could have been a fair few people," added Churchill. "Do you remember Inspector Mappin telling us how many complaints he'd received?"

"I suppose he'll start questioning everyone who complained about her now," said Pemberley.

"And that includes us! Oh dear, I'm not looking forward to that. He'd better not start entertaining the idea that you or I had something to do with this, Pembers. Cutting the brake cables... Goodness! What a cold, calculated thing to do. How does someone who could carry out such an act go to sleep at night?"

"Whoever it was must have been extremely angry or upset with her," said Mrs Thonnings.

"Indeed they must," replied Churchill. "It's all so horrible."

"Well, like the newspaper said, we're lucky we have Monsieur Legrand staying in the village," said Mrs Thonnings. "He'll have it sorted out in no time."

"That's quite an assumption," said Churchill. "What if the man wants nothing to do with the case? He may be hiding in his cottage hoping no one will come knocking on his door to bother him about this."

"Do you think so?" asked Pemberley.

"He's retired, isn't he? I imagine he'll be rather annoyed that this murder's happened, and now even the local newspaper is writing about the high hopes everyone has that he'll solve the case. There's a weight of expectation resting on his shoulders. I wouldn't like that myself."

"I'm sure he'll rise to the challenge," said Mrs Thonnings. "He strikes me as that sort of man."

"Well, it'll be interesting to see what happens," said

Churchill. "Imagine how amused Monsieur Legrand will be by Inspector Mappin's attempts to investigate!" She gave a low chuckle.

Chapter 9

CHURCHILL, PEMBERLEY AND OSWALD MADE THEIR WAY UP Grindledown Hill a short while later. Pemberley carried a bunch of white carnations.

"I still can't believe it," she said. "It was only a few days ago that you and Mrs Cobnut had that stand-off in the tea rooms."

"I wouldn't call it a stand-off, Pembers. It was merely an exchange of words."

"A *heated* exchange of words."

"It was barely even that."

"Oh, but it was! Don't you remember? She called you a trout face or something similar. Then you called her a jug worm, wasn't it?"

"I really don't recall our conversation descending into name-calling."

"But it did! Surely you remember? Or perhaps you'd prefer to forget."

"I would absolutely prefer to forget, Pembers. It wasn't my finest hour, and now the woman's been murdered I'm worried people will go mentioning my name to Monsieur Legrand."

"Why on earth would they do that?"

"Oh, you know the routine, Pembers. When someone's murdered, the detective immediately sets about trying to find out who the victim fell out with."

"But surely he won't suspect you."

"I should think my name will appear somewhere on the list after a supposedly heated exchange of words took place in the tea rooms, as witnessed by the Compton Poppleford Ladies' Bicycling Club along with all the other customers and the staff there."

"He'd be foolish to think that you would murder Mrs Cobnut over something so trivial."

"Yes, he would. I suppose it all depends on the other motives he uncovers."

"Mrs Harris's loaf was squashed."

"I shouldn't think he'd pay any attention to that."

"You never know."

"No, you're quite right. People have been murdered over far less. Is this the place?"

A gate in the hedge offered a view of a steeply sloped field.

"Yes, I think this is it," replied Pemberley. "Let's go through the gate."

"Righto. I feel quite out of puff. It's rather a steep hill, isn't it?"

The two ladies walked through the gate and began making their way up to the far end of the field. Oswald scampered to and fro, sniffing around in the long grass.

"Is that someone walking up there?" asked Churchill, peering up at a pale-coloured figure at the top of the field.

"Yes, it looks like someone's laying flowers just in front of the hedge," replied Pemberley.

"The hedge Mrs Cobnut crashed through. And just beyond it is where the road bends, I imagine."

They continued walking until they came to an area of grass that had been disturbed. Tufts of displaced earth and grass lay scattered about.

"Gosh," said Churchill suddenly feeling cold and shivery. A sadness began to weigh heavily on her as she considered how Mrs Cobnut's bicycle must have left the road and tumbled down into the field.

"It's a strange thing," said Pemberley, her voice a little choked. "I can't help but think about how terribly annoying the woman was when she shouted at us to leap out of the way, and the manner in which she boisterously conducted herself in the tea rooms. Still, she didn't deserve this."

"I agree," said Churchill sombrely.

The two ladies turned to survey the view across Compton Poppleford, the spire of St Swithun's church rising above the huddle of houses.

"What a lovely last view she would have had," commented Pemberley.

"Lovely indeed. Although she would only have appreciated it very briefly before realising her brakes weren't working."

"How awful. I suppose she would have pulled at them, then pulled at them again before it dawned on her that nothing could be done. Then I imagine she would have put her feet down to stop herself."

"And that would have unbalanced her at the speed she generally liked to travel at, the silly billy. One can stop oneself with one's feet when going slowly but, given that she liked to hare along at great speed, it would have made little difference."

"It would have made it worse, in fact."

"Well yes, it might have done. It would most likely have interrupted the momentum of the bicycle."

"And then the bike would have left the road and flipped over."

"Tumbling a number of times, judging by the dents we saw in the grass."

"Oh, how awful!"

"And terrifying!"

"If it ever happened to me, I'd be maintaining some hope that I might escape with a few bumps and bruises."

"As would I, Pembers. I'd probably expect that a bone would be broken here or there. But to lose one's life? It really is terribly tragic."

Churchill turned to look at the figure standing beside the floral tributes. She was wearing a straw hat and a pale blue dress. Even from a distance Churchill could see that she had brightly rouged cheeks.

"Any idea who that pink-faced lady is, Pembers?" she whispered.

"Mrs Twig. Pink?"

"The rouge."

"Ah, yes."

"Do you know her well?"

"No, but I think she was among the bicycling gang in the tea rooms."

"I see. Well, it would be rude not to speak to her, wouldn't it? Besides, she might be able to tell us something interesting."

Oswald reached Mrs Twig before Churchill and Pemberley could, immediately jumping up at her legs.

"Hello, little dog." She bent down and patted him on the head. Then she stood up to greet the two ladies. "And hello, Miss Pemberley."

"Good morning, Mrs Twig," said Pemberley. "Please accept our condolences."

"Thank you, Miss Pemberley," she replied sadly. Then she turned to Churchill. "And you're Mrs Churchill; the lady who argued with Mildred in the tea rooms."

"Indeed I am," said Churchill. "I fear I'll always be remembered for that sorry incident after this."

"People will soon forget about it," replied Mrs Twig. "Mildred was an argumentative person. I think she quite enjoyed it."

"I see. Were there other people in the village she argued with?"

"Oh yes! Myself for one. In fact, if it hadn't been for our mutual love of bicycling, Mildred and I wouldn't have got on well together at all."

"Is that right?"

"Yes. The power of two wheels and a couple of pedals is quite astonishing, isn't it?"

"Is it? You'd know that better than me, Mrs Twig."

The ladies fell silent for a moment as Pemberley laid her white carnations alongside the other flowers.

"Can you recall any specific arguments you had with Mrs Cobnut, Mrs Twig?" ventured Churchill once a respectable period of silence had passed.

"Oh yes, lots."

"Would it be impertinent for me to ask what they were about?"

"Not at all. They were about all sorts of things: our favourite music, places to holiday, which farm had the best eggs... that sort of thing."

"Just about anything, then?"

"Yes."

"And, dare I say it, largely trivial matters?"

"I suppose now I'm looking back on them, yes, but

at the time they seemed very important indeed. But then again, everything seems very important until someone dies. And then nothing seems important at all, does it?"

"I understand what you mean, Mrs Twig."

"And we often argued about money, too."

"Why's that?"

"Oh, she happened to lend me a small sum once, and I must admit that I was rather slow in repaying it. I repaid some of it, just not quite the full amount."

"You borrowed money from her?" Churchill was taken aback that the seemingly well-presented lady standing in front of her might have found herself in need of money. "Do you mind me asking what for?"

Mrs Twig scratched the back of her neck. "Well, it's a little embarrassing, but I had quite run out of funds. It's my husband, you see. He likes a drink. Each week he gives me my housekeeping money and I put it in my drawer. At least, that's what used to happen until things took a turn for the worse and he began taking it out of the drawer again."

"What a scoundrel!"

"It reached the point where there was no money left in there."

"Did you ask your husband for it back?"

"There was no point; he'd drunk it all."

"So there was no money at all?"

"I thought we still had our savings, but when I visited Mr Burbage at the bank he told me there was nothing in the account. He'd drunk all that as well."

"Oh dear. How awful!"

"So I had no choice but to turn to Mrs Cobnut and ask her for a little something to tide me over."

"And she willingly lent you the money?"

"Yes, but then she became rather impatient with me about paying it back."

"I see. What did she do?"

"She kept mentioning it every week or so. I agreed to pay a set amount back each week, and then she requested that interest be paid on the outstanding amount."

"Oh. From the sound of things, you might have received more sympathy from Mr Burbage had you chosen to borrow from the bank instead."

"Possibly, but we'd borrowed from him before."

"Oh, I see."

"That's what we did the last time my husband got bad with the drink."

"Was it just you Mrs Cobnut lent money to or was she a general lender to other people as well?"

"I heard she'd lent money to Mrs Thonnings, which was why I asked her in the first place. Mrs Cobnut wasn't short of a few bob, you see. In fact, she was really quite wealthy."

"How very interesting. How much of the money did you manage to repay her?"

"About half. But even though I'd managed half she grew increasingly insistent about it."

"In what way?"

"She started calling on me once a week for the money, and then a young man took her place."

"What did he want?"

"He was demanding repayment."

"Oh right, of course."

"Large, he was. Tall and broad. Heavy jaw, big fists. A cousin of the Flatboots, I believe. He told me he would take away all my valuable items if I couldn't repay the money: jewellery, antique vases, that sort of thing. Not that I own many valuable items, as it happens. I inherited a few family heirlooms, but those are of greater sentimental than financial value."

"And did he take them?"

"No, because that was last week and he hasn't been back since. I was expecting him this morning but he didn't turn up."

"Because of Mrs Cobnut's death, do you think?"

"Well, yes. That's the only explanation I can think of."

Chapter 10

"There is another possibility to consider, Pembers," said Churchill as the two ladies walked back to the village with Oswald.

"Which is?"

"That Mrs Cobnut cut her own brake cables."

"Decided to take her own life, you mean?"

"I know it sounds rather unbelievable, but it's a possibility that shouldn't be completely overlooked. This may not be a murder case after all."

"But would a woman who was planning to take her own life have bothered to pursue Mrs Twig so relentlessly for the money she owed her?"

"That's a very good point, Pembers."

"And surely Inspector Mappin would have found the cutters in her shed if she'd had a pair."

"Pfft! We can't always rely on Inspector Mappin to find these things, can we?"

"But if there was no sign of the cutters in the shed it would suggest someone had deliberately concealed them."

"The murderer, you mean?"

"Yes. If Mrs Cobnut had cut her own brake cables, she would most likely have left the cutters lying nearby. It would have been irrelevant to her whether they were hidden or not."

Churchill gave a nod of agreement. "Yes, Pembers, I see what you're saying. You have quite the sleuthing mind these days."

"What do you mean by *these days*? I've always had a sleuthing mind."

"Another thing we should consider is that the murderer must have had an excellent knowledge of a bicycle's components. The culprit must have known which cables to snip in order to disable the braking mechanism."

"Not necessarily. It would have been easy to work that out."

"I should have found it quite impossible."

"Not at all, Mrs Churchill. Let's find a bicycle and I'll show you."

Churchill and Pemberley reached the high street a short while later.

"That hoof up the hill has completely worn me out, Pembers. I need some restorative tea and a plate of cheerful jam tarts."

"Not before we've looked at the braking mechanism on a bicycle, Mrs Churchill."

"Oh yes. How about we look at it after the tea and jam tarts?"

"No need. There's a bicycle right here." Pemberley pointed at one propped up outside the tea rooms.

"So there is."

The two ladies walked over to it.

"Look," said Pemberley. "There's a brake lever on this side of the handlebars and another on this side."

"Yes, I can see those."

"One is for the brake on the front wheel and the other for the brake on the rear wheel."

"Even I can remember that."

"I told you it was straightforward, didn't I?"

"Shall we have tea in the tea rooms or back at the office?"

"I haven't finished yet. Now all you need to do is follow the cables from the levers on the handlebars. See where they're clipped to the frame there?"

"Yes, I see that." Churchill's stomach grumbled.

"And you can see that the two cables go their separate ways here," said Pemberley, pointing to where they were clipped together above the front wheel. "One leads to the brake on the front wheel, you see?"

"That's the brake?"

"Yes."

"That little bit of rubber?"

"That's right."

"It doesn't look like much."

"No, but it has an important job."

"Hence why Mrs Cobnut is no longer with us."

"And this brake is actually quite worn down. The owner really needs to replace it. Anyway, the other cable is clipped to the frame of the bicycle and leads to the brake on the back wheel. Can you see it there?"

"Yes."

"All the murderer had to do was snip the cables. I don't know where he snipped them. If I were the murderer, I probably would have snipped them quite close to the brakes so Mrs Cobnut would have been less likely to notice."

"A very good point. If he'd snipped them up at the handlebars she would have noticed as soon as she climbed onto her bicycle."

"Exactly."

"Excellent. I can clearly see now that the murderer did not require any expert knowledge of bicycles. Jam tart time?"

"There's still plenty of prune cake left."

The door to the tea rooms opened and Inspector Mappin stepped out. "What are you doing with my bicycle?"

"Your brakes need replacing," replied Pemberley. "Didn't you advise everyone to check that their bicycle braking mechanisms were in full working order? We read your words in the *Compton Poppleford Gazette* this very morning."

"Yes, but I haven't had a chance to check my own," he fumed. "I'm too busy investigating a murder!"

"In the tea rooms, Inspector?" asked Churchill.

"Regular sustenance is an essential requirement during such busy times." He patted his stomach.

Monsieur Legrand stepped out through the door behind him and exchanged greetings with the two ladies.

"I see you've enlisted the assistance of a renowned detective, Inspector," said Churchill. "Mrs Cobnut's case will soon be solved."

"Indeed. Monsieur Legrand has offered to help, and it would be foolish of me to refuse."

"Indeed it would."

"Ah, my favourite little dog!" gushed Monsieur Legrand, greeting Oswald. "Roll over!" he commanded.

The little dog did as he was told.

"It seems rather opportune that you happened to be

waiting for us outside the tea rooms, Mrs Churchill," said Inspector Mappin.

"We weren't waiting for you."

"Well, it seems rather opportune all the same, as I wanted to ask about the recent to-do you had with the late Mrs Cobnut inside these very same tea rooms."

Churchill sighed. "That mild disagreement will haunt me forever. What have you heard, Inspector?"

"I'd like to hear an account of the incident in your own words, Mrs Churchill."

Churchill's stomach gave another grumble as Inspector Mappin readied himself with his notebook and pencil.

"Do you think I might have cut the cables on Mrs Cobnut's bicycle because we'd had an exchange of words in the tea rooms, Inspector?"

"Not at all."

"Then why are you asking me these questions?"

"We're asking similar questions of a lot of people, as I'm sure you'll appreciate."

"Let me say this now, then. I was angry that Mrs Cobnut almost hit us on Grindledown Hill and I told her as much in the tea rooms, but I had nothing whatsoever to do with sabotaging her bicycle."

"Thank you, Mrs Churchill. Now perhaps you could tell me what happened in the tea rooms."

Churchill reluctantly recounted the incident. "And that, Inspector, is all I have to say on the matter," she added once she had finished. "I only ever met Mildred Cobnut twice. The first time on Grindledown Hill and the second in the tea rooms. I didn't see anything more of her and then I heard this morning that she had died."

"Thank you, Mrs Churchill."

The inspector scribbled down a few more sentences in

his notebook, while Monsieur Legrand simply stroked his moustache.

"Don't you like to write things down, Monsieur Legrand?" Churchill asked.

"Me?" he replied. "Non."

"You remember everything everyone says, do you?"

"Not everything, no. Only the most pertinent things."

"But how do you know what's pertinent and what isn't?"

He gave a shrug. "I just know."

"And how do you remember what each person has told you?"

"Most of what a person tells me is not so helpful."

"Oh?"

"It is what they do *not* say that is most important," he replied. "When people choose their words they are trying to make a certain impression upon the listener. I am able to find the disparity between the impression they are trying to make and the impression they are really making."

"Goodness, are you?"

"Sometimes there is little disparity, sometimes there is much."

"And if there's a big difference you know they're guilty, do you?"

"Not necessarily. It all depends on the character."

"Oh, does it indeed? This is all making me feel very self-conscious about my speech, Monsieur Legrand. I'm not sure I like being analysed in such a way."

"It is not for you to like or dislike, Mrs Churchill. You are merely presenting us with a set of facts. Perhaps they are not the facts you intended to present, but all the same that is what you have done."

"Marvellous."

Churchill didn't like the way his eyes were resting upon

her. The thought that he might be weighing up her guilt or innocence felt disconcerting.

"Right, well I need some sustenance of my own," she stated. "If there's anything else you need, Inspector, you know where to find us."

Chapter 11

"WHAT DO YOU THINK ABOUT MRS TWIG, PEMBERS?" asked Churchill once they had restored themselves with tea and prune cake back at the office. "Is she a possible suspect?"

"Removing Mrs Cobnut would certainly have put an end to her debt."

"Rather a strong motive, wouldn't you say?"

"Very strong. Especially when you consider that Mr Twig had drunk all their savings. Mrs Twig had been left with nothing and then Mrs Cobnut hired that Flatboot cousin to demand repayment. It must have been a very worrying situation for Mrs Twig."

"She was under duress. Forced to act."

Pemberley nodded.

"I shouldn't think Mappin has found as strong a suspect as Mrs Twig yet, even with that expert detective helping him," said Churchill. "Monsieur Legrand has a certain way about him, doesn't he? I wish I knew what was going on in his mind. I think I'd like to read his first memoir in order to understand a little more about him. Shall we take a trip down to the library, Pembers?"

Compton Poppleford Library was a small, crooked building leaning up against the town hall on the high street. The two ladies stepped into the cosy interior where a sign next to the bell on the librarian's desk read: "Ring bell quietly and once ONLY."

"No sign of Mrs Higginbath," whispered Churchill to Pemberley. "She'll be close by, though, lurking behind the shelves somewhere."

Pemberley nodded.

"I'm sure she does it on purpose," continued Churchill in her lowest whisper, "just so she can leap out from behind a shelving unit and take people by... Yikes!" She clasped a hand to her pounding chest. "Good grief, Mrs Higginbath, you frightened the living daylights out of me!"

A lady with a square face and long grey hair was staring at her impassively. "Did I?" she responded. "I was just tidying behind this bookshelf."

"So I gather. We've come to... I mean, Miss Pemberley has come to borrow a book. I'm merely accompanying her as I don't possess a reading ticket."

"Which book might that be?" asked Mrs Higginbath.

"Monsieur Legrand's memoir."

"There's been quite a bit of interest in his memoir recently. We have two copies, but both are out at the moment."

"May I ask who has borrowed them?"

"Only patrons with reading tickets are allowed to ask me that."

Churchill looked at Pemberley.

"May I ask who has borrowed them?" asked Pemberley.

"Borrowed what, exactly?" replied Mrs Higginbath.

"The two copies of Monsieur Legrand's memoir."

"Ah, yes. Inspector Mappin and Mrs Thonnings."

"Thank you, Mrs Higginbath," said Pemberley.

"It looks as though we'll need to make our way to the haberdashery shop, then," said Churchill.

"It's my duty to remind you that sub-lending a library book is expressly forbidden," said Mrs Higginbath. "Any attempt on your part to persuade Mrs Thonnings to lend you her copy would be a serious offence. If you wish to read Monsieur Legrand's memoir, I shall put your name on the waiting list for when the book is returned."

"Of course, Mrs Higginbath," said Churchill.

"My words were directed at Miss Pemberley, who is the only reading ticket-holder standing in front of me."

"Of course, Mrs Higginbath," said Pemberley.

"Oh, hello ladies," said Mrs Thonnings as they stepped into her haberdashery shop. "I'm just putting out some new ribbon to cheer myself up. Do you like it? It's come all the way from my London supplier."

"What a lovely shade of red," said Churchill.

"It's vermilion."

"How fancy."

"And quite lovely for trimming a bonnet, wouldn't you say? It would put a new lease of life into an old, dull piece of headwear."

"That sounds like a lovely idea."

"You'd like to buy some, Mrs Churchill?"

"Possibly. I'll have a look at my hats when I go home and see which it would suit the best."

"Marvellous. I can put a yard to one side for you if you like."

"I'll check my hats first, Mrs Thonnings."

"Right you are."

"How are you feeling after this morning's upset?"

"Rather wobbly, I'm afraid. I'm mostly able to distract myself by arranging the new stock on the shelves, but then an awful reminder of what's happened comes crashing over me and I have to have another little cry." She pulled a handkerchief from her pocket and dabbed at her eyes.

"That's totally understandable, Mrs Thonnings. This has been a terribly shocking incident. Anyway, we heard from Mrs Higginbath that you've borrowed a copy of Monsieur Legrand's memoir from the library."

"That's right, I have."

"Is it any good?"

"It's all right, I suppose. A little on the boring side, to be honest. He talks about himself a great deal. I was hoping to read all the details about the Murderer of Marseille, but I haven't got to that bit yet."

"May we have a quick look at your copy?"

"Oh yes, it's just over there." Mrs Thonnings walked behind the counter and pulled out two books from beneath it. "I keep these here for when it's quiet between customers."

"What's the other book?"

"Oh, just one of those romance novels I like. Makes a change from Monsieur Legrand talking about his academic achievements in Geneva."

She handed them the memoir, entitled *Inside the Mind of a Detective: the Famous Cases of Monsieur Pascal Legrand.*

"Do you think you'll finish it, Mrs Thonnings?"

"Probably not. I'm more interested in the other book, *Forbidden Obsession.*"

"Good grief." Churchill felt herself blush. "It sounds rather racy to me."

"Oh, it is. You can have a borrow when I've finished it if you like."

"I fear it might get me rather hot under the collar."

"Mrs Higginbath said that sub-lending was expressly forbidden," said Pemberley.

"Well, I only need to borrow Legrand's memoir for a few days," replied Churchill. "Besides, do you always do what Mrs Higginbath tells you to do, Miss Pemberley?"

"I did when we were at school, and I suppose the habit has stuck with me."

"I can imagine her being a very bossy schoolgirl."

"Oh, she was. Even the headmistress was wary of her."

"You're rather interested in Monsieur Legrand, then, Mrs Churchill?" asked Mrs Thonnings.

"Yes, he's an intriguing character. I'd like to understand how he intends to investigate Mrs Cobnut's death, and I thought a quick read of his memoir might enlighten me."

"It's not a quick read, Mrs Churchill." Mrs Thonnings laughed. "You'll be yearning for a bit of *Forbidden Obsession* before you reach the end of chapter one."

"We'll see about that. I did manage to plough through *Wuthering Heights* once."

"That's quite different altogether," exclaimed Pemberley. "It's a masterpiece!"

"A little too wordy for me," said Mrs Thonnings. "Anyway, I'm sure Monsieur Legrand will have Mrs Cobnut's murder solved in no time, and then we'll all be able to rest easy again."

"If you say so," replied Churchill. "Sometimes such people can be a little talked up, don't you find? They have one successful case and suddenly everybody thinks they're an expert sleuth. We had a nice chat with Mrs Twig this morning, didn't we, Miss Pemberley? She told us she'd borrowed some money from Mrs Cobnut after hearing that you had done the same."

"Indeed I did, and what a mistake that was. It was only fifty pounds for some new shelving and carpet in here, but you wouldn't believe her repayment terms! She wanted a shocking amount of interest with very little time to repay the money. She threatened to send her thug round if I didn't oblige. I managed to pay it all back on time but it wasn't a pleasant experience. I hear Mrs Twig got in quite a mess with it all."

"Yes, she did."

"Mrs Cobnut never was the lenient type. She may have been rather beastly to Mrs Twig about the money," continued Mrs Thonnings. "All the same, it's awfully sad that she's dead. I wonder how Mr Cobnut's faring. He must be terribly upset."

"I expect he's in rather a bad way."

"He will be. It'll be interesting to see whether he gets the old housekeeper back."

"I remember Inspector Mappin telling us she had recently left the Cobnut household. Do you know why?"

"It was all Mrs Cobnut's doing. Something about Miss Plimsoll not cleaning the hearth or polishing the silver properly. Something small. But I suppose enough small things not being done properly could easily add together to become something much larger, couldn't they?"

"They might well do."

"And then there were the rumours."

"Rumours?" Churchill said curiously.

Mrs Thonnings waggled her painted eyebrows up and down suggestively.

"What rumours?"

"Oh, you know." She waggled her eyebrows again.

"I won't know unless you tell me, Mrs Thonnings."

"Well, I'm rather reluctant to elaborate because rumours aren't always based on fact, are they? And I'd be very hesitant to repeat a piece of gossip that somehow became treated as fact."

"I know the difference between gossip and fact, Mrs Thonnings! Can't you at least give me a hint?"

"All I can tell you is what I witnessed with my own eyes."

"Which was?"

"Stolen glances between Mr Cobnut and Miss Plimsoll when we attended Haggerton Cottage for the recent Compton Poppleford Ladies' Bicycling Club meeting."

"Stolen glances, eh? Do you think they were romantically entwined?"

"Gosh, I don't know if it ever came to that. There was plenty of gossip, of course, but I can only tell you what I saw."

"That's very interesting indeed. Thank you, Mrs Thonnings."

"Not at all. Enjoy the memoir, if such a thing is possible."

"Thank you again. Please don't mention to Mrs Higginbath that you've lent us this book, Mrs Thonnings. We'll be in terrible trouble if you do."

"I won't breathe a word. And I'll drop *Forbidden Obsession* in to you as soon as I've finished it."

Chapter 12

"Whereabouts does Miss Plimsoll live, Pembers?" asked Churchill as they drank tea in their office the following morning.

"I think she lives in a cottage near the cricket field."

"It's possible Ramsay could have strayed that way, wouldn't you say?"

"Ramsay?"

"Mr Pyeman's missing goat."

"Oh! I'd completely forgotten all about him."

"That's not surprising. So much has happened since Mr Pyeman came to visit us."

"You think we should look for the goat in the cricket field, do you?"

"Yes, and if we happen to bump into Miss Plimsoll as we're doing so, that could be useful."

"Why would that be useful? We're not investigating Mrs Cobnut's death, are we? Surely we're leaving the case up to Inspector Mappin and his expert detective."

"Of course we are. But I'm anticipating a little more interest in my good self from Mappin. My card is marked after that slight disagreement I had with Mrs Cobnut in the tea rooms."

"He can't possibly suspect you, Mrs Churchill."

"No, he can't. But he accosted us outside the tea rooms yesterday, and I wouldn't be surprised if we were to receive another visit from that fool inspector sometime soon. I like to be forearmed in these situations."

"By investigating the case?"

"It'll be nothing more than a conversation or two with a few people we meet along the way, Pembers. Now, have you got your nice stout walking shoes with you?"

"They're in my drawer. I'll just put them on."

"I made a start on Monsieur Legrand's memoir last night," said Churchill as she waited. "Mrs Thonnings wasn't wrong; it's not terribly exciting."

"Is this a piece of prune cake in my drawer?"

"Is it?"

"That's what I was asking you, Mrs Churchill."

"How odd. Does it look like prune cake?"

"Yes."

"Well, I imagine it must be, then. How very strange indeed."

"How on earth did it get in there?"

"I have no idea. Perhaps you accidentally left the drawer open while you were serving up the cake and some accidentally fell in."

"I'm quite sure I would have noticed that."

"Perhaps you were distracted at the time. Come along, Pembers, we need to find this goat."

"To speak to Miss Plimsoll, you mean."

. . .

73

The two ladies and their dog found themselves strolling along a lane that led to the village cricket pitch a short while later.

"If one has solved cases such as the Naples Heist, the Cologne Kidnapping and the Murderer of Marseille, one should at least make an attempt to write one's memoirs in an entertaining fashion," said Churchill. "I haven't even got to the case-solving bit yet, and neither am I likely to if he continues in the same vein. Perhaps I should skip a few chapters."

"Oh no, you must never skip chapters, Mrs Churchill!"

"Even if they're boring?"

"Even so. The book was intended to be read as a whole, with each chapter tackled in consecutive order. And besides, you might miss a nugget of interesting information."

"There hasn't been a single nugget yet. Is that the cricket field up ahead?"

The two ladies approached the emerald-green expanse, which was encircled by a tidy hedge. A white wooden pavilion with a little clock tower on its roof was positioned over on one side of the field.

"They're not playing today, then," commented Churchill. "Detective Chief Inspector Churchill always enjoyed the crack of leather on willow. I suppose it is rather a nice sound, isn't it? If only they didn't have to complicate it with all these runs and innings and overs and whatnot. I think I'd quite enjoy watching it if they got rid of all that. Now, where's Miss Plimsoll's place?"

"I think it's one of those over there." Pemberley pointed toward a row of little cottages with gardens backing onto the field. "I think we should poke about where the hedge borders the gardens. That should flush out a few occupants."

"I like your way of thinking, Pembers."

Oswald led the way as Churchill and Pemberley strolled onto the cricket field and began to loudly examine the hedge. It wasn't long before someone appeared.

"Do you mind?" asked a red-faced man with pale hair. "You're staring straight into my garden!"

"We're looking for nibbled leaves in your hedge," replied Churchill. "Have you seen any nibbled leaves?"

"What the jiggins are you talking about, woman? Are you raving mad?"

"We're just looking for an escaped goat. Have you seen him?"

"No I haven't, and you need to watch where you're standing. The groundsman will be after you if you're not careful. That cricket field is private property."

"There's no need to threaten us with a groundsman, sir. We're carrying out official business on behalf of Churchill's Detective Agency. We've been tasked with finding a goat, and that's precisely what we're doing."

"But you're peering into my garden!"

"Your pelargoniums are wilting," responded Pemberley. "They need a bit of water."

"Well said, Pembers," muttered Churchill as they moved on. "That impertinent man should be watering his pelar-whatsits rather than being rude to us."

"Oh, hello," said a stout lady as she hung her washing on the line.

"We're terribly sorry to bother you," said Churchill. "Have you seen a goat around here?"

"I'm afraid not."

"Never mind. Sorry for troubling you."

"I'd like to, though."

"Would you?"

"Yes, I like goats."

"Do you happen to know if they can swim?"

"Oh yes, they're good swimmers."

"Thank you. Well, if you do see a goat around here, please call in to Churchill's Detective Agency and let us know. We're just above the bakery on the high street."

"The bakery? I like bakeries."

"They're good, aren't they? Right, we should be getting on."

They walked on quickly, leaving the woman to continue with her washing.

"Odd people in these cottages, aren't they, Pembers?" muttered Churchill. "Is this the quirky side of the village?"

Chapter 13

"Can I help you?" came a voice from the other side of the hedge.

The two ladies peeked over the shrubs to see a fair-haired lady in a floppy summer hat sitting on a garden bench with a book in her lap.

"Good morning, Miss Plimsoll," said Pemberley.

"Ah, Miss Plimsoll!" said Churchill, pleased they had finally encountered the person she wished to speak to. She introduced herself and the detective agency before adding: "I don't suppose you've seen a lost goat around here, have you?"

"Not that I recall."

"Mr Pyeman has lost his goat, and my trusty assistant Miss Pemberley and I are busy searching for him. What a lovely garden you have here, Miss Plimsoll."

"Thank you." She placed her book down on the bench next to her and stood so she could chat to the ladies over the hedge more easily. She had a freckled face and wore a floral apron over a dark green dress. "I've had a bit more time to spend on it recently."

"Why recently, may I ask?"

"I lost my employment."

"Oh dear, I am sorry. What was your employment?"

"I was a housekeeper."

"I do hope you'll be able to find a new position soon."

"So do I. Initially I feared that I wouldn't, but I suspect it'll be a little easier now."

"How so?"

"Well, the lady I worked for is no longer around. In fact, I'll be honest with you, Mrs Churchill, it was Mrs Cobnut."

"Oh, gosh! The bicycling accident lady?"

"Yes, the very same. I must be careful what I say, as I don't like to speak ill of the dead."

"Indeed, no."

"But she dismissed me, you see, and when she did so she threatened to ensure that I would never work for any household this side of Dorchester again."

"Strong words."

"I'm pleased you think so, Mrs Churchill. That's what I thought, too. It's one thing to dismiss someone from their job and quite another to threaten that they'll never work again. That's taking my entire livelihood away, that is!"

"It was certainly quite the threat. Have you any idea why she decided to be so heavy-handed?"

"We fell out, I can't deny that, and she decided she didn't want me to work for her any more. But there was no need to threaten me. That was a step too far, in my book."

"And in many other people's books, I suspect, Miss Plimsoll. May I ask what you fell out about?"

"Oh, the usual. My work wasn't up to the standard she expected. She'd been grumbling about it for a while. I missed a bit of dusting here or I forgot to wash something properly there. Laundry wasn't put away neatly enough. That sort of thing."

"Did she have high standards?"

"Extremely high. Impossible to meet, if you ask me. I've worked for some very fussy people in my time, but she was beyond the pale. She told all her friends what a dreadful person I was, which stopped any of them taking me on. And then she began complaining to just about everyone she met in the village about what a disgrace I was, and so on. I should think a fair number of people think less of me on that account."

"If it's any consolation, Miss Plimsoll, let me just tell you that no such words or sentiments reached our ears."

"That is kind of you to say. Thank you, Mrs Churchill. Are you looking for a housekeeper, by any chance?"

"Not at the moment. I'm only renting a small cottage, you see. There's barely enough room to swing a cat if one were cruel enough to do such a thing."

"That saying refers to the cat o' nine tails," interrupted Pemberley.

"That whip thing they use on sailors?"

"Yes."

"Why would anyone want to use something like that in my cottage?"

"I don't suppose anyone would. But when someone mentions there not being enough room to swing a cat, they're referring to an instrument of punishment rather than a domesticated animal."

"Although your little digression has nothing to do with our current conversation, Miss Pemberley, I'm quite pleased to have that one cleared up. Now, where were we? Ah yes, my cottage is a little small to warrant employing a housekeeper at the present time, Miss Plimsoll, but should the need arise I certainly know whom to ask."

"Thank you, Mrs Churchill."

"Now, the long and the short of it seems to be that Mrs Cobnut's demise may make it easier for you to find a new position given that she's no longer around to tell the rest of the village not to employ you."

"That's right, Mrs Churchill. I hope to find another position soon."

"I see. May I ask how long you worked for Mrs Cobnut?"

"Three years."

"Do you have any idea who might have cut her bicycle brake cables?"

"None whatsoever. She wasn't a pleasant lady but sabotaging her bicycle in such a way took things a step too far."

"I quite agree with you there, Miss Plimsoll. What about Mr Cobnut? Have you any idea how he's faring?"

"He's holding up as well as he can. I visited yesterday to offer the poor chap a bit of comfort."

"You get along well, do you?"

"Very well indeed. He always treated me kindly and told me not to mind his wife's fussiness. It's all well and good to say such things, but sadly he wasn't able to put a stop to it. She wore the trousers in their house."

"Those unsightly bicycling breeches?"

"Yes! She wore them all the time."

"Are you a bicyclist, Miss Plimsoll?"

"No. I can't say it's ever been of interest to me."

"I've heard tell that Mr Cobnut disapproved of his wife's new hobby."

"He didn't really understand her reasons for doing it. It kept her out quite a bit and he didn't like it."

"Why not?"

"He thought it rather embarrassing to have his wife riding around like that. Then when I was dismissed, he had no one to wait on him while she was out on her long bicycle rides."

"Now, now, now. This won't do!" a voice behind them scolded.

Churchill turned to see a white-whiskered man in a shabby woollen suit and straw hat regarding them coolly.

"I beg your pardon?" she responded.

"This won't do!" He pointed his finger first at Churchill and then at Pemberley, ignoring Oswald, who was jumping up at his legs.

"*We* won't do?" queried Churchill.

"I said *this*!"

"We were simply speaking to Miss Plimsoll."

"It won't do. You shouldn't be standing on the cricket field!"

"Ah, now I have a better understanding of the transgression that has angered you so."

"That's one way of putting it. No one is allowed on this cricket field."

"How do people play cricket on it, then?"

"I suppose you consider that a funny remark."

"Well, it was slightly more amusing than anything you've said so far, don't you think?"

He pointed a finger at the ground. "This is the private property of Compton Poppleford Cricket Club and, as I maintain the grounds here, I'm ordering you to leave. Only members are permitted on the cricket field."

"How do you know we're not members?"

"Because you're women!"

"Oh, it's that simple, is it?"

"Yes, it is."

"Well, thank you, my good man, for your warm welcome to Compton Poppleford Cricket Club. We'll be on our way." Churchill turned back to Miss Plimsoll. "And thank you, Miss Plimsoll, for the pleasant chat. I hope you find a new position soon and do let us know if you spot our missing goat."

Miss Plimsoll bid them farewell before the groundsman marched the two ladies and their dog off the field.

"Did you say missing goat?" he asked once they reached the edge.

"Yes. If you'd given us a chance to explain ourselves we would have been able to tell you we're looking for Ramsay the goat, who has escaped from his owner, Mr Pyeman."

"Is he brown?"

"Are you referring to the goat or Mr Pyeman?"

"The goat. Is he a brown goat?"

"Yes. With one horn."

"He was here about two days ago, in that case."

"Thank you. You've been most helpful."

"Miss Plimsoll didn't let on that there was anything untoward between herself and Mr Cobnut, did she?" said Churchill as the two ladies walked back to the office with Oswald.

"I don't suppose she'd readily admit to it if there was, though."

"No, I don't suppose she would. There's a possibility Mrs Thonnings is mistaken. Perhaps she just imagined the stolen glances between them. I'd say that was quite likely given that she spends most of her time reading racy stories."

"Miss Plimsoll seems too nice to wreak havoc on a marriage."

"It's always the nice ones you've got to watch, Pembers. At the present time, however, we can't be sure whether there was a little ardour between the two or not. We'll just have to continue our investigations to find out."

"But we're not supposed to be investigating the case."

"Aren't you just a little bit interested, Pembers?"

"Oh yes, of course. First, we have Mrs Twig, who owed money to Mrs Cobnut, and now we have Miss Plimsoll, who was dismissed. Two people who were recently aggrieved by her."

"And were possibly seeking revenge."

Chapter 14

Inspector Mappin called in on Churchill and Pemberley shortly after they arrived back at their office.

"Good morning, Inspector. How's the investigation progressing?"

"It's progressing, Mrs Churchill." He hung his hat on the hat stand. "I'm awaiting Monsieur Legrand, whom I've arranged to meet here."

"You've arranged to meet him at our offices? It seems rather presumptuous to make arrangements on our premises. I expect you'll be wanting tea and cake, too."

"Monsieur Legrand is more of a coffee man."

"I imagine he would be, coming as he does from the continent."

"I'll make some tea," said Pemberley. "And there's plenty of prune cake left."

"There's really no need," replied the inspector. "Our enquiries won't take long." He was just reaching into his pocket for a notebook and pencil when a knock sounded at the door.

"Enter, Monsieur Legrand!" chimed Churchill.

The smartly dressed detective stepped into the room with a demure smile. He removed his panama hat to reveal neatly parted hair.

"Bonjour, Mrs Churchill, Miss Pemberley. And the delightful little Oswald, of course." He gave the dog a small bow. "Roll over!" Oswald did as he was told. "There's a good dog. And bonjour, Inspector Mappin. Did you enjoy your apple this morning?"

The inspector took a step back and gave a puzzled frown. "I did, actually. How did you know about that?"

"I have observed, Inspector, from the apple cores in the wastepaper basket in your office, that you enjoy an apple each day. I also observe that you have a smudge of white paint on the left sleeve of your uniform this morning. You have attempted to rub it off with your handkerchief, no doubt, but the paint used to decorate a doorframe can be quite stubborn."

"It is," agreed the inspector. "I caught it—"

"Ah." Monsieur Legrand raised a finger. "Allow me to finish your sentence for you. You caught your sleeve on the freshly painted doorframe of the greengrocer's shop this morning. I saw the man painting it when I took my morning stroll. You visited the greengrocer to purchase your apple."

Inspector Mappin smiled and shook his head in admiration. "Simply marvellous, Monsieur Legrand. You don't miss a thing, do you?"

"Wonderful powers of observation," agreed Churchill. "Do please take a seat, gentlemen. Do you have any opinion on who might be responsible for the murder of Mrs Cobnut yet, Monsieur Legrand?"

"It is much too early to form any sort of opinion, Mrs Churchill. We must first of all speak with everyone involved in this matter."

"Naturally. You already spoke to me outside the tea rooms, remember?"

"That's correct," said Inspector Mappin, consulting his notebook. "However, we also need to discuss an incident you reported to me before Mrs Cobnut's death, when you claimed to have almost been struck as she rode her bicycle down Grindledown Hill." He readied his pencil. "Tell me about it again, Mrs Churchill."

"Again? Weren't you listening the first time?"

"Please just explain what happened so Monsieur Legrand can also hear the details."

Churchill sighed before recounting the incident on the hill a second time. Monsieur Legrand observed her closely as she spoke, smoothing his moustache on occasion. As she told her tale, Churchill recalled the detective saying he was more interested in what people didn't say than in what they did say. The manner in which he was observing her made her feel horribly self-conscious.

"Thank you, Mrs Churchill," said the inspector once she had finished. "That will be all for now." He closed up his notebook.

"For now? Do you intend to question me again?"

"I may need to, and I may not."

"Do you believe that I might have had something to do with Mrs Cobnut's death?"

"There's still a lot for us to find out, Mrs Churchill."

"That suggests you're still keeping an open mind with regard to me. I consider all this most disconcerting when I had absolutely nothing to do with Mrs Cobnut's demise. I barely knew the woman! In fact, I didn't know her at all. We've encountered several people who had fallen out with Mrs Cobnut. Have you spoken to them yet?"

"Probably. Which people are you referring to?"

"Mrs Twig and Miss Plimsoll, but I'm sure there are more. Have you considered the husband?"

"The poor man is extremely upset."

"Yes, I can imagine he would be. Are you considering him as a suspect?"

"The poor man has just been widowed!"

"Yes, we know that. But come now, Inspector. You're well aware that we can't allow emotion to get in the way of the facts when investigating these matters." Churchill glanced at Monsieur Legrand to see whether he would acknowledge this common detective sentiment, but his face remained impassive. "Surely you can't rule Mr Cobnut out just because he's upset?" she asked the inspector.

"Of course not, but you must also appreciate that it would be rather insensitive of me to question him at this juncture."

"I understand, Inspector. No doubt you'll question him at a time you consider appropriate. However, the fact remains, don't you think, that he could be a suspect? And quite an important suspect, I should think, because he would have had access to his wife's bicycle and been able to cut the cables undetected."

"There's no doubt that he could have done so," replied Mappin, "but we would need to find the evidence to prove it, and a motive, too."

"Apparently, he disapproved of his wife's new bicycling hobby because it took her away from the fold and meant he had to make his own tea."

"I'd heard there was some dissatisfaction on that part."

"There you go, then. There's your motive."

"It would be rather drastic to commit a murder over something so trivial, wouldn't it?"

"Murder is always a drastic measure, Inspector! Every

murder there has ever been was an overreaction to something."

"It's a line of enquiry I shall pursue if and when I deem it appropriate to do so, Mrs Churchill. As Monsieur Legrand and I interview people I'm sure we'll uncover a host of possible motives from all sorts of bitter and twisted people."

Churchill sighed. "It's always the way, isn't it? What are your thoughts with regard to Mr Cobnut's possible guilt, Monsieur Legrand?"

He spread his palms apologetically. "It is impossible to say at this stage, Mrs Churchill."

"You might want to speak to Miss Plimsoll about her recent dismissal from the Cobnut household," continued Churchill. "There may be more to it than meets the eye." She waggled her eyebrows the way Mrs Thonnings had when she mentioned the topic.

"I must point out that there's a vast difference between a thorough police investigation and idle gossip," Inspector Mappin said scornfully as he and Monsieur Legrand rose to their feet. "Thank you for your time this morning, Mrs Churchill."

"Sometimes there is an element of truth behind the rumours, Inspector."

"That's what the village gossips would have us believe, isn't it?"

"Don't you think a little overfriendliness between Mr Cobnut and Miss Plimsoll might have been the reason for the housekeeper's dismissal?"

"It's mere tittle-tattle, Mrs Churchill. And besides, I don't discuss the details of my cases with civilians."

"We're detectives, Inspector, just like Monsieur Legrand here. In fact, we're even more detectivey than he is because we have our own detective agency and he's supposed to be writing his memoir. Volume two, I should add. I'm currently reading the first volume, monsieur."

"Are you indeed?" he said, smiling appreciatively. "And enjoying it, I hope?"

"You've put a lot of detail in there."

"Oh, yes. Detectives like detail, Mrs Churchill, as you well know!"

Chapter 15

"THANK YOU FOR TELEPHONING US TO REPORT YOUR sighting of Ramsay the goat, Mr Spakes," Churchill said the following day. "Have we missed him?"

She and Pemberley stood in Mr Spakes's garden, almost breathless with exertion after hurrying over from the office. Mr Spakes was a white-haired man with a large, beak-like nose.

"Yes, you've missed him all right."

"That's a shame," replied Churchill. "He can't have got far, though. Where did you see him?"

"Just over there, nibbling the cherry laurel. Look, you can see the half-eaten leaves, and there are some little cloven footprints in the flowerbed. He's had a go at the astrantia, too. I can't say I'm impressed by that. It was a lot of work to protect the new shoots from the slugs, and now a blimmin' goat's got at them."

"You have my deepest sympathy, Mr Spakes. How did the goat get in here?"

"Through the gate, I expect. It's always left open."

"And how did he get out?"

"Back through the gate, proberly."

"You didn't think to close the gate and keep the goat in here until someone was able to collect him?"

"No. The gate's always left open, you see."

"And by the time we arrived Ramsay had walked off again."

"I suppose he must've done. He's not here now is he?"

"He isn't, more's the pity."

"I'm beginning to think I should have closed the gate now."

"It certainly would have kept him in your garden while we made our way over here."

"I suppose it would have, wouldn't it? I didn't think, you see."

"Clearly not. Nevertheless, you took the time to telephone us about the goat, and that's the important thing."

"I saw your notice in the *Compton Poppleford Gazette*."

"I'm pleased to hear it. Thank you, Mr Spakes."

"You could try the allotments; they're close by. Lots of fresh vegetables there for a hungry goat."

"That's a very helpful suggestion, Mr Spakes. Thank you."

"As the crow flies, the allotments are just over there." He pointed toward a row of trees at the bottom of his garden. "But you'll have to walk the long way round."

"The allotments, Pembers!" said Churchill as they walked along the sunny lane. "Why didn't we think of them sooner? They must contain a plentiful supply of food, mustn't they? And a little tastier than your average garden, I'd say. Although my diet is not that of a goat, I imagine garden plants to be a little bitter and tasteless compared with the delights of cabbages, carrots and tomatoes down at the allotments. Juicy tomatoes! I can imagine a goat being particularly partial to those."

"I think goats like everything."

"With a bit of luck, Ramsay might be there at this very moment. It's no use us being one step behind him. We need to be a step ahead."

"Or on the same step, at the very least."

"Indeed. I think that's actually the best approach, because then we'll all be there at the identical moment. I do hope thinking of the allotments has put us on the same step. We might find one of the gardeners up there who can tell us about nibbled vegetables and the suchlike."

It wasn't long before the two ladies arrived at the allotments, with their neatly planted rows of vegetables and little tool sheds. The only person in sight was an elderly gentleman who had dozed off in his deckchair next to a scarecrow with a robin sitting on its hat. Oswald ran over to him, sniffed his legs and then slunk away, as if disappointed to have received no response.

"I suppose we could wake him if we really needed to, Pembers," whispered Churchill. "It's rather frustrating that there's no one else here to ask about the goat. With any luck, Ramsay will simply emerge from the woods over there and begin helping himself to some of those runner beans. They look tasty, don't they? Are you allowed to help yourself to allotment produce, Pembers?"

"No. It belongs to the allotment holder."

"I don't suppose the holder would notice a couple of missing beans, would he?"

"He might not but imagine what would happen if everyone had the same thought. His beans would be stripped bare."

"True. But not everyone thinks the same way, do they? Otherwise there wouldn't be any beans here."

"It would be stealing, Mrs Churchill."

"Really? It's only a couple of beans."

"I can hear voices."

"Oh good, someone else to ask. Where are they?"

"I think they're coming from the overgrown path," whispered Pemberley.

Churchill also lowered her voice. "The overgrown path? Where on earth is that?"

"It's almost impossible to find now, but I remember that it emerges from the hedgerow over there. I never understood why anyone would use the overgrown path when the lane provides a quicker and easier route."

"Why would someone be walking along the overgrown path today?"

"To be secretive, I suppose."

"Secretive? Oh gosh, Pembers, how exciting! I think we should be secretive, too." Churchill glanced around quickly, looking for a place to hide. "Let's squeeze behind this water butt," she urged. "And you'd better grab hold of Oswald. We don't want him giving us away."

Pemberley did so, and the two ladies and their dog just managed to hide themselves before a figure emerged from the hedgerow. It turned out to be a broad-shouldered man with a thick wave of grey hair. His features were handsome, if a little stern.

"Mr Cobnut," whispered Pemberley.

"Really?"

He wore a sleeveless green pullover in a cable knit over a white shirt and smart tweed trousers. He placed his hands on his hips and surveyed the allotments. His eyes fell on the sleeping old man for a moment, then he called over his shoulder toward the hedge from which he'd just emerged: "All clear!"

Moments later, a fair-haired lady in a floppy summer hat pushed herself through the hedgerow to join Mr Cobnut. She brushed the foliage from her cotton dress before giving him a broad smile.

"Miss Plimsoll!" gasped Churchill in a whisper.

The two ladies watched in horror as Mr Cobnut and Miss Plimsoll shared a quick embrace before parting. She walked off toward the lane, while he checked his watch and paced alongside the hedgerow for a minute or two. He examined the runner beans Churchill had previously admired, picked a few, checked his watch again, then headed off in the direction of the lane himself.

"Did you see that, Pembers?" hissed Churchill. "Absolutely shocking behaviour given that his wife is only recently deceased. Mrs Thonnings was right all along. I knew there had to be an element of truth behind all the gossip. And then he went and stole those runner beans. The man is a disgrace! He and Miss Plimsoll have no scruples at all. What a brazen pair!"

"I wouldn't say brazen, exactly. They thought no one could see them."

"I suppose so. They wouldn't have expected anyone to be watching from behind the water butt, would they?"

"Bonjour, ladies," came a voice from behind them.

Churchill's heart leapt into her mouth and she spun around.

"Monsieur Legrand!" she exclaimed. "You surprised us!"

"Have you seen something interesting?"

"Oh, erm, well... We were looking for Ramsay the goat, you see, and we heard he might be here."

"I see." He raised an eyebrow, then smiled at Oswald.

Pemberley released the dog from her arms and he jumped up at the detective.

"Hello again, my little friend. Hold out a paw."

The dog did as he was told.

"Now two paws."

Churchill and Pemberley watched enviously as Monsieur Legrand performed another impromptu routine with their wayward dog.

"How's the investigation into poor Mrs Cobnut's demise going?" Churchill asked him once he'd finished.

The detective gave a wry smile. "It is most interesting."

"What a tantalising reply. I can only guess that means you've gathered a great deal of information, which you're now trying to make sense of."

"Something a little like that. I am trying to accustom myself to the quirks of this village."

"It's such a relief to hear someone else say that, Monsieur Legrand. It can be quite tricky when one is an outsider, can't it? I'm quite fortunate that I have my aide-de-camp, Miss Pemberley here. She knows the ins and outs of just about everything in Compton Poppleford. I can always rely on her to explain things to me."

"Am I really that helpful?" Pemberley asked.

"Yes, of course you are. Not bad for a fixture and fitting, eh? Pemberley was included as one of the fixtures and fittings when I bought Atkins's Detective Agency, Monsieur. And she has proved herself to be very useful indeed."

"I have heard all about your legendary incident board," he said. "I must take a look at it sometime."

"Oh, that old thing?" Churchill gave a humble laugh. "Well, it helps two old ladies get their minds around important matters, that's for sure."

"I heard that it has helped you solve many crimes."

"The word 'many' may be overdoing it a little, I fear, but it has helped us with one or two cases. They were nothing at all compared with the Naples Heist, the Cologne Kidnapping and all those other great cases you've worked on, Monsieur."

"Oh, sometimes it is a case of luck rather than design."

"You think so? That's rather reassuring to hear. I can't deny that one sometimes finds oneself bumbling along feeling a little unsure as to where the answers lie. It's encouraging to hear that even one of the world's greats can find himself in such a situation. I'd be interested to hear who your main suspects are at the moment."

"That is really Inspector Mappin's business."

"I realise that, and we understand he must be left to get on with investigating it all. But what about your hunch at the present time, Monsieur? There must be a few people who are of interest to you? Are you willing to share any names with us?"

He laughed. "Oh no, I would never do such a thing, Mrs Churchill. In fact, I rarely have a strong idea until I am practically at the conclusion of my investigation. A detective cannot make up his or her mind too soon, of course. It tends to prejudice the thought process."

"Ah yes, absolutely. I agree with you entirely, Monsieur. An open mind must be retained until you reach the point of no doubt whatsoever. Just let us know if we can be of any help."

"Oi!" cried a voice that startled the three of them.

The sound had come from the other side of the allotments.

"Get out of here!" came the voice again, followed by a heavy thudding sound.

"Is he talking to us?" asked Pemberley.

"I don't think so, and thankfully he can't have been

addressing Oswald on this occasion because he's here with us."

There was another thudding sound, followed by several curse words.

"Sacré bleu!" exclaimed Monsieur Legrand. "What has happened?"

Chapter 16

THE OLD MAN, WHO HAD PREVIOUSLY BEEN ASLEEP IN HIS deckchair, was marching around his allotment shaking a fist. He wore a checked shirt tucked into a pair of filthy trousers.

"Is something wrong?" Churchill called out.

"Yes, something is very wrong!" he fumed. "Some accursed goat has just been eating my chard!"

"Aha!" replied Churchill. "Was he brown?"

"Yes. What's that got to do with anything?"

"One horn?"

"Yes."

"That'll be Ramsay, the escaped goat."

"You know him?"

"Yes."

"Are you planning to recompense me for the chard he's eaten?"

"I'm afraid you'll have to take that up with his owner, Mr Pyeman. He simply asked us to find Ramsay for him. Where's that blasted goat got to now?"

"Up that way." He pointed toward the woods beyond the allotments. "I had to throw some stones at him to send him away."

"How cruel!" retorted Pemberley. "He was only trying to find himself some lunch."

"It was all I could do to get him off my allotment. There were plenty of other things to eat around here. He didn't have to eat all my veg!"

"I believe it's rather characteristic of the goat species," said Churchill. "But how wonderful that we've found him at last. We'd better go and fetch him from the woods. Do excuse us, Monsieur Legrand. I can't imagine you'll be interested in helping us capture our goat."

"I hope you catch him, Mrs Churchill," replied the detective. He stroked his moustache thoughtfully and looked around. "This is all very interesting," he added. "Very interesting indeed."

"What do you think he means?" muttered Churchill to Pemberley once they were out of earshot. "What's so interesting?"

"Oh, these renowned detectives like to say vague things like that because it makes them seem more enigmatic."

"That can't be the only reason, Pembers. He must have seen something that made him feel extra thoughtful."

"Perhaps he also spotted Mr Cobnut and Miss Plimsoll."

"I thought they had already departed before he arrived."

"I thought so too, but we don't know how long he'd been hanging around the allotments, do we? Perhaps he observed them from a different vantage point. Maybe he'd been expecting to see them there, and that's why he was at the allotments in the first place."

"That's a very good point, Pembers. Why else would he have been there? No doubt he has an interest in Mr Cobnut because he's the murder victim's husband. Therefore he guessed, or perhaps even knew, that Mr Cobnut would be meeting his fancy lady and walking up to the allotments along the overgrown path. Perhaps he's been following them."

"I wonder if he suspects Mr Cobnut."

"I'd say that he must do if he's been following him. He might suspect Miss Plimsoll, too. They're both strong suspects now, aren't they? No man in his right mind would be consorting with his housekeeper on an overgrown path only days after his wife had been murdered."

"Perhaps there's an innocent explanation," suggested Pemberley.

Churchill gave a cynical laugh. "I'd like to hear it if there is. It would be interesting to ask one or both of them about the other to see what answers they give. If they admit to walking up the overgrown path together perhaps, they have nothing to hide. If not, we'll know there's some dishonesty afoot. Now, where's that goat got to?"

"There are some recently nibbled leaves here," said Pemberley, pointing at a sapling. "I think he must have come this way."

"Right then, let's continue. I thought Oswald would be sniffing out the trail for us, but he doesn't seem interested, does he?" Churchill glanced down at the scruffy little dog who was biting at some long blades of grass at the foot of the hedgerow. "Let's be on our way."

They walked on into the dappled shade, looking out for any sign of the goat. "Mustn't it be wonderful to enjoy eating almost anything, Pembers?"

"I'm not sure."

"Oh, come now, it must be. Imagine if all this verdant greenery we see around us now tasted as delightful as a vanilla sponge cake with a thick layer of jam in the middle? That must be what it's like to live as a goat. How marvellous that would be. You'd find yourself just wandering about all day nibbling the hedgerow if that were the case; never more than a few feet away from another delicious bite. Unlimited, too! And surrounded by nature's bountiful larder. I feel quite envious of goats, Pembers."

"Look!" Pemberley grasped Churchill's arm. "Is that him up ahead?"

Churchill stopped and peered along the path. "It could be. It's difficult to see with the sunlight filtering down through the trees. I've got my field glasses in here some-where." She started rummaging about in her handbag.

"Oh, don't worry about those. They never work."

"I spent quite some time the other evening adjusting them, Pembers. I think I had them on a funny setting before. Now, where are we? Ah yes, here we are." Churchill raised her field glasses to her eyes. "Where is he?"

"Straight ahead of us, I think. I can just make out his head and his rump."

"Ah yes, I can see his rump."

"You're not even looking in the right direction, Mrs Churchill."

"How am I able to see his rump, then?"

"I have no idea. Swing them around so they're pointing straight ahead." Pemberley placed her hands on Churchill's shoulders and moved her into position.

"Now I've lost his rump," she protested.

"He's on the move again," said Pemberley. "Let's go!"

She scurried off with Churchill stumbling along behind her.

"Not so fast, Pembers!"

"You'll find it easier to run if you put your field glasses away, Mrs Churchill."

"Ah yes, I forgot I was still looking through them."

As Churchill followed after Pemberley, she caught a flash of brown ahead of them.

"Oh, I see him now!"

"Yes, that's him, and I think he knows we're after him. He's speeding up!"

"Clever, you see," replied Churchill, beginning to feel out of breath. "Where will this path lead us, Pembers?"

"It comes out near the duck pond."

"I could have sworn that all the paths in this village come out near the duck pond."

"It means one rarely gets lost."

"Indeed. Must we really keep moving at this speed? My legs are feeling a little heavy."

"You can walk if you like, Mrs Churchill. I'll carry on after him and you can catch us up."

"I wasn't suggesting slowing to a walk. I merely meant we could perhaps move at a slightly gentler pace."

"If we go any slower, we'll lose sight of him. Don't worry if your legs can't manage it; I've got it in hand."

"Oh, they can manage it all right."

They continued on down the little path through the woods, dashing over tree roots and around patches of mud.

"Are you all right back there, Mrs Churchill?" Pemberley called out.

There was no response.

"Mrs Churchill?"

"Yes…" Churchill had no breath left to form a reply.

"I think he's sped up," said Pemberley. "I can't see him any more. Shall we keep running?"

More silence ensued.

"Mrs Churchill?"

"Wha…?"

"I think we should stop," said Pemberley.

The change in speed was so abrupt that Churchill stumbled into the back of her assistant.

"Oh dear, Mrs Churchill, I fear you've overdone it a little."

Churchill simply stared at her assistant, unable to reply. She gasped for air, rivulets of perspiration running down her hot face. Extreme exertion had been replaced by an odd floating sensation as her heart pounded heavily in her ears. She felt the urgent need for a glass of water.

"I didn't know…" she said.

"Didn't know what?"

"Goats."

"You didn't know goats?"

"Ran… that fast."

"It seems they can, given that Ramsay has managed to outrun us. Perhaps he's nibbling something down by the duck pond. Let's go and see."

Churchill hobbled along behind Pemberley. "My legs," she puffed. "They've seized up. Oh, the pain!" Her mouth was dry and her head was spinning.

Oswald skipped alongside her merrily.

"Here's the duck pond," announced Pemberley as they stepped out of the woods and into the bright sunshine.

"Bench!" Churchill cried out with relief.

In all her years she had never seen a bench as welcoming as the one beside by the pond. It gave a loud creak as she sank down onto it.

"No sign of Ramsay, though," said Pemberley as

Oswald plunged delightedly into the pond. "Perhaps he didn't stay on the path. He could have turned off, I suppose. Shall we head back to the woods and take a look?"

"No," replied Churchill resolutely.

"But we're so close to catching him!"

"You go then, Pembers. If I have to move within the next half-hour, I fear that I may keel over and die."

Chapter 17

"ARE YOU ALL RIGHT MRS CHURCHILL?" Mrs THONNINGS paused beside the bench, shopping basket in hand. "Your face is all red."

"I'm quite all right, thank you. Just a little overexerted, that's all."

"You should go careful at your age." She sat down next to Churchill and placed her basket on the ground beside her feet. "It's quite nice sitting here by the duck pond, isn't it? I never think to sit here. I'm always too busy marching on past it with some errand in mind. Where are the other two?"

"They're in the woods looking for Ramsay the goat. We almost caught him, but it turns out he can move quite swiftly."

"Goats can be very fast."

"I realise that now."

"I've just remembered I have something for you, Mrs Churchill. I've been carrying it around in my basket meaning to pass it on." Mrs Thonnings reached into her basket and pulled out a well-thumbed paperback. "*Forbidden Obsession*," she said.

"Oh, really?" Churchill gave the risqué book a wary glance.

"Go on," said Mrs Thonnings with a nudge of the elbow. "You'll enjoy it, Mrs Churchill. It's an easy read."

"I can manage difficult reads as well, you know."

"Can't we all? But you've got to admit they can be rather tiresome. One chapter of this and you won't be able to put it down."

"Righty-ho." Churchill took the book and tucked it into her handbag. "Talking of romances," she said, "you'll be very interested to hear what we've just witnessed." Churchill proceeded to tell Mrs Thonnings about the surreptitious meeting between Mr Cobnut and Miss Plimsoll.

Mrs Thonnings gave an affirmative nod once Churchill had finished. "I knew it," she stated nonchalantly.

"Do you think Mrs Cobnut knew?" asked Churchill.

"She must have had her suspicions, and that may well be why she dismissed Miss Plimsoll. She didn't discuss it with any of the Compton Poppleford Ladies' Bicycling Club members, though."

"No, I don't suppose she would have done. She didn't seem the type to air her dirty laundry in public."

"Oh, no. She'd never have admitted there was anything wrong. Her approach was always to soldier on. There were whispers among the bicycle club members, of course, and we all realised the Cobnuts didn't have many kind words to say about each other."

"What did she say when she spoke about her husband?"

"Well, she didn't. Not very much, anyway. And when

she did it was usually to grumble about muddy boots in the scullery or hairs in the butter."

Churchill grimaced. "How very unsavoury. So your view, Mrs Thonnings, is that there was little love lost between Mr and Mrs Cobnut."

"That was my impression, but I couldn't vouch for it."

"Of course not. It makes one wonder, though, doesn't it? Perhaps Mrs Cobnut became superfluous to Mr Cobnut once Miss Plimsoll came along."

"It does make me wonder that." Mrs Thonnings eyes widened and she lowered her voice. "Do you think he might have done it?"

"I think a number of people might have done it, but there's no doubt Mr Cobnut had a strong motive. As did Miss Plimsoll, for that matter."

"Gosh, yes! What a thought, Mrs Churchill!"

"Enjoying a nice sit down, I see," puffed Pemberley as she re-emerged from the woods. Her grey cardigan was tied around her waist and numerous pieces of foliage covered her hair and blouse.

Oswald skipped past her and splashed into the duck pond again.

"Hello, Pembers! There's still room for a little one on this bench if we budge up."

Churchill made way for Pemberley, who flopped down beside her.

"How did you get on with Ramsay?" she asked.

"I nearly caught him four times," Pemberley replied.

"Golly, really?"

"Yes, but he managed to run off each time. I could have done with a bit of help." She gave Churchill and Mrs Thonnings a pointed glance.

"I was spent, Miss Pemberley. I did warn you I might die if I remained on my feet."

"Goodness! You must have been in quite a bad way, Mrs Churchill," commented Mrs Thonnings.

"Well, he got away," replied Pemberley sullenly. "And all that hard work was for nothing."

"Never mind. We'll come up with a plan to trap him," said Churchill.

"A trap?" said Pemberley. "We mustn't hurt him!"

"Of course we won't hurt him. It'll be a friendly trap of some sort. In other news, Mrs Thonnings and I have just been discussing the murder of Mrs Cobnut."

"Without me?"

"Don't worry, Pembers, you haven't missed out on much." Churchill told her their thoughts regarding the affair between Mr Cobnut and Miss Plimsoll. "We have a few suspects to consider," she added.

"Who are the others?" asked Mrs Thonnings.

"Mrs Twig seems a bit fishy if you ask me, although I do feel terribly sorry about the situation she's in."

"Yes, absolutely," agreed Mrs Thonnings. "It can't be nice having an errant son. He's been a terrible financial drain on the Twigs, and an emotional drain, too."

"Errant *son*?"

"Yes, I think she feels quite a sense of shame about it all. He's the reason she had to borrow money from Mrs Cobnut."

"Because of her son?" queried Churchill. "I thought it was because of her dastardly husband."

Mrs Thonnings laughed. "Mr Twig? Dastardly?"

"Yes! He's been drinking all their money away."

"Mr Twig a drinker? Impossible! I've never met such a nice, well-mannered chap."

"Really?"

"Yes. Why do you look so surprised, Mrs Churchill?"

"I'd heard quite a different description of Mr Twig."

"That he's a drinker?"

"Yes."

"We should speak a little more quietly. They only live just over there, you know."

"Over where?" Churchill glanced around at the little houses abutting the green next to the duck pond.

"It's that white one with the green shutters," replied Mrs Thonnings in a hushed voice.

Churchill peered at it.

"Don't stare too much, Mrs Churchill, she might see you. I've seen Mr Twig enjoying a drink at various parties and celebrations over the years, but I've never seen him the worse for it at any point. In fact, I'd go so far as to say that Mrs Twig drinks more than him, and she's not much of a drinker either."

"Perhaps he does all his drinking in private."

"*All his* drinking? I don't think there is any drinking. I have never once seen Mr Twig in a state of inebriation. He always seems to be smartly turned out with a pleasant word to say, and he has an important job in Dorchester. He travels there by train every day, you know. I really can't think why anybody would say such derogatory things about him."

"Me neither. Let's forget that his drinking was ever mentioned."

"Good idea. I haven't heard a single rumour that he's a drinker."

"I must have misinterpreted what I was told."

"I've never even seen him buying liquor."

"Good."

"In fact, I don't think I've ever seen him at the Wagon and Carrot either."

"Excellent. We can probably forget about Mr Twig and

his drinking – or rather the lack of it – altogether now, Mrs Thonnings."

The haberdasher shook her head thoughtfully. "I'm trying to think who would even say such a thing."

"But there's an errant son, you say. Do you know much about him?"

"No, not even his name."

"How mysterious."

Mrs Thonnings picked up her basket. "I'd better get back to my shop. I put a sign on the door saying I'd be back in ten minutes, and that was about half an hour ago."

She bid Churchill and Pemberley farewell and went on her way.

"Well, there's a bit to think about now, isn't there?" said Churchill as they watched Mrs Thonnings amble off toward the high street. "Did Mr Cobnut cut his wife's bicycle cables? Or did Miss Plimsoll do it? Perhaps the two conspired together."

"Getting rid of her would have paved the way for a happy future together, wouldn't it?" replied Pemberley.

"It certainly would."

"I can't imagine either of them doing such a brutal thing, though."

"I agree. Although doing something as sneaky as cutting a brake cable isn't quite as brutal as committing the awful act of murder in person, is it? I should think it would be a little easier for the culprit to distance him or herself from the act."

"To almost convince themselves they hadn't done it after all, you mean?"

"Yes. But if Mr Cobnut did it, why would he break into the shed? Surely he would simply have used the key. Why go to all the trouble of moving and upturning the urn when you have a key?"

Pemberley nodded. "And as the former housekeeper, Miss Plimsoll would surely have known where to find the shed key as well."

"Very true. Although they both have a motive, the damage caused to the shed counts in their favour. And I must say I'm rather baffled about the Twigs. Who are we to believe with regard to Mr Twig's drinking? Mrs Twig or Mrs Thonnings?"

"Mrs Thonnings has no reason to lie to us."

"You're right there, although she could be repeating a lie she was told herself."

"Yes, she could be. It sounds as though Mrs Twig has either lied to her or lied to us."

"Which doesn't paint Mrs Twig in a particularly good light, does it?"

"Either that or she's been telling everyone the truth and she's unfortunate enough to have a drunken husband *and* an errant son."

"It's not unheard of. Troublesome fathers often begat troublesome sons."

"Be*get*."

"Is that right?"

"I don't know."

"Begotten? Anyway, I think you catch my meaning, Pembers. I should like to meet this Mr Twig so we can judge for ourselves."

"It might seem rather odd if we merely turn up on the Twigs' doorstep."

"You're right, it might indeed. It would be helpful if we could speak to him without Mrs Twig around, if possible. We could intercept him on his way to or from the train station. Mrs Thonnings told us he has an important job in Dorchester, so all we have to do is pounce on him while he's travelling to work or back home."

"Pounce?"

"We'll obviously need to be a little more subtle than that. We'll have to engineer some sort of interaction with him."

"I think we should do it on his way back from the train station. He won't want to stop and talk to us in the morning or he'll be worried about missing his train."

"Excellent thinking, my trusty assistant. What's the time?"

"Four o'clock."

"Now, let's suppose Mr Twig finishes his Dorchester job at five o'clock. I would say that he'd probably be on the branch line by half-past five, wouldn't you?"

"Yes."

"And knowing the speed of that branch line, he'd most likely arrive in Compton Poppleford during the early hours of the following morning!"

"It's not quite that slow, Mrs Churchill. There's a train that leaves Dorchester at twenty-past five and arrives here at thirty-five minutes after six."

"Do you have the whole train timetable in your head, Pembers?"

"Yes."

"I see. Very useful. Thirty-five minutes after six, you say?"

"Yes."

"Right then, we'll find ourselves hanging about outside the station at around that time this evening. Do you know what he looks like?"

"Yes, I've seen him from afar."

"Excellent."

Chapter 18

Later that day, Churchill, Pemberley and Oswald stood loitering near Compton Poppleford train station. The stone ticket office glowed a warm gold in the evening sunlight and a tall white fence separated the platform from the street. The station master's peaked cap was visible just above the fence as he paced up and down the platform.

"What's the time now, Pembers?"

"Two minutes after you last asked."

"We're getting closer."

"I'd be worried if we weren't."

"That train should be arriving any moment."

"What are we going to say to Mr Twig?"

"Oh, I'll think of something spontaneous. If we plan it out too much it'll look rehearsed. We don't want it to sound as though we're following a script."

"I agree. It might remind him of a performance from the Compton Poppleford Amateur Dramatic Society."

"That certainly wouldn't make a good impression. I shall think of an excuse to intercept him, then you can follow my lead."

"What do we do if he's not on the train?"

"Oh gosh, I'd made the assumption that he would be. What time's the next one?"

"There's only one an hour after six o'clock."

"Which would mean having to wait here for another hour. Oh well, I suppose that's what real detective work is all about."

"It would give us enough time to fetch a bun or two from somewhere."

"Pembers, I feel quite sure that you're thinking more and more about your stomach these days."

"It's true. I didn't think about it much at all until I met you, Mrs Churchill."

"Well, the bakery will be shut by now."

"Yes, of course. Oh dear."

"Although Simpkin sometimes hangs about after closing time, doesn't he? We might be able to knock on the back door and pick something stale up. Hark! Is that the sound of a train?"

"I hope so."

The two ladies turned their heads in the direction of the train station as the steam engine appeared, puffing clouds of smoke and steam into the still evening air.

"Here we go, Pembers. Brace yourself!"

"If he's on it, that is."

"Let's hope he is."

The train slowly pulled away a few minutes later, and a smattering of people emerged from the station building before dispersing in different directions.

"Are you sure he would walk this way, Pembers?"

"This way is the most direct route to his home."

"Let's hope he follows his usual route and doesn't make a detour via the Wagon and Carrot if his wife's stories are to be believed."

The two ladies watched each person as they left the station and grew hopeful when one or two began walking in their direction.

"I think this may be him," said Pemberley.

"Really?"

"Actually, it's not. It's rather confusing when they all wear the same thing, isn't it? All in bowler hats, dark suits and briefcases. Oh, I think the next one along is him."

"The next one along?"

"Yes, there are about four who look exactly the same to me. I think it's the second of them."

"Which one are you calling the second, Pembers?" asked Churchill as she scrutinised the four suited men walking toward them.

"Not the first one, but the second one. It's quite simple."

"Simple to you, maybe. Do you mean the one with the chin?"

"They all have chins."

"I realise that, but that one has a larger chin."

"You mean the one with the largest chin of the four? I can't see the chin of the man right at the back."

"Neither can I quite yet, Pembers. Deary me. This is getting me all rather flustered now."

"The fourth one may have a large chin for all I know."

"He may well have, but given that we can only clearly see the chins of the first two men... Actually, the third chin is becoming a little clearer now, but it's less pronounced than number two, I'd say. Right then, number two with the large chin?"

"Yes, that's him."

"Right, we need to pretend to be conversing amongst ourselves now, Pembers, or all four of them will grow suspicious."

"What shall we say?"

"I don't know, we'll just make something up. What a lovely evening it is, wouldn't you say?"

"Yes indeed."

"I see the train from Dorchester has arrived on time."

"So it has."

"Can't you think of a longer response than that, Pembers? Why must I be the one thinking of all the words to say? It's quite tiring, you know."

"It appears to come more naturally to you, Mrs Churchill."

"I suppose it does, but there's no harm in you doing a little more of it."

The first suited man was upon them. Churchill gave him a polite nod. "Good evening." Then she focused her attention on the second man with the large chin who was closing in on them. "Are you sure this is him, Pembers?" she whispered.

"It's Mr Twig all right."

Churchill observed the tall, lean man striding toward them. He appeared quite intent on marching swiftly to his destination, and as he approached them Churchill found her mind emptying of all thoughts. With great horror she realised her plan of spontaneous conversation was unlikely to work in light of this. The sudden realisation that she had to think of something pertinent to say to a complete stranger and somehow detain him to get all the information she needed was thoroughly daunting.

"Erm…" she said.

"Are you all right, Mrs Churchill?"

"What are we going to say to him?" she whispered. "He doesn't look like the chatty sort."

He was only a few steps away.

"You need to speak to him *now*, Mrs Churchill, or he'll walk past."

"Righty-ho. Yes. Here we go. What to say? What to say? What to say? Erm… Good evening!" she said with a beam as she realised the moment was about to be lost. Mr Twig acknowledged her with a nod but maintained his steady stride.

"I don't suppose you've seen a goat around here, have you?" she asked, panicking that she was just about to lose him.

To Churchill's relief he stopped, even if her question did draw a scowl.

"A goat?"

"Yes. Mrs Pyeman's goat, Ramsay, has been missing for a few days now and we're on the lookout for him."

"Sorry, no." He began to walk on.

"Only I thought you might have, you see."

He stopped and turned. "Why would I have seen him?"

"Because… he was last seen in your garden."

"In my garden? How do you know where my garden is?"

"It's Mr Twig, isn't it?"

"Yes." His scowl deepened. "What do you want?"

"We want to know if you've seen the goat."

"I've already told you I haven't and, if it's been in my garden, I sincerely hope it hasn't done any damage. In fact, I don't even know how it got in there."

Churchill's mind scrambled for more words to detain him.

"Why don't you ask my wife if she's seen it?" he continued. "She's the one who's at home all day while I'm out busy working."

"We have asked her, actually... Or have we, Miss Pemberley?"

"We did speak to her, but I can't remember whether we asked about the goat."

"Indeed. Sad news about Mrs Cobnut, isn't it, Mr Twig? Your wife seemed quite upset about her passing."

"Yes. Very sad indeed." He checked his watch. "I'm afraid I must be on my way but do ask my wife about the goat if you haven't already. I'm not sure why you'd think that I might have seen it."

He turned to walk away.

"Perhaps your son has seen him," suggested Pemberley.

Mr Twig turned again, clearly irritated by the further detention. "My son?" he queried. "I don't have a son."

"Oh, I do apologise. I thought you and Mrs Twig had children."

"No, no children. Good evening, ladies."

The two elderly detectives watched him march away.

"He's rather insipid, wouldn't you say, Pembers?"

"He's not the friendliest of gentlemen, but then he does seem rather busy and important."

"And no son. No children at all, in fact! So Mrs Twig lied to Mrs Thonnings about the errant son! Do you think she lied about her husband's drinking as well?"

"It's difficult to say. He doesn't look much like a drinker, does he? He doesn't have a drinker's nose."

"You're right, he doesn't. That's when it goes all red and knobbly, isn't it?"

"Nor does he have a drinker's ruddy face or heavy jowls."

"You're right. He has the air of a teetotaller, in fact. If you ask me, the man could do with a good stiff drink to relax him a little. He seems rather uptight, doesn't he?"

"He does indeed."

"It's difficult to know what to make of the chap. That said, Mrs Twig seems to have told several large fibs, and I think we need to go and find out why."

Chapter 19

"Is that the horse we saw running down the high street the other day, Pembers?" asked Churchill as they walked back to the office. The skewbald horse was tethered to a stationary cart standing outside the town hall.

"It is indeed," replied Pemberley. "It looks as though it belongs to Farmer Glossop. Is that Monsieur Legrand he's talking to?"

"By golly, so it is," said Churchill. She observed the well-built farmer in his straw hat and shirt sleeves standing beside the horse's head and talking to the diminutive detective. "Perhaps he's thanking Monsieur Legrand for catching the poor animal."

Monsieur Legrand gave the farmer a nod and continued on his way. The two ladies drew close to Farmer Glossop, who was about to climb onto his cart.

"Is he behaving himself today?" called Churchill to the farmer, who was red-haired with a wide moustache and thick beard. With his heavy brow and bright, steely eyes, he reminded Churchill of the pictures she had seen of Viking warriors.

"Be'avin'?"

"Your horse. We saw him running along this very street the other day."

"Ah." He gave a nod. "That's right. 'E got scared off."

"Oh dear. By what?"

"By that woman." He jabbed the air with his thumb, as if to gesture in someone's direction.

"Which one?"

"The one what's died."

"Oh, you mean Mrs Cobnut?"

"That's the one."

"What happened?"

"Me cart were loaded up with veg, an' old Jasper 'ere were pullin' it. 'E's worked for me for thirty year, 'as Jasper. Reliable as they come. Don't move too fast, as a rule, but when 'e does, 'e don't 'alf move."

"So what happened?"

"We was just comin' up Dunley Lane, an' that's when I 'eard it."

"Heard what?"

"A buzzy, whirry sound, it were. I thought it were a fly in me ear, but then it got louder an' louder. Now, there ain't nothin' much as bothers Jasper, but I pulled him up all the same. 'Woah!' I says to him so we can stop an' find out where the noise is comin' from, see. Well, no sooner 'ad we stopped, I seen a bicycle and that woman on it. Travellin' much too fast, mind."

"Sounds familiar." Churchill tutted.

"Came right up be'ind us, almost deliberate, like! Well, Jasper were off. He weren't gonna let a silver machine get 'im, that's for sure. Never known him move so fast in thirty year! Trouble is, when an 'orse starts goin' like that there ain't much that'll stop 'im. We went through Mrs Graggles's back 'edge and out through 'er front 'edge. This is all with the cart still attached, mind, and meself and Flaley bouncing round on it."

"Flaley?"

"The boy what 'elps me. And he 'ad the dog under 'is arm, too. Did a good job 'anging on to 'er, 'e did. Anyways, we went on down Barfby Lane, sheddin' vegetables all the way. No sign o' the bicycle by this stage, but there were still no stoppin' Jasper. Down Barfby Lane we went, narrerly missin' Mr Browngage in 'is motor car. Then we've took a sharp left at the end o' the lane, an' that sent the cart flyin' right over. What were left o' the veg all rolled down the slope there an' ended up on the railway line. Jasper fell too, poor blighter, but 'e soon got 'imself free and took off along the 'igh street.

"Meanwhile, the station master on the platform saw what'd 'appened and come runnin' down the track wavin' his flag and blowin' his whistle at me – as if that's gonna change anythin' – and tells me to get me veg off the tracks 'cause the ten-fifteen from Dorchester's due any moment. I told 'im in no uncertain terms that if the ten-fifteen from Dorchester's due any moment I didn't wanna be down on them tracks pickin' up me veg. Me and Flaley did what we could to save 'em, but then we seen the engine comin' at us and we 'ad to 'op out the way. Most of me veg were ruined after that."

"You must have lost a lot of vegetables altogether."

"Too right I did. I was 'opin' to sell me cartload for eight pound. By the time all that palaver were over and done with I 'ad practicly nothin' left. Me cart were broken an' all. That cost a pretty penny to fix."

"You must have felt rather annoyed with Mrs Cobnut."

"Livid, I were! Absolutely fumin' livid, like you wouldn't believe, Mrs Churchill! Once I learned it was 'er on that silver machine I marched right round there and told 'er exactly what I thought of 'er."

"Did she apologise?"

"Apologise, my eye! She's always gave as good as what she got, that woman. Told me I shouldn't of 'ad such a skittish 'orse! Well, there ain't nothin' skittish about that 'orse, let me tell you. I ain't never seen 'im move faster than a trot the 'ole thirty year. Not even when 'e were in a field with Farmer Jagford's brood mare. He 'ardly moved at all that day. Quite a disappointment to all of us, that were."

"So, in summary, Mrs Cobnut caused you to lose your takings and damage your cart. And then she refused to apologise."

"Yeah."

"And how is Jasper faring now?"

"Oh, 'e's fine. Forgot all about it once that detective got 'old of 'im. Seems to 'ave a way with animals, that fellow."

Chapter 20

"Have you seen the *Compton Poppleford Gazette* this morning, Mrs Churchill?" asked Pemberley back at the office the following day.

"No, I've successfully managed to avoid it so far."

"There's an article about the wire cutters in there." She placed the newspaper on Churchill's desk.

Cobnut Bicycle Murder: A Plea to Persons Handing in Wire Cutters

By Smithy Miggins

There is no longer any space at Compton Poppleford Police Station to store all the wire cutters that have been handed in since the murder of Mrs Mildred Cobnut. Inspector Mappin made a plea to anyone who happens to find a pair of wire cutters to seriously consider whether they might have been used to cut the brake cables on Mrs Cobnut's bicycle.

"Only one pair of cutters would have been used in the incident," he told our reporter. *"However, we have received in excess of thirty pairs of wire cutters so far. While I realise many have been handed to me in good faith, some are too bent or rusty to function properly and one pair even had a broken hinge.*

"I would like to remind the public that we're looking for a pair of wire cutters in good working order, which have been reasonably well maintained, with sharp blades and an oiled mechanism. The cutters are likely to have been discarded somewhere, which means we must give more consideration to those found in a hedgerow or a body of water; the sort of places a murderer might have disposed of a murder weapon. I urge people to think carefully about the provenance and condition of any wire cutters found before handing them in to the police station.

"Having to discount irrelevant wire cutters from the investigation takes up valuable police time and creates a great deal of paperwork when we could be out there apprehending the culprit."

"How amusing," commented Churchill. "Poor Inspector Mappin grumbling about having too much police work to do! A lot of it must be rather tedious, I suppose. He should simply accept that and be grateful that members of the public are trying to be helpful. Now, let's consider our suspects. We already had Mrs Twig, Mr Cobnut and Miss Plimsoll, and now we also have Farmer Glossop. The list of possible suspects is growing by the day, Pembers."

"Do you think Farmer Glossop could have done it?"

"He has a motive, doesn't he?"

"I can't imagine him cutting the brake cables on Mrs Cobnut's bicycle."

"He lost his takings and had to pay for his cart to be repaired, and he was very angry with her. I think he needs to be considered a suspect until we can rule him out. What a perplexing case."

"And we're not even supposed to be working on it."

"Exactly, yet it still perplexes me. How I wish I could pay it no heed at all and spend my time enjoying *Forbidden Obsession* instead."

"You must be enjoying it, Mrs Churchill. I can see it there on your desk."

"Oh yes, I'd better hide it."

"Why?"

"It's rather embarrassing to have a book like that lying on one's desk, isn't it? One might expect something a little more highbrow. Something by Thomas Hardy or similar. He was a Dorset fellow, wasn't he?"

Pemberley groaned. "Yes, he was. But nothing happy ever happens in his books."

"Does it not? What a shame! Perhaps I'm better off with *Forbidden Obsession* after all. It's generally quite happy and… er…" Churchill wiped her brow. "Well, all sorts of things happen in it."

"I'll make us some tea," said Pemberley. "Would you like a nice slice of prune cake?"

"There's still some left, is there?"

"There's plenty left."

"Hasn't it gone off by now?"

Pemberley lifted the lid of the cake tin and examined its contents. "No, for some reason it doesn't seem to go off."

"Quite astonishing."

Churchill watched, with lacklustre enthusiasm, as Pemberley cut her a slice of the cake. Then she picked up her paperback, but footsteps on the stairs prompted her to reluctantly put it down again.

"Good morning, Inspector," she said as Inspector

Mappin stepped in through the door. "Oh, and Monsieur Legrand as well."

The two men gave her a polite nod.

"You're just in time for tea and prune cake," she added.

"Tea would be nice, thank you, though I'd say it's a little too early for cake."

"I see. You have rules about cake, do you, Inspector?"

"Very much so."

"Please take a seat."

The two men did so.

"Any arrests in the case of Mrs Cobnut yet?" asked Churchill.

"Not yet."

"You must be finding it rather a tricky one."

"It's complicated, but nothing we can't handle, Mrs Churchill. I hope you don't have any designs on this case yourself."

"Absolutely not."

"Good." He retrieved his notebook from his pocket and settled himself in a manner that suggested he intended to remain there for a fair while. He cleared his throat and began: "I'm trying to establish where everyone was on the night Mrs Cobnut's brake cables were cut."

"I assume everyone was at home, Inspector. Apart from the culprit, that is."

"A sensible observation. You were at home yourself that night, were you, Mrs Churchill?"

"Of course I was."

"Do you have an alibi?"

"A what? Someone there with me, you mean? What an impertinent question, Inspector!" Churchill felt her face flush.

"Why would that be impertinent? I realise you're a

widow, Mrs Churchill, but you may have had a visitor or two staying with you that night. Or perhaps you have staff."

"I'm not so grand as to have staff, Inspector."

"Any visitors, then?"

"None. I live alone and no one was staying with me at the time."

"I see."

Inspector Mappin wrote something down in his note-book and Monsieur Legrand stroked his moustache.

"What are you writing down, Inspector?" she asked.

"I'm just making a note of your alibi, Mrs Churchill, or lack thereof. Did you go anywhere that evening?"

"No, I was at home all evening. Though I wish I'd been somewhere or had visitors staying now." She glanced across at Monsieur Legrand, fervently hoping her apparent lack of alibi wouldn't lead him to think that she could be guilty of vandalising Mrs Cobnut's bicycle.

"Perhaps there was someone you made a telephone call to," suggested Inspector Mappin. "Someone who could vouch for the fact that you were home for at least part of the evening."

"Farmer Drumhead's cottage doesn't have a telephone, Inspector. I have to go to the farmhouse if I wish to make a telephone call."

"And did you?"

"No, I didn't. Although, once again, I now find myself wishing I had done so. I remained at home alone all evening and all night, which is quite usual for me, to tell you the truth. And besides, Inspector, how would I even get to Mrs Cobnut's cottage? It's about three miles from my house."

"Walking there wouldn't be beyond the realms of possibility."

"How about a taxi?" suggested Pemberley.

"Whose side are you on, Miss Pemberley?" asked Churchill.

"No one's side," replied her secretary, looking perplexed. "It was just a thought."

"I've made enquiries with Mr Speakman, the taxi driver," said Mappin, "and he confirmed that he didn't take anyone to Haggerton Cottage that night. I suppose you could have bicycled there, Mrs Churchill."

"I did not ride a bicycle to Mrs Cobnut's cottage in the middle of the night, Inspector. And besides, I would never have made it up Grindledown Hill."

"You could have dismounted and walked up."

"If I'd tried to bicycle to her home that's probably what I would have done, but I didn't. I was tucked up in bed! Why are you asking me for an alibi, anyway?"

"Because you were on less than friendly terms with Mrs Cobnut."

"As were most of the people around here! There's Mrs Twig for one. And Farmer Glossop. And what about Mr Cobnut and Miss Plimsoll? They're all very fishy, Inspector. Wouldn't you agree, Monsieur Legrand?"

The Swiss detective gave a polite nod.

"I don't disagree that Mrs Cobnut was on unfriendly terms with a number of people," said Inspector Mappin, "but we have our list of suspects now, Mrs Churchill, and your name happens to be on it."

Chapter 21

"The cheek of it, Pembers! That absurd Inspector Mappin grilling me about an alibi, and all the while there's that renowned detective eying me up and down, no doubt making all manner of deductions based on what I was saying."

"Well, if he's as brilliant as they say he is he'll know you had nothing to do with it, Mrs Churchill."

"Yes, that's true. But it doesn't stop him doing all that assessing and scrutinising while I'm talking, does it? Have you noticed the way he stares at people? It's rather like being an exhibit in a freak show. And I was particularly bothered when the inspector kept mentioning that alibi business. I don't know how he can expect someone who lives alone to have an alibi in the middle of the night!"

"He doesn't know what else to ask you about, that's all."

"There's only one thing for it, Pembers." Churchill got up from her chair. "It's high time we put our trusty incident board together."

"But it's not our job to investigate this case!"

"True, but I'm not having that hapless inspector or that pensive detective suspecting I'm somehow responsible for cutting Mrs Cobnut's brake cables. Now that I'm a suspect I can feel the screws tightening. I may be forced to prove my innocence if things continue in this vein. It's quite ridiculous, really. It makes you wonder whether that so-called expert detective is all he's really cracked up to be. It's quite obvious they're not on the right path, isn't it? And besides, I've never read anything quite so boring as *The Famous Cases of Monsieur Pascal Legrand.*"

"Perhaps he's just calling our bluff. Isn't that what renowned detectives do?"

"Oh yes, they play all sorts of games like that, but as we can't be exactly sure what he's up to, it makes sense to carry out a few investigations of our own." Churchill marched over to a map hanging on the office wall next to a portrait of King George V. "Where is Mrs Cobnut's house on here?"

"Here," replied Pemberley, joining her at the map and sticking a pin into the board.

"Jolly good. I see Grindledown Hill now."

"Yes, the accident occurred on that first bend, by Sloping Field." Another pin went in.

"Good. Now we need some pictures of our suspects. We need Mrs Twig up there."

"Do you really think Mrs Twig could have killed Mrs Cobnut?"

"I realise she doesn't look like the violent sort, Pembers, but let's remember that the method used meant the culprit didn't have to do anything quite so direct as pull the trigger of a gun or inflict injuries with a blade. No, this was a fairly non-violent, sneaky sort of murder. Rather like a poisoning. The culprit laid a trap, then merely waited for the victim to succumb."

"Ah yes, scheming and sneaky. I can imagine Mrs Twig being both of those things."

"Indeed. So let's put her up there. And I think we need to consider Farmer Glossop, too. You saw how enraged he was about the upended cart incident and, seeing that Mrs Cobnut was unrepentant, he probably feared a repeat performance. What better way to put a stop to it than by vandalising her bicycle?"

"I suppose the murderer may not have intended to murder Mrs Cobnut. The perpetrator may have hoped she would simply endure a nasty fall."

"Yes, we shouldn't discount that theory. The culprit may be as horrified as we are that she ended up dead. But removing a bicycle's braking capability is quite a serious business, especially when you consider the speed she was in the habit of travelling at on downhill gradients. I think the culprit must have known she would come to serious harm. Now then, who else? Ah yes, we also have the housekeeper, Miss Plimsoll."

"Because Mrs Cobnut dismissed her?"

"Yes, that could be the motive, couldn't it? Revenge. And then we have Mr Cobnut."

"The suspicious husband."

"Indeed. He's the one who had easiest access to the bicycle in the shed. The other three suspects would have had to sneak their way in there, while he could have simply got up in the middle of the night, unlocked the shed and attacked the bicycle without anyone knowing."

"But the culprit got in through the window."

"Perhaps the break-in was staged by Mr Cobnut."

"Oh, I like that idea."

"Well it's not an idea one should really like, as such, because we're talking about murder here. However, it is the sort of thing a scheming murderer would do to put people off the scent, isn't it?"

"Yes. He may be hoping that if people assumed the murderer had been forced to break into the shed it couldn't possibly have been him because there would have been no need for him to damage his own shed to gain access."

"Indeed. Four suspects, then."

"The snippers must be somewhere, too."

"Snippers?"

"The ones used to cut the wire."

"Ah, yes. They're probably sitting among that huge pile handed in at the police station, only Mappin has no clue which ones they are. It's possible they have fingerprints on them, although it's also possible the culprit wore gloves. I'd say that was very likely, in fact, because a lot of planning seems to have gone into all this. Whoever it was moved the urn, broke the window and carried out their act of sabotage. It was all carefully thought out. Oh dear, I've just remembered there's a little toolbox in the cupboard under the stairs at my place that will undoubtedly have a pair of cutters inside it. Can you imagine what would happen if Inspector Mappin were to discover it? Especially seeing as I don't have an alibi for the night Mrs Cobnut's bicycle was vandalised! He'd put two and two together and make five. Oh Pembers, I could be in terrible trouble this time!"

"Inspector Mappin wouldn't be allowed to search your home without a warrant," said Pemberley.

"But he could search it if I allowed him to, couldn't he? If he politely asked to search my home and I refused he would assume I had something to hide!"

"I don't think it'll come to that, Mrs Churchill."

"It's got every chance of coming to that, I'm on his list of suspects. You heard the man say so himself!"

"There is one way you can prove that you didn't vandalise Mrs Cobnut's bicycle."

"Brilliant, Pembers. How?"

"The culprit climbed in through the shed window."

"Yes?"

"And…" Pemberley trailed off for a moment, saying nothing further but glancing up and down at Churchill's large frame.

"Spit it out, then."

"Well… do you recall when you got stuck in the window at the offices of the *Compton Poppleford Gazette*?"

"Yes, although I don't see why you feel the need to remind me of that now. Oh, I see!" Churchill glanced down at her vast bosom. "Yes! I got stuck in that office window, which is presumably much larger than the window of a shed."

"That's what I was thinking."

"Only someone skinny like you could clamber through a shed window, Pemberley."

"Well, we don't know the exact size of the shed window. Perhaps the Cobnuts' shed has a particularly large window, though it's not common for them to be big."

"There's only one way to find out, isn't there? We shall have to go over there and take a look at the shed window."

"I can't see Mr Cobnut liking that."

"Well, we can ask him and see what he says. I can't face walking all the way up that hill, though. Shall we travel by taxi?"

Chapter 22

Pemberley telephoned the taxi driver, and a short while later she and Churchill were in a cab travelling up Grindledown Hill toward Haggerton Cottage.

"You got business with Mr Cobnut?" asked Mr Speakman, the heavy-jowled taxi driver.

"Yes, we're visiting him."

"Interviewin' 'im for your detective agency, are you?"

"Not as such. We're leaving all that to the police."

"Shame about 'is wife," continued the taxi driver. "They reckon one of 'em in that bicycling club done it."

"Is that so?" asked Churchill. "Who is 'they'?"

"Dunno any specifics; it's just what people's sayin'. She weren't popular with 'em. Made 'em go up steep 'ills, she did."

"They could have refused."

"No they couldn't of. She made 'em."

"I see."

"I reckon one of 'em did it, any'ow."

"To stop her making them bicycle up steep hills?"

"Yeah. It were either one o' them or Miss Garthorn."

"Who's she?"

"She went off an' set up the South Bungerly Ladies' Bicyclin' Club."

Churchill gasped. "A rival club?"

"You could say that. 'Ere's the Cobnuts' place." The taxi stopped outside Haggerton Cottage. "Or *Mr* Cobnut's place, I should say."

Churchill peered out to see a long, low, white building hugging the top of the hill.

"Would you be able to wait for us?" Churchill asked Mr Speakman. "We won't be long."

He shook his head. "I gotta pick up Mr and Mrs Grafts from the station."

"Ah. It's times like this when I wish there happened to be more than one taxi car in the village."

"Won't take me long, then I'll come back up the 'ill and pick you up, Mrs Churchill."

"That would be most kind of you."

The two ladies and Oswald got out of the car and surveyed the cottage.

"Mr Cobnut certainly enjoys a nice view from up here, doesn't he?"

"As did Mrs Cobnut prior to all this," replied Pemberley.

"Quite true." Churchill made a full rotation as she took in the view of rolling hills and distant church spires. "Quite a panorama. A little windy, though."

"I'm nervous about what Mr Cobnut might say. I don't think he'll want us here."

"I'm sure he won't but let's try to talk him round. I feel confident that we'll achieve a promising result if we approach this in an upbeat manner. An orange fence?"

Churchill gave the picket fencing a bemused glance. "What an odd choice of colour."

They proceeded down the garden path toward the front door.

"I think we need to speak to Miss Garthorn after we've finished here," continued Churchill. "Do you know anything about the South Bungerly Ladies' Bicycling Club, Pembers?"

"I've never heard of them, but then they are based in a different village."

"And judging by what Mr Speakman just told us, Mrs Cobnut and Miss Garthorn had a falling out. Let's take a look at the Cobnuts' shed window and find out a little more."

A long silence followed Churchill's knock at the door, during which the wind moaned around the cottage. She noticed the curtains were drawn at every window.

Churchill knocked again. There was more silence, but then the door gave a crack and a jerk before opening slightly.

The handsome yet stern face of Mr Cobnut appeared. His wavy grey hair was neatly parted.

"Can I help you?"

"Good morning, Mr Cobnut. We're so sorry to trouble you at this difficult time. I'm Mrs Churchill and this is Miss Pemberley. We're private detectives."

"The police are seeing to everything, thank you."

"I realise that. How reassuring for you."

He gave a sad nod.

"I must say that I've been placed in the rather tricky situation of becoming a suspect."

Mr Cobnut's eyes widened, as did the gap between the door and its frame.

"Really, Mrs Churchill?"

"Yes. Your wife and I exchanged a few choice words, you see, but it was nothing more than that."

"Oh, she was like that."

"So I gather. The thing is, Inspector Mappin seems to think there's a possibility that I could have squeezed myself through your shed window!"

Mr Cobnut politely looked her up and down.

"I'm fairly sure I wouldn't fit through your shed window. Don't you agree, Mr Cobnut?"

"Well, I... I don't think it's my place to say. I will say, however, that I know what it's like to be a suspect. I've been on the receiving end of a few tough questions from Inspector Mappin myself."

"How awful for you, given that you're a grieving widower."

The door opened wider still and Mr Cobnut leaned against the doorframe, seemingly warming to the conversation. He wore the same sleeveless green pullover he had been wearing when Churchill and Pemberley spied him down at the allotments.

"It's an odd thing indeed," he mused. "I keep expecting Mildred to march back into the house in her bicycling breeches and make me a cup of tea."

"How terribly sad," sympathised Pemberley.

"You must miss her very much," added Churchill. "It's such a terrible thing. Were your wife's suspicions not aroused at all when she discovered the broken window and upturned urn?"

"They were, but we assumed it was an attempted burglary. We had a good look around the place but when we saw nothing had been taken, we decided they must have given up. There were a few gardening tools in the shed they could have stolen, but for some reason they left them behind. Well, I know the reason they didn't now, but at the time I couldn't really fathom it. The bicycle was too big to be taken out through the window, of course.

"In the end we decided it was probably just bored youths messing about. Mildred told me she would report the damage to Inspector Mappin when she arrived in the village, and we left it at that. Neither of us thought to check whether her bicycle had been tampered with. I think she was simply relieved it was still there after the break-in. She rode off and…" He swiftly pulled a handkerchief from his pocket and held it over his eyes.

"I'm so sorry, Mr Cobnut," said Churchill. Then she recalled him climbing out of the hedge with his house-keeper and felt a little less sympathetic. "Miss Plimsoll must be rather upset too," she added.

"Yes, she is," he responded, his handkerchief still covering his eyes. "Mildred dismissed her but Miss Plim-soll was very forgiving about it all. She's terribly upset so I've decided to reinstate her to smooth things over." He removed the handkerchief, folded it up and placed it back in his pocket. "I need someone to look after the house and she needs employment. It was a silly falling out, really. I'm sure Mildred would have taken her back anyway."

"Really?"

"Yes. You seem surprised about that, Mrs Churchill."

"Well, we happened to speak to Miss Plimsoll while we were looking for a lost goat and she said that your wife seemed determined to make life difficult for her; even going to the lengths of telling all her friends not to employ her."

He gave a sad laugh. "Oh, that was just Mildred for you. Miss Plimsoll knew what she was like, but she always came round in the end. She fell out with a lot of people and then she made up with them again. Our marriage was the same. She would have made up with you eventually, too."

"Would she?"

"Oh yes. You'd have found a little gift on your doorstep before long."

"Left by your wife?"

"Yes! A bottle of Mrs Gollywood's elderflower wine or something like that, I should think. That was Mildred, I'm afraid. Confrontational one moment and then apologetic the next. And very much missed…"

The handkerchief came out again and Churchill waited patiently while Mr Cobnut dried his eyes and blew his nose.

"Yet after all I've been through, Inspector Mappin still asks me such harsh questions," he added bitterly.

"That's Inspector Mappin for you," responded Churchill. "I suppose harsh questioning is something he simply has to do."

"But isn't it obvious that there would have been no need for me to break into my own shed?"

"Very obvious, Mr Cobnut."

"There were some rather lovely petunias in that urn, and somebody tipped them out on the ground! No thought at all for the plants."

"Or for your wife's life," added Pemberley.

"Exactly! That just shows you the sort of person we're dealing with."

"Who knew that your wife kept her bicycle in the shed?"

"I don't know. I couldn't name anyone specifically. Perhaps she mentioned it to someone or perhaps they saw her moving it in and out of there. Or perhaps it was merely an assumption. The shed is the only outbuilding we have here, so the culprit wouldn't have to have been a genius to establish that the bicycle would be kept there."

"True. I heard that you didn't entirely approve of your wife's bicycling hobby, Mr Cobnut."

"I didn't *not* approve. In fact, I would have wholly approved if it hadn't taken over her life in the way that it did."

"So you *slightly* disapproved?"

"I suppose you could say that, yes."

"And did this slight disapproval of her bicycling hobby create any disagreements between you?"

"Yes, a few. I was a little annoyed that I had to do more for myself around the house, especially after she'd sent Miss Plimsoll packing."

"And you took umbrage at that?"

"A little. But I reasoned that Mildred would grow tired of bicycling before long and bring Miss Plimsoll back, and then everything would return to how it had been before."

"That rarely happens in life," said Pemberley.

"An interesting point, Miss Pemberley," said Churchill.

"It never does, though, does it?" continued Pemberley. "I can't tell you how many times I've hoped life would return to how it was before, but it never has done. I've learned not to expect it now."

"That's certainly been true in my case," said Mr Cobnut, "because now my wife is dead."

"Indeed, Mr Cobnut, and we really are terribly sorry about that."

"I won't deny that there were a few disagreements between us, but that's quite normal, isn't it? And besides, we spent a very pleasant few days in the Peak District not so long ago."

"Oh, how lovely. My late husband and I enjoyed several breaks there. Whereabouts did you stay?"

"Just a little place. You won't have heard of it."

"Try me. You never know, Mr Cobnut."

"Cresswell End."

"Never heard of it."

"It was a delightful place. Little did I know that it would be our last ever excursion." He wiped his brow with his handkerchief.

"I'm so sorry, Mr Cobnut. Now, I wonder... would you mind awfully if we had a quick look at your shed?"

"I'd rather you didn't."

"It would be terribly helpful if you'd allow us to, Mr Cobnut. If I can prove that there's no possible way I could have fitted through the window, I can be ruled out as a suspect."

"That may suit you, Mrs Churchill, but what about me? How do I get myself ruled out as a suspect?"

"By the very fact that someone forcibly gained entry to your shed. As you say, there was no need for you to break into it. Now, if I could just see if..."

"I would prefer it if you stayed away from the shed, Mrs Churchill. There have been enough people poking around it over the past few days, and each time they do it reminds me of the terrible tragedy that's occurred." His voice became choked once again.

Pemberley gave Churchill a sad glance and Churchill realised it would be unfair to ask a third time.

"Oh, all right, then. Thank you for taking the time to speak to us, Mr Cobnut. I feel sure that the culprit will be caught very soon. Especially with Monsieur Legrand on the case."

"I hope so. He seems a pleasant enough chap, and he doesn't insist on questioning me the way Inspector Mappin does."

"He's an observer."

"I see."

"Are you sure there's no chance at all that we could just have a tiny little peek at your…"

"I'm afraid not, Mrs Churchill. I need to go and have a lie down now, my head hurts."

"Of course, Mr Cobnut. Thank you anyway."

Chapter 23

"WELL, I SUPPOSE THAT SETTLES IT, PEMBERS."

The two ladies and their dog walked back down the garden path.

"Now we'll have to wait for Mr Speakman to fetch us again," said Pemberley. "I suppose we could start walking and meet him as he comes up Grindledown Hill."

"Yes, that's a good idea. Better than milling around here while we wait. Oh, how frustrating that Mr Cobnut wouldn't let us look at his shed! It was the last chance we had to prove my innocence to Inspector Mappin."

"Not necessarily the last chance, Mrs Churchill. There may be other opportunities."

"Such as? Oh, isn't he an annoying police inspector? If he hadn't gone and asked me all those questions about alibis and so on, I wouldn't have felt the need to prove him wrong. How infuriating."

The two ladies walked toward the hill and turned a bend in the road that ran alongside the periphery of the Cobnuts' garden.

"Cresswell End," mused Churchill. "I really haven't

heard of it at all. I shall have to look it up on a map. Oh, look!"

A large wooden shed loomed into view as they walked past the garden.

"There it is, Pembers. Just ten yards away!"

"But where's the window?"

"It must be on the other side."

"Are you sure it's the right shed?"

"I can't see any other shed in the garden, can you? And Mr Cobnut said they only had the one outbuilding. Oh, how tempting!"

"Tempting?"

"To go and have a look!"

"Oh no, Mrs Churchill. You mustn't."

"What's between us and the shed at this moment, Pembers? Just a scrap of grass and a little low fence, which would be easily stepped over. I can see how straightforward it would have been for the culprit to tamper with the bicycle now. It's very accessible."

"Once he or she had broken into the shed, that is."

"That was easily achieved through the smashing of the window. Oh, it must be just over on the other side. And look how far the shed is from the house. I'd say it was an easy forty yards. Fifty, even!"

"We really shouldn't go over there, Mrs Churchill. Mr Cobnut forbade us, and it's his private property. Besides, he's a grieving widower. It would be terribly rude to upset him even more than we already have."

"But he'll never know, Pembers. He's up there in that house with the curtains drawn, and the shed is just a hop, skip and a jump away from us. I'd wager that I could nip over there, take a peek at the window and be back here in two shakes of a lamb's tail."

"Which is how long, exactly?"

"Two minutes. A mere two minutes."

"What happens if he spots you?"

"He won't. He can't even see out of his house with the curtains drawn. Oh, come on, Pembers. We didn't pay a shilling's worth of taxi fare for nothing. And it'll be another shilling to get back to the village again. I know I can prove Inspector Mappin wrong in just two minutes' time."

"And what if the window is enormous?"

"It's unlikely, isn't it? And if it is, I'll just have to think of something else. But for the time being, it's just over there and we're just over here, and I feel certain it can be quickly investigated with no disruption to Mr Cobnut whatsoever."

"I see that nothing I could say or do will persuade you otherwise, Mrs Churchill."

"Of course it couldn't. Now, you wait here with Oswald and I won't be a moment."

Churchill checked all around her to make sure nobody was watching, then tiptoed through the long grass toward the low fence. Before stepping over it, she peered up at the house at the top of the garden just to ensure that every window was covered. Feeling sure that it was, she hitched up her tweed skirt, raised one leg and stepped over the fence.

As soon as her foot touched down on Mr Cobnut's lawn Churchill felt an excitable tingle of anticipation. She brought the next foot over and scampered over to the rear of the shed in order to stay out of view of the house.

Once she had reached the back of the shed, she turned to face Pemberley and Oswald and gave them a thumbs up signal. Then she proceeded to make her way around to the other side of the shed to examine the window.

Churchill's heart thudded heavily, and she felt the hairs on the back of her neck prickle as she continued her way around it, knowing she wasn't supposed to be there. She suddenly remembered playing truant from her grammar lessons at Princess Alexandra's School for Young Ladies.

As soon as she turned the corner of the shed, Churchill saw, with great delight, the upturned urn on the ground. Around it lay countless small shards of shattered glass. As she glanced upward, she saw the smashed window. Churchill smiled to herself as she observed how untouched the crime scene was. It was completely as the culprit had left it, with no tidying up carried out. Trying to avoid the broken glass, she stepped closer to the broken window and peered inside to see various dusty garden implements basking under heavy cobwebs in a ray of sunshine. At the centre of the shed was a space where Mrs Cobnut's bicycle must once have stood.

Turning her attention back to the window, Churchill mentally tried to ascertain the size of it. Then she fetched a measuring tape from her handbag and began to measure. There was barely any glass left in the windowpane, and she imagined the culprit wearing thick gloves to smash out as much of the glass as possible. Churchill figured the intruder had done well to achieve it without the Cobnuts hearing anything. As she glanced back at the house, she saw that it was a reasonable distance away; perhaps a little too far away for the sound of breaking glass to be heard.

"Twenty-five by twenty-five inches," she muttered to herself as she measured the windowpane. "It must have been rather a slender murderer." She smiled as she put her tape measure back in her handbag, knowing there was no possible way she could have fitted through the window. Then she looked at the little windowsill and the ground around her feet for any clues the culprit might have left that Inspector Mappin and his men hadn't yet spotted.

"What do you think you're doing?" came a voice from

behind her. It sounded far away, somewhere up near the house, but it was unmistakably Mr Cobnut's.

Churchill jumped, wondering whether to try to explain her presence or to simply run away without another word. She decided to face him and saw that he was striding down the sloping garden toward her.

"Oh hello, Mr Cobnut! I was just walking past your shed, and I thought that as it was so nearby there wouldn't be any harm done if I quickly looked in."

She wasn't close enough to see his face clearly, but she detected a scowl.

"I'm just leaving!" she called out, scurrying away. "Bye!"

"This is trespass!" he shouted after her.

Churchill launched one leg over the low fence. The other was about to follow when she realised she had been brought to an instant halt. She glanced down to see that her skirt was caught on a rusty nail.

"Oh, darn it!" Her fingers fumbled with the material as she hastily tried to unhook it. The knowledge that Mr Cobnut was swiftly catching up with her made her fingers fumble more than ever. "Curse this Harris tweed!" she fumed. "It's so strong I can't free it!"

"I'm calling the police!" threatened Mr Cobnut.

Churchill brought her other leg over the fence and lurched away with as much strength as she could muster. She closed her eyes with bitter regret as she heard the sound of her skirt ripping. Once she was free, she dashed through the long grass to where Pemberley and Oswald were waiting.

"Everything all right?" asked Pemberley.

'Why don't you try asking my skirt?"

"Whatever for?"

"Look at the state of it! It got caught on the fence.

Come on, let's move. Cobnut's after us." Churchill began scampering down the hill.

"He saw you?" lamented Pemberley, hurrying after her.

"Yes, I have no idea how. I really don't know how he saw me with all the curtains closed."

"He probably decided to peer through a gap so he could keep an eye on us as we left."

"Well, that's just strange."

"But also understandable. We were poking about and being nosey, weren't we? Knowing that we'd pass his shed on the way down the hill, he probably decided to watch us."

Churchill stopped and glared at her assistant. "Telling me all this now isn't very helpful, Pembers. If you thought he was likely to look out for us, why didn't you tell me that before I decided to look at the shed?"

"I tried to talk you out of it. And I only thought of those other things after he saw you. It's the benefit of hindsight, I suppose."

"Hindsight is so terribly annoying. I wish people didn't have to refer to it. There's nothing to be gained from it whatsoever, other than a deep sense of regret that one did what one did. Come on, we need to keep moving down this hill."

The two ladies and their dog trotted on.

"The good news is that I'm much too big to fit through the shed window," puffed Churchill.

"That's very good news."

"So for the purposes of our no doubt imminent conversation with Inspector Mappin, I could see that it would have been completely impossible for me to fit through it."

"Then you're in the clear!"

"Yes, but then I always was, wasn't I? With that expert

detective on hand there's no way I could reasonably have been suspected of something I hadn't done. I simply wanted to prove Inspector Mappin wrong so he would stop asking me for alibis. But Mr Cobnut said he intended to call the police, so that fool inspector will have something new to berate me about. I think I can hear Mr Speakman's taxi approaching. Thank goodness for that."

Chapter 24

"Stop here, please, Mr Speakman!" ordered Churchill.

"But why?" asked Pemberley. "We haven't reached our office yet."

The taxi halted beside the duck pond.

"I realise that, but I want to know who *he* is," said Churchill, pointing out of the window.

"Who?"

"The gentleman stood at the Twigs' front door," replied Churchill. "Do you know him?"

The two ladies and the taxi driver stared at the squat, dark-suited man. He wore a trilby hat and had bicycle clips around the bottom of his trousers. A bicycle was leaning up against the Twigs' front fence.

"That's Bobby Storks," announced Mr Speakman.

"And who might he be?"

"He's a well-known local face."

"Just his face?"

"And the rest of 'im."

"And how is his face, and the rest of him, well-known?"

"'E does various things of what you might call a shady nature."

"A criminal visiting the Twigs?"

"Nothin' too serious, mind, but nothin' entirely above the law, neither. Though you never 'eard it from me."

"It looks as though he's pocketing something," said Churchill. "Has Mrs Twig just given him something?"

"Proberly," replied Mr Speakman. "How long you plannin' on waitin' 'ere? I got another job."

"Right, we'll get out, then."

Churchill, Pemberley and Oswald clambered out of the taxi and paid Mr Speakman his fare.

"Let's pretend to walk around the duck pond, Pembers," whispered Churchill.

"Pretend to walk around it or actually walk around it?"

"Oh, all right. Let's *actually* walk around it."

"So we're not pretending at all."

"No. I don't really know why I used that word now I come to think of it."

The two ladies began a circuit around the duck pond while keeping half an eye on Bobby Storks, who remained chatting on Mrs Twig's doorstep. Oswald jumped into the pond, setting a number of ducks quacking with alarm.

"What do you know of this Stork chap?" Churchill whispered to Pemberley.

"Not much. He's the sort of chap who seems to have a finger in every pie."

"I know the sort you mean."

"*Criminal* pies."

"I wonder what criminal pies taste like. Mind you, I don't think I'd like to know if his fingers have been inside them."

The two ladies paused and observed Bobby Storks from their position on the other side of the duck pond.

They could just make out the form of Mrs Twig in the doorway as he appeared to bid her farewell. Bobby made his way over to the bicycle leaning against the fence, and Churchill and Pemberley continued on their way.

"I wonder if his visit was a one-off or whether it's a regular thing," whispered Churchill. "I suppose there's only one way to find out."

Pemberley groaned. "Surveillance?"

"Absolutely."

"But I hate doing surveillance. It's boring and we always get caught."

"What would you rather, Pembers? Should we simply ignore the fact that a known criminal has just called upon Mrs Twig? A lady who may have been involved in the murder of Mrs Cobnut?"

"I suppose we can't just ignore it. Perhaps we could ask her about him instead."

"What would we ask?"

"We could ask what he was doing visiting her. We could say we're concerned because we saw a known criminal calling at her home."

"And what do you suppose she'd say to that?"

"She'd either tell us it's none of our business or she'd tell all and find it a great relief to get everything off her chest."

"I think any sort of explanation from Mrs Twig is likely to complicate the situation even further. Given her track record, she'll only concoct another story to confuse us once again. Asking Mrs Twig isn't the answer."

"What do we do, then?"

"We speak to this Storks fellow."

Pemberley shuddered. "I wouldn't much like to speak to him myself."

"I can't say that I particularly relish the idea either. But we need to be able to explain why a middle-aged, middle-class lady bicyclist would have a known crook calling at her door."

"Maybe it was something to do with bicycles."

"What makes you say that?"

"Bobby Storks bicycled here, so maybe they share a mutual love of bicycles."

"They might, I suppose. But why would he call on her and pocket something she had given him? It's all a bit suspicious if you ask me, especially when you consider that she's been telling a fair few fibs lately."

Chapter 25

"Trespassing is a serious offence, Mrs Churchill," said Inspector Mappin as he stood in front of her desk.

"I can think of far more serious offences, Inspector."

"Yes, there are plenty of those, but you can't use them to somehow diminish the seriousness of what you've done yourself."

"I merely took a peek at Mr Cobnut's shed, Inspector."

"Which happens to be on Mr Cobnut's land, after he had expressly forbidden you to do so."

"At least I tried to seek his permission first."

"That doesn't lessen the impact of the offence."

"It would demonstrate good character in a court of law."

"It would demonstrate better character if you hadn't trespassed in the first place."

"I was driven to it, Inspector, don't you see?"

"Driven to it?"

"By you, with all your questioning of me. I felt quite perturbed that you thought I might be guilty of Mrs Cobnut's murder. All that business about an alibi when I didn't have one. I thought if I demonstrated that I couldn't possibly have fitted through the shed window you'd realise I must be innocent."

"There was no need for you to investigate for yourself, Mrs Churchill."

"I think there was. If I'd suggested checking the window size you'd have merely replied that you didn't have time to go around measuring shed windows because you had too much on your plate, or words to that effect."

"And how big is the shed window?"

"Twenty-five inches by twenty-five inches."

"And may I ask your personal measurements?"

"No you may not! But I'm sure you can see from the width of my shoulders that I wouldn't be able to fit through a window of that size. Do you recall the time when I found myself stuck in a window at the *Compton Poppleford Gazette* offices?"

"Ah yes, another trespass incident. It never looks good when a defendant has committed previous offences of a similar kind."

"Mr Trollope decided not to press charges, Inspector, so in the eyes of the law there was no offence."

"It still doesn't look good."

"I don't suppose it does, but my hand was forced, Inspector, and there we have it. I stepped about four yards onto Mr Cobnut's land, measured a broken window and then returned to the public lane close by. I was there for approximately three minutes in total. I also ruined a thoroughly decent skirt. If you'd like to make a big song and a dance about it, please do, but I'm not sure what the residents of Compton Poppleford will make of your harsh pursuit of a vulnerable old lady when there's a murder to solve."

Inspector Mappin sniffed and rubbed at his whiskers.

"You do realise Mr Cobnut is a widower and your actions have caused him severe upset, don't you?"

"What I did was far less upsetting than the fact that the culprit who murdered his wife is still at large. I imagine Mr Cobnut might feel a little consoled once the killer is caught. Where's your Swiss detective friend this afternoon, Inspector?"

He folded up his notebook. "I don't know. We don't live in each other's pockets, you know."

"I've become quite accustomed to seeing the pair of you together."

"I am capable of investigating Mrs Cobnut's murder without him, if that's what you're alluding to, Mrs Churchill."

"I'm sure you are, Inspector. Did I say anything to the contrary?"

"No, but it was implied in what you didn't say."

"Golly, you're beginning to sound more like the great detective every day. Returning to the subject of Mr Cobnut, you are aware of his friendship with his house-keeper, Miss Plimsoll, are you not?"

"*Former* housekeeper."

"Ah, but he's taken her back. Did you know that?"

Inspector Mappin reopened his notebook and made a quick note on a blank page. "No, I can't say I did know that."

"Rather interesting, wouldn't you say?"

"I don't see why you've got it in for Mr Cobnut all of a sudden. He's a grieving man."

"With his devoted housekeeper consoling him."

"Why ever not? The poor chap needs someone to comfort him. I'm not sure why you've set up an incident board for this case either when you're not supposed to be meddling in it."

"I had no choice, Inspector. That incident board is my defence!"

He tutted and put his notebook away. "I'm going to issue you with a warning, Mrs Churchill. If you go near Mr Cobnut or his property again, I shall have no other option than to arrest you."

"How near is *near*, Inspector?"

"Must you always make me split hairs? Twenty yards. Will that do?"

"I suppose so."

"Good. Now stay out of it!"

"Can I be disregarded as a suspect now that it's obvious I couldn't possibly have fitted through the shed window?"

"I shall have to visit the place myself with a tape measure before I can confirm that."

"I'd be grateful if you would do so at your earliest convenience. I should like to be disregarded as soon as possible."

"A nice piece of prune cake will cheer you up, Mrs Churchill," said Pemberley once Inspector Mappin had departed.

"I'm not sure it will on this occasion, Pembers. My mind has become entirely consumed by this case."

"By the way, I found some prune cake in your wastepaper basket when I was emptying it yesterday."

"Really? I can't imagine how that happened."

"You must have put it in there."

"Ah, I remember now. It must have been the piece I accidentally dropped on the floor, so I put it in the bin. Anyway, where does Miss Garthorn live?"

"The lady the taxi driver told us about? The one who set up the South Bungerly Ladies' Bicycling Club?"

"Yes."

"I think she lives in one of those houses down by the river."

"She doesn't live in South Bungerly?"

"No."

"Interesting. Right, well we need to have a little chat with her this afternoon. And before we leave, I think we need to find out which hotel Mr and Mrs Cobnut stayed at when they visited the Peak District."

"Why?"

"If I can speak to a hotel manager who may have witnessed a dreadful disagreement between the two it would strengthen the case for Mr Cobnut being a suspect, wouldn't you say? We could make a telephone call to that new directory enquiry service and find out how many hotels there are in Creswell End. As I've never heard of the place, I'm hoping it's rather small with only a few hotels."

"What a good idea," said Pemberley. "I'll telephone them and find out."

"Thank you, Pembers. And could you please ask your friend Mrs Frosling if we can borrow her bicycles again?"

"Really, Mrs Churchill? After the disastrous situation we found ourselves in the last time?"

"Why do you always feel the need to bring that up? It was far from a disaster; merely a minor collision with Colonel Slingsby's car. Besides, it was all his chauffeur's fault."

Chapter 26

"THERE ARE ONLY TWO HOTELS IN CRESSWELL END," mused Churchill as the two ladies and their dog left the office to visit Miss Garthorn. "I shall telephone the managers to find out whether they can tell us anything more about the Cobnuts. And let's call in on Mrs Thonnings on the way to Miss Garthorn. She'll be able to fill us in on a few handy details before we meet her. It always pays to have a bit of background."

They stepped inside the little shop, where the red-haired haberdasher was seated behind the counter reading a tired-looking paperback.

"Mrs Churchill! Miss Pemberley!" Mrs Thonnings put down her book. "You can borrow this one when I've finished it, Mrs Churchill. *Reckless Enchantment*. How are you getting on with *Forbidden Obsession*?"

"I've finished it."

"Good, isn't it? And I think you'll enjoy *Reckless Enchantment* even more. It's a little racier."

"Golly. Well, that's not the reason I usually read books."

"Oh, come on, Mrs Churchill. It's the only reason to read books! And quite enjoyable, too, with some of Mrs Gollywood's elderflower wine." She pointed at a half-full glass beside her. "Would you like some?"

"No thank you, Mrs Thonnings. We're on duty."

"That makes you sound very official indeed. I suppose I'm on duty, too." She glanced around her little shop. "But I find a little tipple of something never does any harm. Are you here to collect the vermilion ribbon I set aside for you?"

"The whatty?"

"You were going to check your hats, remember?"

"Oh yes, so I was. I haven't checked them yet, but I shall do so this evening."

Mrs Thonnings's face fell. "Oh, I could have sold it to Mrs Higginbath earlier. She was after a bit of vermilion ribbon but I told her I'd sold out."

"Right, I'll take it in that case. Thank you for putting it to one side for me. Now, what do you know about Miss Garthorn?"

"The lady who left the Compton Poppleford Ladies' Bicycling Club in disgrace? That'll be eight pence for the ribbon, please."

"Eight pence? That seems like quite a lot."

"It's vermilion."

"I see." Churchill rummaged about in her purse and handed Mrs Thonnings the relevant coins. "Now, back to Miss Garthorn. Why did she leave the club?"

"Would you like your ribbon rolled or folded?"

"Could we leave the ribbon particulars until the end of our conversation, Mrs Thonnings?"

"I thought I could roll it or fold it while we were talking, you see."

"All right. Rolled, please."

"And shall I pop it in a paper bag for you?"

"Thank you, Mrs Thonnings. Why did Miss Garthorn leave the bicycling club?"

"She wanted to be in charge. Miss Garthorn and Mrs Cobnut founded the club together but then a power struggle ensued."

"I take it Mrs Cobnut won."

"Yes. I don't have any little paper bags left. Will a medium-sized one do?"

"Yes, thank you. Any bag will do. In fact, no bag is required as I can just pop it inside my handbag. So Miss Garthorn left the Compton Poppleford Ladies' Bicycling Club in disgust and founded a rival one?"

"That's right. She went over to South Bungerly in the next valley and started one there. There weren't many ladies in South Bungerly who enjoyed bicycling, so a number of Compton Poppleford ladies joined the South Bungerly club."

"Much to Mrs Cobnut's annoyance, I imagine."

"Oh yes. She wanted the Compton Poppleford club to be as big as possible so she could prosper from the subscriptions. But with a number of Compton Poppleford ladies switching to the South Bungerly club, Mrs Cobnut began losing out. She was most annoyed that they had been enticed away by promises of cheaper subscriptions and flatter bicycle rides. She used to scoff that the South Bungerly Club was for softies who couldn't stomach riding up hills. She prided herself on heading up a bicycling club for more serious lady cyclists. Sometimes on our rides she'd take us over to the next valley and we'd race through the village just to intimidate the South Bungerly club members."

"Goodness! And were they intimidated?"

"I don't know, to be honest. I always thought bicycling

was meant to be a fun pastime, and that there was no need for rivalry between bicycle clubs or racing through each other's villages. To be honest with you, Mrs Churchill, I was this close to leaving." Mrs Thonnings held up her thumb and forefinger with just a tiny space between them. "And then Mrs Cobnut died, which put an end to it all anyway."

Churchill and Pemberley found Miss Garthorn in a workshop adjoining one of the little houses on the river.

"Oh, hello," she said, wiping oil from her hands with a rag. "I'm just doing a little upkeep."

She had sharp green eyes and wore oil-spattered over-alls, her hair tied up in a headscarf. An upturned bicycle sat at the centre of the workshop, and various tools and bicycle parts were lying about on workbenches and shelves.

"It's Mrs Churchill, isn't it?" she asked, hands on hips. "And Miss Pemberley, of course."

"It's a pleasure to meet you, Miss Garthorn," said Churchill.

"And this must be your dog," she said, pointing at Oswald who was sniffing around in a dark corner of the workshop. "Is he a ratter?"

"Not that we're aware of," Churchill replied.

Miss Garthorn gave a disappointed shake of the head. "I need a ratter, you see. You should see the size of some of the river rats we get in here. Twice the size of your dog, some of them are."

"Oh, goodness!" exclaimed Pemberley. "They might hurt him!"

"Not necessarily. If he's a quick thinker and gives them a quick bite to the throat he'll be fine."

Churchill winced.

"Oswald would never bite anything on the throat," said Pemberley. "In fact, he has never bitten another living creature."

"Has he not?" Miss Garthorn surveyed him, her hands still on her hips. "There's not a lot of use in a dog who doesn't kill things."

"He's a detective dog," replied Pemberley in a wounded voice.

"Right. So what can I help you with?"

"The unfortunate demise of Mrs Cobnut," replied Churchill.

"Oh?" Miss Garthorn folded her arms.

"Having been placed in the embarrassing position of being considered a suspect, I'm keen to find out anything I can," she explained.

"You two ladies run the detective agency, don't you?"

"Yes."

"But you're not officially investigating?"

"No. That's all down to Inspector Mappin."

"Yes, I've spoken to him. And some detective chap with a very wide moustache."

"Monsieur Legrand."

"Is that who he is? The pair of them came sniffing around down here a few days ago. I told them what I could, of course, which was next to nothing."

"Oh."

"But you're also interested in the case?"

"Purely to clear my own name, you understand."

"So the inspector can blame me instead of you, you mean?"

"Oh no! No, I don't mean that at all. I—"

Miss Garthorn laughed. "I'm only joking, Mrs Churchill. Well, half-joking at least."

"Oh good. Only half?"

"Don't look so worried. Why does the inspector suspect you?"

"Because of a minor to-do in the tea rooms; nothing more than that. Oh, and also because Mrs Cobnut almost ran Miss Pemberley and me over last week."

Miss Garthorn gave a sympathetic nod. "Who didn't she almost run over? It's rather ironic that she died because someone cut her brake cables when she wasn't given to using her brakes much!" She laughed, then checked herself, as if realising murder wasn't an appropriate matter to laugh about. "It's not nice to be a suspect," she added, "but I'm sure Inspector Mappin will soon realise you had nothing to do with it."

"He will. And if not, the renowned detective will surely work it out."

"Oh yes! In which case we can all rest easy. Now, what did you want to ask me? You'll probably know by now that Mrs Cobnut and I had our differences, so I can't exactly go around pretending she was my best friend."

"I'm not sure she was anyone's best friend by the sound of things. You co-founded the Compton Poppleford Ladies' Bicycling Club with her, is that right?"

"Yes, about four months ago. We had both recently bought bicycles and regularly used to encounter one another on our jaunts around the village and its environs. The Compton Poppleford Bicycling Club has been going for about thirty years, and that's what gave us the idea."

"That's the men's version, is it?"

"Yes."

"Why isn't it called the Compton Poppleford Men's Bicycling Club?"

"Because they got there first, I imagine. It's often the way, isn't it? Anyway, we were mindful of the fact there was already a men's bicycling club in the village, so we decided to set one up for the ladies."

"And there was some disagreement over how it should be run, was there not?"

"It was all fine to begin with, for about a week, and then things turned sour. Mrs Cobnut wanted to be in charge, you see."

"And you also wanted to be in charge?"

"Not necessarily, but I didn't think that she was the right person to be in charge, and as the club only had two members at that time I accepted it would be better if someone other than Mrs Cobnut were in charge."

"You, then."

"Yes, albeit a little reluctantly because I'm not terribly bossy. But Mrs Cobnut was a little too bossy. Anyway, we reached an uneasy truce and she remained in charge while I set about recruiting more ladies. It wasn't much of a bicycling club with only two members."

"Understandably."

"So I concentrated on the recruiting and Mrs Cobnut did the bossy things."

"Which were?"

"Collecting the weekly subscriptions and leading the bicycle rides."

"I imagine the members must have enjoyed themselves or they would have left."

"I suppose they did, although I think many of them stayed out of fear. Once you were in, you were in. And some of them stayed in the club because they liked associating with Mrs Cobnut. She was a good person to have on your side, you see, and the members had a lot of loyalty for one another. If someone picked a fight with one member of the Compton Poppleford Ladies' Bicycling Club, they picked a fight with the whole group of us, if you know what I mean. The trouble was, old Cobnut took it extremely personally whenever someone left the club, as if they had personally insulted her."

"When did you leave the club?"

"I stuck it out until about three months ago."

"So you were only a member for about a month."

"Yes. Cobnut took it badly. She made my life very unpleasant indeed."

"What on earth did she do?"

"She put a large spider in my bicycle basket on one occasion."

"Goodness! That sounds like the sort of trick one might carry out as a schoolgirl."

"Another time she let down the tyres on my bicycle while I was in the tea rooms."

"Oh dear."

"And she heightened my saddle once so I thought my legs had shrunk."

"Not very nice. And you didn't immediately realise that someone had heightened your saddle?"

"No. It never occurred to me that someone would wish to do such a thing, so I simply assumed my legs had shrunk. I was most upset about it. On another occasion she removed the little dinger from my bell so that nothing happened when I rang it."

"How inconvenient."

"Especially so when I was once approaching the vicar from behind and relying on my trusty bell to warn him. When it failed to ring I floundered about, trying to get it to work, and then I got too close to him and had to bail out."

"Oh dear! You threw yourself off your bicycle?"

"I had no other choice. The first the vicar knew about it was when I made a loud exclamation as I hit the ground.

He turned to see me and my bicycle lying on the ground just behind him."

"That must have been a concerning moment for him."

"It was! Quite concerning for me, too, and it was all Mrs Cobnut's fault."

"How do you know Mrs Cobnut was behind all this?"

"She used to send me notes taunting me about it afterwards. Things like: 'I hope your eight-legged passenger enjoyed his ride today' and 'I hear the vicar lives to see another day'."

"What a bully!" fumed Pemberley.

"Oh, she was beastly. The woman was a fiend."

"And what did you do about this bullying behaviour?" asked Churchill.

"I called on her and politely asked her to stop it."

"And did she?"

"No, of course not. So I chose to ignore her and threw myself into the South Bungerly Ladies' Bicycling Club instead. We all enjoy ourselves very much. We bicycle at a leisurely pace to suit everyone, and hills are optional."

"That sounds just the way a bicycling club is meant to be."

"Yes, it is. I took as many of the Compton Poppleford Ladies' Bicycling Club members with me as I could. The brave ones, mainly."

"And a rivalry between the two clubs developed?"

"Yes, I'm afraid it did. It's most regrettable, but I tried not to think about the rivalry too much. Instead, I tried to set an example of how a bicycling club should be run. Once I had set the standard, I hoped other local clubs would follow suit. I think Mrs Cobnut had begun to tire of the rivalry shortly before her death. She realised the pranks and insults weren't making any difference, and that the

South Bungerly Ladies' Bicycling Club was to continue no matter what she thought about it."

"Given this rivalry, does Inspector Mappin consider you a suspect?"

"Probably. But I told him I had no interest in cutting anyone's brake cables. I also happened to be in Italy at the time of her death."

Chapter 27

"How lovely," replied Churchill. "Whereabouts in Italy did you go, Miss Garthorn?"

"I spent a glorious couple of weeks on the shores of Lake Garda. Quite delightful."

"Have you any idea who might have cut the brake cables on Mrs Cobnut's bicycle?"

"It could have been a number of people. There were many who bore her ill will."

"Who wished her dead?"

"Not dead, no. That would have been rather extreme. Just ill will."

"Did you bear her ill will?"

"Of course!"

"Tea, Polly?"

Churchill and Pemberley jumped on hearing this unexpected voice behind them.

"Oh, I'm so sorry. I didn't realise you had visitors." The woman had the same sharp green eyes as Miss Garthorn and would have looked remarkably similar to her had she been wearing overalls instead of a canary yellow dress.

"Margaret, this is Mrs Churchill and Miss Pemberley. This is my sister, Mrs Heston. She manned the fort here while I was in Italy and decided to stay on for a few weeks before heading home to Shropshire."

The ladies exchanged pleasantries, and Mrs Heston asked Churchill and Pemberley whether they would like some tea.

"That would be delightful, thank you." Churchill glanced first at one woman and then the other. "Identical twin sisters?" she queried, instantly feeling a little foolish for asking such an obvious question.

"Of course."

"People must muddle you up all the time."

"Indeed they have over the years," said Mrs Heston. "Polly and I had great fun at school confusing everybody."

"It was a hoot," agreed Miss Garthorn. "The main difference between us now is that I ride bicycles and Margaret detests the machines. So when you see one of us bicycling around you can be certain it's me."

"An excellent way to tell you apart. Did you know Mrs Cobnut, Mrs Heston?"

"Not really. I only heard about her from Polly, but she sounded like a frightful horror. I'll go and fetch the refreshments."

After a pleasant cup of tea with Miss Garthorn and Mrs Heston, Churchill, Pemberley and Oswald went on their way. They followed the path beside the river, which led back to the centre of the village. Oswald took a brief dip before climbing out and shaking himself beside Churchill's legs.

"Now my stockings are all damp, you cheeky doggy," she said. "I know Mrs Cobnut is no longer with us, Pembers, and I don't wish to dishonour her memory, but the more I hear about her the less I like her."

"It's a terrible shame," replied Pemberley. "I'm beginning to think it would be good to hear someone say something nice about her."

"I'm inclined to think that the person who murdered her would probably choose to be a little more flattering."

"Ah, yes! Because that would hide any possible motive they had for murdering her."

"Exactly, my trusty assistant. It wouldn't do for them to go around moaning about her too much, would it?"

"In that case, we can ignore the people who have been complaining about her loudly and concentrate on the ones who aren't talking about her with quite as much disdain."

"Indeed."

"That could work. Unless someone happens to be bluffing."

"Oh dear. Do you think they might be?"

"Yes. They may be one step ahead of us, assuming we would immediately discount anyone who spoke openly about how much they hate her."

"I see. Then that's another reason not to rule anyone out, isn't it? It's quite frustrating that each time we come up with a clever theory to discount certain people there's always a reason not to follow it. What about Miss Garthorn, Pembers? Do you think she could have had a hand in Mrs Cobnut's death?"

"Not if she was in Italy at the time."

They approached a riverside bench, where a man sat reading a newspaper.

"But do we have any evidence that she was in Italy?" continued Churchill. "We only have her word for it."

"And Mrs Heston's."

"Mrs Heston could be covering for her or may have been misled. Miss Garthorn may simply have told her sister she was going to Italy, when she was really hiding out somewhere nearby for two weeks in order to cut the cables on Mrs Cobnut's bicycle. Quite ingenious really, if that's what she did."

"There's nothing to suggest that she didn't do that, so I suppose we must consider her a suspect along with Mrs Twig, Mr Cobnut, Miss Plimsoll and Farmer Glossop."

"That's quite a list."

"Bonjour."

"Oh, gosh!" Churchill's heart seemed to bounce up into her throat before plummeting back down again. "You frightened me, Monsieur Legrand!"

The man on the bench lowered his newspaper and rose to his feet.

"What on earth are you doing here, Monsieur?" she asked.

"Enjoying a read of the newspaper in the sunshine."

"That does sound rather pleasant."

"It also gives me a good opportunity to observe the comings and goings."

"I can imagine it does. Are you observing anyone in particular?"

"Non." He folded up the newspaper and tucked it under his arm.

"You just decided to sit here and see what happened?"

"Yes. One can learn a lot of things from sitting in one place."

"I can imagine so. You're in quite a sneaky position, if I may say so. I suppose you're able to overhear countless conversations before people realise you're here."

"Absolutely." He tapped the side of his nose and

smiled. "You have just visited Miss Garthorn, is that right?"

"Yes," replied Churchill a little disconcertedly. "How did you know?"

"I heard you discussing her when you walked past me earlier."

"Oh. We passed you earlier?"

"Yes."

"And you were sitting here?"

"Yes, all the time."

"We didn't notice you at all, which is rather worrying seeing as I like to consider myself to be quite observant."

"Few people take any notice of a gentleman reading a newspaper on a bench."

"You're right, few people would. Such a mundane activity makes you blend in with the wallpaper a little. There isn't any wallpaper out here, of course, but I think you understand what I mean."

"Yes, I completely understand. The trick is, if you do not want people to notice you, you just act as though you don't want anyone to notice you."

"Is that all?"

"It is quite simple."

"I don't think I could quite pull it off, perhaps because of my generous size. I think the larger you are the harder it is not to be noticed."

"It is nothing about size, Mrs Churchill; it is merely your bearing. Ah, but here is my favourite little dog!" The detective grinned as Oswald pulled himself up against his legs. "Now, stand," he commanded. Oswald did as he was told, and the two of them performed another little routine of tricks.

"I wish I could do that," said a sulky Pemberley once they had finished.

"But you can!" smiled the detective. "All it takes is a little patience and practice. What a good boy, Oswald. Lie down." The dog did as he was told.

"Have you interviewed Miss Garthorn yet, detective?" asked Churchill.

"Yes. Inspector Mappin and I paid her a visit."

"Is she one of your suspects?"

He replied with a laugh. "We are still at the information-gathering stage, Mrs Churchill."

"Still? I thought you were doing that several days ago."

"These things take time."

"Yes, I suppose they do. And what of the suspects?"

"There are some who appear to be more suspicious than others."

"And who might they be?"

"I really could not possibly say, Mrs Churchill."

"Well, perhaps you could tell Inspector Mappin to rule me out. It would have been physically impossible for me to climb through the Cobnuts' shed window to snip the brake cables. I'm much too big to fit through it."

"I see."

"Yet Inspector Mappin still doesn't see fit to rule me out. I say this because I know you must be considering a number of suspects, and I'm merely trying to make the investigation easier for you. I realise you've most likely heard a number of guilty people plead their innocence over the years, so what I'm saying probably comes as no surprise. But if you choose to believe me – and I sincerely hope you will, because word has it you're a clever judge of character – you will surely believe me when I say that we are entirely innocent of any wrongdoing. In fact, we're happy to help with your investigations. We've offered our assistance to Inspector Mappin in the past but he's always been rather dismissive of it. I put it down to a clash of character, because we've certainly proved ourselves in the field of solving murders. Wouldn't you say so, Miss Pemberley?"

Her secretary nodded.

"And I'm sure that if we'd been in Naples or Marseille when you were carrying out your investigations there, we would have had a good crack at those cases, too."

"That is most useful to know, Mrs Churchill."

"I've been enjoying *Inside the Mind of a Detective: the Famous Cases of Monsieur Pascal Legrand* very much."

"Have you indeed?" He gave an appreciative nod.

"Yes, it's a very interesting read indeed."

"Did the outcome of the Munich case surprise you?"

"I haven't got to that bit yet."

"Ah, you must be quite early on in the book, then."

"Yes I am, but it's still a wonderful read."

"Why, thank you, Mrs Churchill."

"And I'm very intrigued to find out about the Munich case."

"I hope you enjoy it."

"So, any word you could have with Inspector Mappin about removing me from his list of suspects would be greatly appreciated."

"I see." The detective's eyes moved to a distant point above Churchill's left shoulder. "Yes, I think I do see now…"

"See what?"

Churchill turned to look in the direction of the detective's gaze but saw nothing more than the path beside the river and the row of cottages where Miss Garthorn lived in the distance.

"It makes me wonder…" he continued. "Ah, never mind!" He picked up his hat from the bench, put it on his head and bid the ladies a good day before heading off in the direction from which they had just come.

Chapter 28

"CAN YOU REMEMBER HOW TO PEDAL, MRS CHURCHILL?" asked Pemberley as they clambered aboard their bicycles outside the office the following day.

"Of course I can! What do you take me for, Pembers? Surely you remember me telling you about my advanced bicycling proficiency during my youth? It's only in my latter years that I've found it all rather cumbersome, but that's simply because I don't do it enough."

"Well, it's nice to see that you've become interested in bicycling again, Mrs Churchill."

"I'm not interested at all! This is merely my duty. We must find out more about that Storks fellow, and the only way to do so is to follow him and his bicycle at a safe distance."

Oswald poked his head out of the basket on the front of Pemberley's bicycle.

"I can already see that someone likes bicycles," commented Churchill, admiring the little dog. "Doesn't he look adorable?"

The two ladies cautiously pedalled off, bumping their

way down the cobbled high street. After a few minutes they reached a lane that led down to the church.

"I found it quite amusing when you told Monsieur Legrand how much you were enjoying his memoir," said Pemberley as they rode. "A nice little fib to curry favour with him!"

"He seemed quite flattered when I mentioned it, didn't he? I should really get on and read it in case he refers to anything else from the book in conversation. Mrs Thonnings put *Reckless Enchantment* in my postbox yesterday and I must confess I've been a little distracted. He's a funny little man, isn't he? What do you suppose he was staring at by the river yesterday?"

"He was probably considering a sleuthing notion of some sort."

"I wish I knew what happened in that mind of his. Right, lead on, Pembers. Let's see if we can find Mr Storks as he bicycles about the village."

Churchill had grown quite accustomed to her machine after ten minutes of bicycling. "Do you know what, Pembers? I'm beginning to see the attraction of joining a bicycling club. It's rather pleasant to feel the breeze in your hair, isn't it? And look at Oswald. I don't think I've ever seen him so happy."

The little dog had hung his head over Pemberley's bicycle basket and his ears were flapping in the breeze.

Five minutes later, Churchill stopped. "That's it, I've had enough. My legs are aching, my back hurts and I've lost all sensation in my posterior. I'm fed up with bicycling about aimlessly looking for this Stork fellow."

"I thought you were beginning to see the attraction of joining a bicycling club?"

"For a minute, yes, but then the feeling passed."

"Do you have any provisions in your basket?"

"Yes, I do." Churchill felt her mood brighten a little. "Thank you for the reminder, Pembers. I've brought a flask of tea and some shortbread. Let's partake of it here." She climbed off her bicycle, lowered the kickstand and began to busy herself with the elevenses.

"Just in the middle of this lane?"

"Yes, I have to stop this very minute. I simply can't go on until I feel replenished."

"But there's nowhere to sit." Pemberley glanced at the high stone wall on one side and the row of cramped little houses on the other.

"We can stand. In fact, I need to stand in order to allow some sensation to return to my—"

"Morning!" A dark-suited man in a trilby hat breezed past them on his bicycle.

"That's him!" hissed Pemberley. "Mr Storks!"

"Oh, darn it! Really?" Churchill watched the retreating figure, aghast.

"Get back on your machine, Mrs Churchill. We need to follow him!"

"Oh, bother!" Churchill flung the flask and shortbread back inside the basket and clambered back onto her bicycle.

The two ladies bicycled off as fast as their aching legs would allow. Fortunately, Mr Storks was travelling at a leisurely pace, and it wasn't long before they had him safely in their sights.

"He's going to notice us following him, isn't he?" said Pemberley.

"Not if we follow at a discreet distance."

"But we never quite manage to be discreet."

"Oh ye of little faith, Pembers! I'll admit we haven't always been terribly subtle when it comes to surveillance, but with each job we learn something new, wouldn't you say?"

"You could say that."

"We learn from what went wrong the previous time and manage things better the next time."

"It doesn't always feel that way."

"Perhaps if you had a little more confidence in our ability to do so we would handle things more effectively, if that makes sense. It's all about self-belief, Pembers. That's all there is to it. Now, I'm setting a good example here. I'm sitting on a bicycle, which I hate, as you well know. However, I'm doing so because I acknowledge that detectives need to be adaptable in their work. Despite my loathing of these machines, I'm willing to get on one for the greater good. And as I sit here, I have a great belief in my ability to acquit myself perfectly. Besides, I can't see anyone paying attention to two old ladies pootling along on their bicycles."

"They paid attention to Mrs Cobnut."

"Because she insisted on zipping about at a hundred miles an hour! If one hadn't paid attention to her, one would be mincemeat. In our case, Pembers, people will simply observe two lady detectives out for a leisurely ride. Mr Storks will think nothing of it."

"He's stopping!" whispered Pemberley.

"Right, then. Let's pause here and observe. We can pretend to take a great interest in the provisions in my basket and then take sneaky, surreptitious glances in his direction."

"Good idea. I think he has designs on that house to his right."

They watched as the dark-suited Mr Storks walked up

to a house and knocked at the door, which was promptly answered.

"Do we know who lives there, Pembers?"

"I think it might be Mr Perret the greengrocer."

"But presumably he'd be at his greengrocer's shop at the minute, so are we to assume that his wife has answered the door?"

"She may well have done."

"Interesting. We're standing next to number nine and the next one is eleven, so Mr Perret must live at number thirteen."

"Fifteen."

"How so?"

"There is no thirteen. It's bad luck."

"Are you sure? Do people really think like that in Compton Poppleford?"

"People think like that in a lot of places."

"I distinctly remember there being a number thirteen in Wisteria Avenue, where I lived in Richmond-upon-Thames."

"And who lived there?"

"The quite delightful Smithson family. He was a doctor. Detective Chief Inspector Churchill and I got to know them quite well. It was a shame they had to leave so suddenly."

"Why did they leave?"

"Their house burned down. Fortunately, they were out at the time, but a lamp they'd left on set the place ablaze. Oh, wait! Goodness, Pembers! Do you think it was because they lived at number thirteen?"

Pemberley gave a shrug. "I wouldn't like to say."

"Oh, golly. I'm starting to think that could be it. Oh look, Mr Storks is returning to his bicycle. I can't wait to find out what the man is up to. He couldn't be delivering something, could he? There's no obvious sign of a delivery item, though he keeps tucking things into his inside jacket pocket. What can it be? Oh, I wish we knew."

"That's why we're here, Mrs Churchill. I'm sure we'll find it out in time."

"I do hope so; the suspense is almost killing me. He hasn't glanced in our direction once. Isn't it marvellous how people care not a jot for two old ladies seemingly going about their business?"

"So you keep saying, Mrs Churchill, but he's paid us so little attention that I'm slightly concerned he knows we're following him and is making a point of showing extreme disinterest so as to lull us into a false sense of security."

"Do you think so? Oh dear. He can't really be that clever, can he?"

"I don't know how clever he is, but I've heard he's a shifty man. And shifty people can be rather cunning and wily, can't they?"

"Now you put it like that, Pembers, I suppose they can. He could be a bit of a sly fox, couldn't he? I must say you have a point there. I think we need to assume that he's a bit of a sly old fox and tread carefully. Oh look, he's off again. Where are my pedals?"

The two ladies followed Mr Storks again. This time a short journey brought them to the duck pond.

"Not the duck pond again, Pembers. I'm sick of the sight of it! We must have bicycled past it at least four times this morning."

"But you know who lives near the duck pond, don't you?"

"Mrs Twig."

"And it looks like he's calling on her!"

Chapter 29

CHURCHILL AND PEMBERLEY STOPPED AND OBSERVED FROM a distance as Mr Storks propped his bicycle up outside Mrs Twig's home and walked along the path to the front door.

"Did you see the look he gave us just now, Pembers?"

"No."

"Exactly, that's my point! He didn't even glance in our direction. It's wonderful how practically invisible we are. If we were young, attractive things he would have been so busy glancing in our direction that he wouldn't have seen where he was going and might well have tripped over the garden path. That sort of thing used to happen around me all the time in my youth."

"Really?"

"Yes, and don't look so surprised. I've told you before that I was quite a beauty back in the day. The fledgling Constable Churchill had a bit of competition on his hands, I can tell you. Now, can we hear what Mrs Twig and her visitor are saying?"

"No, because you're talking."

"Right then, let's hush a moment."

The two ladies strained their ears in an attempt to listen in to Mrs Twig's conversation, and Churchill felt quite surprised to hear laughter.

They watched as Mr Storks returned to his bicycle.

"He still hasn't clapped eyes on us, Pembers," whispered Churchill.

He wheeled his bicycle around, climbed onto it and began to bicycle away.

"Time to go!" announced Pemberley, suddenly taking off after him.

Mr Storks bicycled down the lane that ran alongside Mrs Twig's house, turned right, then swung left into another lane.

"I wonder where he could be going now," commented Churchill.

"We don't know, do we? That's why we're following him."

"Well yes, I realise that. I was just wondering if we could speculate as we bicycle. Oh no, did he signal to turn onto the high street?"

"I think so."

"More cobbles, Pembers. I hate cobbles!"

"You'll be all right, Mrs Churchill. Just pretend they're not there."

"How can I when I'm jiggling around all over the place? My derrière has already suffered enough on this little saddle. Why don't they make bicycles with proper seats?"

"Because you wouldn't be able to move your legs in the right way if they did."

"I'm sure you could if they put the pedals in front of you. I'd like to have a go at redesigning the bicycle with a little comfort in mind... Oh, here come the cobbles now. I hope Storks finishes his bicycling round soon, Pembers.

How will we cope if he does this for the rest of the day? Oh, look at Oswald's little head bobbing up and down. Do you think he minds being bounced about like that?"

"He'd jump out if he did."

"I think you're right. Oh, how funny. Look at his little face."

The two ladies continued along the high street. "I can't believe we have to bicycle past the bakery without stopping," grumbled Churchill.

"It looks as though Mr Storks is turning off to the right after the haberdashery shop."

"Righty-ho. Hello, Mrs Thonnings!" Churchill waved at her red-haired friend through the window before they turned off the high street in pursuit.

"This lane is a little bumpy, and it's all downhill," said Pemberley. "We'd better be careful."

"Thank you, Pembers, but I think I've got the hang of this now. Oh, it is bumpy, isn't it? Still, I survived the cobbles so I'm sure this will be fine."

They trundled down the lane after Mr Storks, which took them past a number of pretty little ancient cottages.

"Watch out, Mrs Churchill, there's a bend coming up."

"I can see it. Mr Storks has just gone beyond it."

"You'll need to slow down a bit."

"Oh, I will, Pembers."

"There's no need to go past me, Mrs Churchill."

"I'm not. I thought I could ride alongside you and look at Oswald's little face again. Oh, isn't he sweet? He absolutely loves riding on a bicycle."

"You should be looking straight ahead, Mrs Churchill."

"I am!"

"Not looking at Oswald."

"I only looked at him briefly."

"Brake, Mrs Churchill."

"I have everything in hand. Don't panic, Pembers. Why are you stopping?"

"I'm braking for the sharp bend. You need to do the same!"

It wasn't until Churchill had slipped past Pemberley and Oswald that she decided to apply her brakes. Her bicycle began to slow as she rounded the bend, but it was still moving at speed.

Out of nowhere, Mr Storks appeared. His bicycle was stationary in the middle of the lane, as though he were waiting for someone. Churchill turned the handlebars to go around him but felt her bicycle begin to lose balance. She tried to correct herself and pass on the other side of him, but this only served to make the bicycle misbehave further.

"What on earth?" was all he managed to say before Churchill's bicycle collided with his and they both went crashing to the ground.

Churchill felt herself tumbling and was sure she had performed a full somersault before coming to rest on her back.

"Mrs Churchill!" Pemberley cried out.

"Oof!" she exclaimed. "What happened?"

"What the…?" demanded Mr Storks, trying to scramble to his feet but seemingly trapped between the two bicycles and Churchill's large frame.

"Oh, goodness!" she exclaimed, desperate to stand and preserve any shred of dignity she had left. But she felt rather dazed by the fall and, although her arms and legs were flailing, she was unable to move herself.

"Get off me!" shouted Mr Storks.

The anger in his voice was vaguely reassuring for Churchill, who took it to mean that he wasn't too seriously injured.

"I'm trying!" was all she could say in response.

Pemberley rushed to her employer's aid. She grabbed hold of Churchill's shoulder and tried to haul her up.

"Good grief!" exclaimed a passer-by.

With Pemberley's assistance he was able to help Churchill to her feet, while Mr Storks remained seated on the floor, nursing his ankle.

"Thank you!" Churchill said to the passer-by, a lean man in shabby clothes whom she now recognised as Mr Pyeman. "And thank you too, Miss Pemberley."

"Are you hurt?" asked Mr Pyeman.

"No, I'm fine, thank you." She clutched her lower back, where a nasty twinge had begun to set in.

"Well I'm not!" fumed Mr Storks, clutching his ankle. His hat had come off in the collision, revealing thinning, oiled hair. His close-set eyes flashed at Churchill darkly. "What on earth were you doing, woman?"

"I'm terribly sorry. I was merely travelling around the bend and found you stopped in the middle of the lane."

"I thought we were done with old ladies speeding about on bicycles," he replied, slowly getting to his feet and wincing as he placed his weight on the injured ankle. "Haven't you learned your lesson after what happened to Mrs Cobnut?"

"The two of us aren't really comparable, and I was barely going any speed at all."

"But you must go slowly around a bend. You never know what's beyond it."

"May I suggest that it isn't entirely clever to stop in the middle of the lane just after a bend?"

"I can stop wherever I like!" He picked his dented trilby up off the floor and tried to knock it back into shape. "It's your responsibility to make sure that you're able to stop safely. Reckless bicycling!"

"I am sorry, Mr Storks."

"How do you know my name?"

"I… you're a friend of Mrs Twig's, aren't you? I know her well."

"No, I'm not a friend of Mrs Twig's."

"Are you sure? I thought I'd seen you visiting her home."

"I'm fairly sure I've seen you sniffing about near there, too. One of those nosey ladies with nothing better to do, I reckon." He smoothed his oily hair across his head and pulled his dented hat back on.

"I'm a private detective," replied Churchill sniffily. "Mrs Churchill of Churchill's Detective Agency. And this here is my trusty assistant, Miss Pemberley, and her dog Oswald."

"What do you want with me?"

"Nothing at all! I merely crashed into you by accident."

"I saw you up by Mrs Twig's place earlier. Were you following me?"

"Why on earth would we do that?"

"I don't know. You tell me."

"We were simply out for a relaxing bicycle ride, and with Compton Poppleford being the tiny village it is our paths have inadvertently crossed a couple of times."

"I'd say they've more than crossed, wouldn't you, Mrs Churchill? They've positively collided."

"That was a little mistake of mine, for which I do apologise."

Mr Storks was beginning to limp about, as if testing his tender ankle. "I think I can just about walk on it."

"That is good news indeed."

"Not at all! It would have been far better news if you hadn't flattened me in the first place!"

"I hardly think *flattened* is a suitable choice of word."

"I think it's a very accurate description of what happened. I merely paused here for a moment to adjust my bicycle clips, and the next thing I knew I was being flattened by you."

"I've already apologised, Mr Storks, and there really is very little more I can do about the matter."

"You're right there, Mrs Churchill." He bent down to disentangle his bicycle from Churchill's before examining it closely for signs of damage. "Hopefully this is still in working order. If it isn't, I shall send the repair bill to Churchill's Detective Agency. Is that right?"

"I suppose so. Although your bicycle looks quite untroubled to me."

"We'll see about that when I start riding it again. I'd be surprised if the wheels weren't misaligned now."

He climbed back onto his bicycle.

"Well, do let me know if they are misaligned, Mr Storks. I hope you'll forgive my little faux pas, and do call in at the agency office if your bicycle requires any repairs."

"Don't you worry, Mrs Churchill, I shall do just that! I have work to be getting on with now, but I shall examine my bicycle carefully as soon as I get home this evening."

"Excellent."

"And mark my words, you'll be hearing from me if anything needs repairing."

"Marvellous."

Churchill picked up her bicycle as he headed off down the lane.

"Goodness, he likes to kick up a fuss, doesn't he?"

"You want to be careful with the likes of him," said Mr Pyeman, who Churchill hadn't realised was still with them.

"Why's that?"

"I dunno, but I've heard he's a bad 'un."

"In what sense?"

"I dunno, like I say."

"But you must have heard something about him in order to deduce that he's a bad 'un."

"I didn't deduce nothin'. I'm just repeating what people's being sayin' about him. He's a bad 'un, apparently, and I can't tell you nothin' more than that."

"Golly. Well, it sounds as though I got off quite lightly, in that case."

"I wouldn't be so sure 'bout that. He might be back."

"I'm sure he'll come into the office grumbling about a bent spoke or something."

"If that's all he's gotta say next time you sees him, Mrs Churchill, you'll have got off real lightly."

"Really? I must say I'm rather worried now."

"It probably ain't worth worryin' about. Jus' be a bit careful. You don't wanna be havin' more than one run-in with the likes of him. Now, have you found me goat yet?"

"Almost."

Chapter 30

"I SUPPOSE WE'RE NONE THE WISER ABOUT MR STORKS'S business," said Churchill that afternoon, "although it appears to be nefarious business of some sort or another. Oswald, you really do become quite heavy after a while. Why does this dog keep climbing on me, Pembers?"

"Because you're lying in the middle of the floor."

"I have no choice. I feel the need to correct something in my back after that awful tumble. And I've also snagged my stockings. Remind me not to wear my best stockings next time I ride a bicycle. Actually, there won't be a next time. I'm never doing that again."

"You were managing quite well until you lost concentration on that bend."

"And that's just the problem. If I'm prone to losing concentration, bicycling probably isn't for me. Now, what could Mr Storks be wanting with Mrs Twig? His visit this morning seemed quite convivial. Did you hear the laughter, Pembers?"

"Yes."

"What could they have been laughing about?"

"The mind boggles. Do you think Mrs Cobnut might have employed him to collect the money Mrs Twig owed her?"

"If that's the case, why is he still collecting the money after she's died?"

"Perhaps Mr Cobnut has taken over the money collection."

"That's an interesting thought. But I hardly think Mrs Twig would be laughing with someone who was demanding payment from her."

"Perhaps it was nervous laughter."

"Possibly, but I don't see why he would also have laughed if that were the case. How on earth are we going to find out?"

"We could ask Mrs Twig if he's been collecting money from her on behalf of Mr Cobnut," suggested Pemberley.

"And if she confirms that to be the case?"

"Mr Cobnut had better be on the lookout if it is. If she murdered Mrs Cobnut over the debt, it stands to reason she'd probably be prepared to murder Mr Cobnut as well."

"That's an interesting thought. Having gone to the lengths of getting rid of one person and failing to solve the problem, she would no doubt wish to ensure that the job was done properly. But I don't know, Pembers. Is Mr Storks really the sort of chap who goes around collecting debts for other people? He has more the air of a self-made man about him. I can't imagine him working for Mr and Mrs Cobnut in that way."

"We could ask Nightwalker."

"That funny investigative journalist chap who helped us with the Piddleton Hotel murder?"

"Yes, him. He seems to know what everyone's up to, and I'm sure he'd know what Mr Storks's business is."

"That's an excellent idea, Pembers. I recall that we had

to place an obscure notice in the *Compton Poppleford Gazette* last time. Isn't that right?"

"Yes, I'll draft something now." Pemberley picked up a pen and paper.

"Do you think there's any chance he could be persuaded to meet somewhere other than that dreadful alehouse, the Pig and Scythe?"

"I doubt it."

"Can't we persuade him to meet us in the tea rooms?"

"No chance."

"Really?"

"Atkins always used to meet him at the Pig and Scythe."

"It's a shame Mr Nightwalker is so set in his ways."

"It's just Nightwalker; there's no 'Mr'. It's a code name."

"Do you know his real name?"

"No."

"He must enjoy being so mysterious, don't you think? If I had my time again, I think I'd craft an air of mystique around myself. There's something rather intriguing about an enigmatic sort of person, don't you think? I've always liked the idea of keeping people guessing. Now, how are you getting on with that note for Mr Nightwalker?"

"*Nightwalker*. I've just written it down here. 'Will Lady who took wrong umbrella from Butcher's Shop, Tuesday afternoon, kindly return?'"

"Ah yes, I remember now. It's some sort of code. He came up with that idea, did he?"

"No, Atkins did."

"Jolly good. Let's get it placed in the local rag, and then I suppose he'll let us know when he's available to meet in that den of iniquity. They don't even wash the tankards in that place; the publican simply spits in them and wipes them out with a rag. I saw it with my own eyes when I was last there."

"Some places are like that."

"Not in Richmond-upon-Thames. Say what you like about folk up there, but at least they've discovered the benefits of soap and water. Do you think the telephone cable will reach down here to me on the floor, Pembers? I've just remembered that I need to speak to those hotel managers in the Peak District."

"No, I don't think it will."

"Darn it. Let's update our incident board, then. Would you be a dear and move the pictures and string about in response to my commands? This position on the floor is really quite comfortable for my back. I'm convinced it's the only position I can adopt at the present time without being in terrible pain. Do we have a photograph of Miss Garthorn? Oh, darn it, someone's coming up the stairs."

There was a brief knock at the glass door before it swung open and the square, stony face of Mrs Higginbath loomed into Churchill's view. She scowled down at Churchill, her long hair framing her face like a pair of shabby grey curtains.

"What are you doing down there?" she asked.

"Recuperating, Mrs Higginbath."

The librarian gave a derisive snort. "Recuperating from what? Another strenuous visit to the bakery?"

"I beg your... ouch!" Churchill tried to sit up but a sharp pain in her back changed her mind. "If you've visited my office to be rude you can leave right away, Mrs Higginbath. There's no need for it, there really isn't."

"I've come to collect some property that belongs to the library."

"Why would there be any library property in here?"

"Books. I'm talking about books."

"Oh, I see. I didn't immediately make the connection. I don't have any of your library books, Mrs Higginbath."

"No?" The librarian pulled a piece of paper from the pocket of her cardigan and read from it: "*Inside the Mind of a Detective: the Famous Cases of Monsieur Pascal Legrand; Forbidden Obsession; Reckless Enchantment; and Clandestine Encounter.*"

"*Clandestine Encounter?*" queried Pemberley. "That's a new one."

"*Four* books, Mrs Churchill," continued Mrs Higginbath. "Four books, which are the property of Compton Poppleford Library, and which you have no business being in possession of!"

"Mrs Thonnings lent them to me."

"That's even worse!"

"Worse than what?"

"A lot of things. Now, no dithering, please. I want the library's property returned without delay."

"Fine," replied Churchill, staring up at the ceiling. "They're in my desk drawer. Miss Pemberley, would you mind fetching the books from my drawer and giving them to Mrs Higginbath?"

"I don't think you realise the gravity of this offence, Mrs Churchill," scolded the librarian. "Sub-lending a library book is a serious breach of library rules. I've already had extremely stern words with Mrs Thonnings about it."

"She did the sub-lending, not me. I'm merely a sub-borrower. Do the rules say anything about sub-borrowing?"

"Not specifically, no."

"There you go then, I'm off the hook. Have you found the books yet, Miss Pemberley?"

"Yes, I've just opened the drawer."

"Good. All four of them should be in there."

"May I state that you're not in the least bit '*off the hook*', Mrs Churchill," fumed Mrs Higginbath. "Any remote chance you had of obtaining a reading ticket for the Compton Poppleford Library has now been revoked for good. Do I make myself clear?"

"Crystal clear, Mrs Higginbath. Now, please fetch the books and leave. Miss Pemberley and I are in the middle of some important detective work."

"While lying on the floor?"

"Are there any rules which state that important work can only be done while sitting at a desk?"

"Don't be ridiculous," scorned the librarian.

"Why is there a slice of prune cake in this drawer?" asked Pemberley.

"Is there?" replied Churchill, staring intently at a crack in the ceiling plaster. "It must have slipped off a plate and fallen in. Who had prune cake recently?"

"You did, Mrs Churchill."

"Yes, and a good number of visitors to this office besides. I suppose the drawer must have been sitting half-open and a bit of cake from a visitor's plate fell in."

"There had better not be any cake on our library property!" warned Mrs Higginbath as she strode over to the drawer.

"Just a few crumbs," replied Pemberley.

"That's more than a few crumbs!" exclaimed the librarian. "It's just as I feared. Library property has been damaged!"

"By a piece of cake?" queried Churchill.

"Yes! The dust jacket of *Inside the Mind of a Detective: the Famous Cases of Monsieur Pascal Legrand* has grease spots on it."

"Won't they rub off?"

"No, they won't!"

"Fine. Then allow me to reimburse the library for it."

"That's no good. The library would still be missing a copy."

"Fine. Then I shall order a new copy direct from the publisher. What's the name of Monsieur Legrand's publisher, Miss Pemberley?"

"Timmins and Hurberry."

"Please make a note of that name for me so I don't forget it, and I shall get on to them right away."

"A new copy may be quite expensive, Mrs Churchill," warned Pemberley.

"Yes, it probably will be. But at the present time I'm trying to come up with the quickest possible way to get Mrs Higginbath out of our office."

Churchill turned her head and watched as Mrs Higginbath gathered up the books. "I shall keep this soiled copy of the detective's memoir until the new copy arrives."

"Right you are, Mrs Higginbath."

"I must say, I still don't understand the widespread fascination in this man."

"He's a renowned detective," said Pemberley.

"That may be so, but even renowned detectives can get things wrong, can't they?"

"Not in Monsieur Legrand's case."

Mrs Higginbath made a scoffing noise. "We hear a great deal about the cases he's solved, but what about the ones he didn't solve? And what about the ones where he wrongly accused someone? Has anyone ever challenged him about those?"

"I don't know," replied Pemberley.

"The danger with these renowned detectives is that whenever they point the finger and do all that *j'accuse* business, everyone takes them at their word."

"But the accused still has to stand trial and face a jury," said Pemberley. "And it's said that Monsieur Legrand is rarely proven wrong."

"What jury would dare to argue with a detective of such renown? Once he's involved, no one could possibly disagree with his version of events. It's all rather fishy, if you ask me. Now, I shall wait to receive the new copy of his memoir; incredibly overpriced, no doubt. Don't ever borrow a library book from someone else again, Mrs Churchill, or I shall have no alternative than to take the matter to the courts."

Chapter 31

"She's a terrible bully that Mrs Higginbath," grumbled Churchill once the librarian had left. "Take me to the courts? I'd like to see her try. She shouldn't be allowed to be a librarian. Help me up, please, Pembers. I've had enough of lying down."

"You should have asked for help while Mrs Higginbath was still here," replied Pemberley, doing her best to haul the portly detective to her feet. "I'm not strong enough, Mrs Churchill. You'll have to roll over and then get onto all fours."

"All fours, Pembers? I tend to avoid that uncomfortable position if I can help it."

"How do you scrub floors?"

"I'm more of a mopper than a scrubber. At least with a mop one can remain on one's feet."

With a little more struggling, and plenty of excitable barking from Oswald, Churchill finally managed to get herself upright.

"I need to sit at your desk to use the telephone," she puffed. "I want to contact the hotels in Creswell End."

"To find out if Mr and Mrs Cobnut spent their days away arguing with one another?"

"Yes. Wouldn't that be a wonderful revelation? It would start to wrap things up rather neatly."

"You'll need to be quick, Mrs Churchill. Don't forget that we need to put the notice for Nightwalker in the newspaper before deadline today."

"Yet another disappointment," grumbled Churchill as the two ladies made their way toward the offices of the *Compton Poppleford Gazette* a short while later. "Although the manager of the Peak View Hotel was able to confirm that the Cobnuts stayed there recently, he had no interesting tales with regard to obvious disagreements between the two. In fact, they reportedly teamed up with another couple, Mr and Mrs Malone, and enjoyed several pleasant walks together. And they played *Scrabble*."

"What a boring holiday," commented Pemberley.

"We can't all go gallivanting around the world with ladies of international travel, Pembers. Now, how long will it take Mr Nightwalker to reply to our notice in the *Gazette*, do you think?"

"He usually telephones the same day the notice appears in the newspaper."

"Perfect. Is that Miss Plimsoll I spy?"

A fair-haired lady in a floppy summer hat was peering through the window of a ladies' fashion shop a little way ahead of them.

"So it is."

"Hello, Miss Plimsoll. How are you faring?"

"Quite well, thank you, Mrs Churchill."

"Have you managed to find yourself a new position yet?"

"Actually, I've been quite fortunate. It looks as though I'll be returning to my old position."

"With Mr Cobnut?"

"Yes. He needs a lot of help at the moment. He told me you called on him the other day, actually." Her eyes narrowed a little. "Something about you being considered a suspect."

"Ah, yes. I just needed to prove that I wouldn't have been able to fit through the shed window."

"He told me he had to telephone Inspector Mappin because you'd trespassed on his land."

"Just a little misunderstanding between us, and all hopefully ironed out now. I'm very pleased to hear that you won't be out of work any longer."

"Thank you, Mrs Churchill. Although I suppose my return to Haggerton Cottage will set tongues wagging again."

"Really? Why?"

"Well, there have been rumours in the past that Mr Cobnut and I are on friendly terms. *Very* friendly terms, if you understand what I mean."

"Gosh. And why would there have been rumours to that effect?"

"I'm not entirely sure. I suppose it's because the two of us get along rather well."

"You have a lot in common, do you?"

"I wouldn't say that exactly, but I've always found him easy to talk to, whereas Mrs Cobnut was a little trickier than that."

"A prickly customer, was she?"

"Definitely a prickly customer."

"Did Mrs Cobnut happen to hear the rumours about you and Mr Cobnut being on very friendly terms?"

"No, I'm quite sure that she didn't."

"Do you think she noticed you were very friendly?"

"We weren't 'very friendly' in reality. Some people simply assumed we were."

"Based on a perceived closeness between you?"

"I suppose it must have been based on that, yes."

"Perhaps Mrs Cobnut also noticed this perceived closeness and that's why she chose to dismiss you."

"I think it unlikely, but I can't say it's beyond the realms of possibility. The reason she gave was that my work wasn't of a high enough standard."

"Which could have been an excuse."

"It may have been, but I decided there might have been some truth to it. Oh, I hope you don't think Mr Cobnut and I are actually on very friendly terms, Mrs Churchill. It really wouldn't do at all. How embarrassing!"

"We can't do a great deal about what people think of us, can we? In a little village like this people are apt to gossip."

"It's so unfair." Miss Plimsoll brought a handkerchief up to her eyes. "Poor Barny has been terribly busy sorting things out since his wife died. There's the funeral and all her affairs to see to, not to mention Inspector Mappin and that Swiss detective visiting him a number of times."

"Have they indeed? Surely they're not treating him as a suspect."

"Not any more. Once they realised there would have been no need for him to break into his own shed, they gave up on the idea. He has a key to the shed, of course. It hangs on a hook by the back door, so there would have been no need to break a window. Thankfully, they're leaving him well alone now, and quite right too! I think he should be allowed to grieve for his wife in peace. Their marriage wasn't perfect, but he certainly didn't want to be rid of her and he never would have murdered her. What a drastic measure that would have been! Even if he had decided to do such a thing, which he wouldn't, it would have been far too obvious that he'd done so, wouldn't it? Poor Barny!"

Miss Plimsoll dabbed at her eyes again.

Chapter 32

Nightwalker telephoned as soon as the notice appeared in the *Compton Poppleford Gazette,* and Churchill soon found herself making her way down to the Pig and Scythe to meet him. The alehouse was a slumped building with dark, mullioned windows. Inside, the dingy bar had sawdust on the floor and an unpleasant stale smell hung in the air. Having visited the establishment once before, Churchill was already accustomed to the room falling silent as she entered.

"Scrumpy?" asked the publican. He wore a collarless shirt, which was as yellow as the few teeth he had left in his head.

"No thank you," she replied, walking briskly over to the far corner of the pub where she had met Nightwalker once before.

The investigative reporter was slumped in the corner with a bent cigarette hanging from his lip. He wore a shabby felt hat and had rough stubble on his chin. He made an effort to prop himself upright when he noticed Churchill approaching.

"Good evening, Mrs Churchill. Not having a drink?"

"No thank you. I've seen how they clean the tankards in this place."

"Right you are." He took a sip from the tankard in front of him. "The scrumpy probably tastes better for it."

"You look rather wary, Mr Nightwalker, if you don't mind me saying so."

"Shush!" He glanced around cautiously. "You mustn't mention my name."

"I am sorry."

"And if I happen to be perching rather anxiously on my seat it's because I'm slightly concerned you might try poking me with your knitting needle again."

"It was a crochet hook, and I only did that because you appeared unresponsive when I arrived the last time."

"Well I'm more than responsive this evening. What can I do for you?"

"I'd like to find out a little more about Mr Storks."

He glanced around again, as if to ensure that no one was listening in. Then he leaned in toward her. "Bobby Storks?" he asked, his voice low.

Churchill also leaned in a little, enjoying the conspiratorial nature of their meeting. "Yes."

He gave a firm nod.

"Can you tell me anything about him?"

"Interesting chap."

"And?"

"He has a finger in every pie."

"We've already established that."

"Oh, well he's also a bit of a transgressor. A vagabond. A miscreant."

"You're still not really giving me anything concrete. I want to know why he's been bicycling around the village visiting seemingly harmless middle-aged ladies."

"Visiting as in *visiting*? Or just visiting?"

"You're not making very much sense, Mr Night—"

"Shush!"

Churchill began to wish she'd chosen to ignore the Pig and Scythe's lack of hygiene and bought a tankard of scrumpy to aid her patience.

"Does he go inside their houses?" asked Nightwalker. "Or does he remain on the doorstep?"

"He remains on the doorstep."

"Ah, yes." He gave a nod, as if this told him all he needed to know. Then he took another drink from his tankard.

"Well?" she asked. "What's he up to?"

Nightwalker leaned forward again. "He's probably taking bets."

"Bets? On what?"

"The greyhounds."

"Greyhound races, you mean?"

"That's the one."

"Why on earth would Mrs Twig be interested in grey-hound races?"

He spread his hands in a gesture of ignorance. "How should I know? Who's Mrs Twig?"

"A middle-aged lady he's been visiting. Can you think of any other reason he might visit her?"

"She might have bought a horse from him."

"I can't imagine her buying a horse."

"Or a gun."

"Goodness, no! A gun, do you really think so? I can't imagine Mrs Twig buying a gun, unless she's planning to shoot Mr Cobnut with it. No, I can't imagine that... but then those sorts of ladies can surprise you. I've discovered that in the past."

"If I knew who you were talking about, I might be able

to proffer an opinion."

"What other reason might there be for their association?"

"Horse. Gun. Greyhounds."

"You've already told me those."

"I can't think of anything else. A bit of jewellery, perhaps?"

"I've never seen her wear any interesting jewellery, and again she doesn't seem the type. She's rather a plain dresser."

He gave a shrug. "How many times has he visited her?"

"My trusty assistant and I have seen him call at her house twice."

He gave another knowing nod. "Then it could be a regular arrangement. I'd say he's collecting the money for the greyhounds each week and then dropping off the winnings, if there are any. You won't get many winnings from bookmakers like Mr Storks. He's a master at setting the odds."

"Mrs Twig betting on the greyhounds? I can't believe it." Churchill mulled this information over a little longer. "I suppose it would explain the money issues. She'd been borrowing money, you see. On one occasion she claimed it was for her husband's drinking and on another she claimed it was for her errant son. However, her husband appears to be one of the soberest people I've ever met, and he told me they don't even have a son."

"She may have a secret son."

"Possibly. But why tell other people in the village about him and not her own husband?"

"That wouldn't be entirely sensible."

"I think she must be gambling all her money on the greyhounds. She's obviously too ashamed to admit she's been doing something illegal and losing all her money in the process, so she pretended she had family members who were frittering away the cash instead. All very interesting. Thank you, Mr Night... Oops, sorry."

"Gamblers are often habitual liars," he replied. "I should know."

"Were you a gambler once?"

"All I'm saying is that I should know."

"Detective Chief Inspector Churchill used to go to the horse races and come back either a little better or worse off for it. Very naughty of him, really."

"I wouldn't admit to being related to a police officer in this establishment, Mrs Churchill. Nor would I admit that he may have involved himself in such things."

"Gosh." She glanced around. "I feel as though there are an awful lot of rules about what you can and can't say or do in places like this."

"Actually, there are. You have to watch yourself around here. And don't go mentioning Bobby Storks's name too loudly."

An orange sunset gave the stone buildings of Compton Poppleford a warm glow as Churchill made her way home. Swifts chattered as they swooped overhead and a happy blackbird sang its evening song. Churchill smiled to herself as she considered the rational explanation for Mr Storks's visits to Mrs Twig.

"Bonsoir, Mrs Churchill."

The Swiss detective materialised from the shadows once again.

"Good grief! Hello, Monsieur Legrand. You startled me again!"

"Oh, I am terribly sorry. I am just taking my evening stroll."

"A very sneaky evening stroll. I didn't see you coming!"

"Just habit, I'm afraid. Perhaps I should get myself some noisier shoes."

"Please do."

"You've just met with the mysterious Nightwalker, I believe."

Churchill jumped again. "What makes you say that?"

"I observe some pieces of damp sawdust stuck to the heel of your shoe."

Churchill peered down. "Ah yes, so there are."

"And there's only one public house I know of in Compton Poppleford that still has sawdust on the floor: the Pig and Scythe. It's a strange English custom."

"It's a strange English public house."

"I can think of no other reason why you would visit the Pig and Scythe other than to meet with the mysterious man they call Nightwalker."

"I shall neither confirm nor deny it. He's a secretive man, you know."

Monsieur Legrand gave Churchill a wink and walked on.

Chapter 33

Churchill told Pemberley all about her meeting with Nightwalker the following day. "So there we have it, Pembers," she said once she had finished. "I'm quite certain Mrs Twig borrowed money from Mrs Cobnut so she could pay off her gambling debts."

"Who'd have thought it? I have no idea how one would even get into placing bets on greyhound races."

"Neither have I. Besides, it's all very well learning what Mrs Twig did with the money she borrowed from Mrs Cobnut, but it doesn't explain whether she was involved in Mrs Cobnut's demise or not."

"I suppose we'll have to keep investigating."

"Yes, we will. And another thing, Pembers, I don't like the way Monsieur Legrand keeps popping up."

"Where does he pop up?"

"All sorts of places. At the allotment, on a bench by the river and then in a shadowy lane yesterday evening. I'm beginning to think he's following me."

"Why would he do that?"

"I don't know. Maybe he considers me a suspect, or

perhaps he's wondering whether I've found out more than him in the course of this investigation. Either way, he makes me feel uneasy. I don't like the way he can look at one's shoes and knows where one has been."

"He can do that?"

"He did it to me yesterday evening."

"Goodness."

"As I'm in the process of getting things off my chest, I also dislike the fact that I have nothing to read now. I was only halfway through *Clandestine Encounter* when Mrs Higginbath snatched it away. Now I won't get to find out what happens between Sophie and Charles."

"You can borrow some of my books if you like, Mrs Churchill."

"Oh, thank you, Pembers. Any of them similar to *Clandestine Encounter*?"

"I'm afraid not."

They were interrupted by a ring of the telephone. Pemberley answered.

"It was someone called Mr Scurridge," she said once she had replaced the receiver. "He says there's a one-horned goat up at the allotments."

"The allotments again? All right, then. Let's hope Ramsay's still there when we arrive. I'm not chasing him again, though; not after my tumble. There's only so much physical duress a lady of my age can endure."

"He went off into the woods," said Mr Scurridge when Churchill, Pemberley and Oswald arrived at the allotments.

Churchill recognised Mr Scurridge as the elderly man who had been asleep in a deckchair the last time they had visited the allotments. He wore the same checked shirt tucked into a pair of equally filthy trousers.

"I've had enough of that goat," he continued. "He's helped himself to quite a bit of my veg now. I've a good mind to get my shotgun out."

"Please don't," said Churchill, "he's only doing what goats do. Mr Pyeman would be most upset if any harm were to come to him."

Mr Scurridge kicked at an empty plant pot. "Well, if Pyeman doesn't catch him soon I'll be left with no other choice. No disrespect intended, ladies, but neither of you looks as though you have the speed to catch a goat."

"I can't disagree with you on that front," replied Churchill. "I can only suggest that some sort of lasso or net is in order. Come along, Miss Pemberley. Let's see if we can find him."

The two ladies and their dog walked up to the woods. As they did so, a lady with brightly rouged cheeks emerged from the trees.

"Mrs Twig!" whispered Churchill to Pemberley.

Oswald ran up to greet Mrs Twig, who patted him on the head before greeting the two ladies.

"I don't suppose you saw a goat while you were in the woods, did you, Mrs Twig?"

"Now you come to mention it, I did, yes."

"Oh good, we'll go and fetch him. By the way, I accidentally collided with your friend Mr Storks yesterday."

"My friend?"

"Yes, Mr Storks."

"Who's Mr Storks?"

"I thought I saw him calling at your home."

Mrs Twig's face reddened. "I don't know who he is, but he has never called at my home."

"Oh, I see. I must be mistaken. How are you faring, Mrs Twig?"

"All right, I suppose. I haven't been able to bring myself to get back on my bicycle."

"Are you worried the brake cable snipper may strike again?"

"No, I don't think he will. I think Mrs Cobnut was very much targeted, if you ask me."

"What makes you say that?"

"I've been giving it a good deal of thought over the past few days and I'm fairly sure I know who did it."

Churchill felt a shiver of excitement. "Really? Who?"

Mrs Twig lowered her voice: "Farmer Glossop."

"Really? Because Mrs Cobnut frightened his horse, you mean?"

"It's not just that. The two of them have been embroiled in a terrible feud that goes back many years. Glossop married Mrs Cobnut's sister, Felicity. And when the marriage turned sour, Felicity Glossop took off to America."

"Gosh, I never knew that."

"Her departure caused all sorts of malicious behaviour between Farmer Glossop and Mrs Cobnut. Before she frightened his horse, Farmer Glossop painted her fence."

"Surely that did her a favour."

"Not when he painted it bright orange."

"I noticed that, actually, but I didn't realise it had been an act of vandalism."

"Before that, Mrs Cobnut let Farmer Drumhead's sheep into Farmer Glossop's turnip field. Their farms are next to each other, you see, and two of the fields are divided only by a gate. Mrs Cobnut snuck over there one night and opened the gate, and the sheep naturally went into the turnip field and ruined the crop."

"Do sheep eat turnips?"

"I don't know, but they certainly trample them with their little hooves."

"Gosh. When I heard about the spooked horse and the upset vegetable cart, I assumed it was nothing more than an unfortunate event. I didn't realise Mrs Cobnut had spooked poor Jasper on purpose."

"Oh yes, she was like that."

"Neither did I realise she was related to Farmer Glossop in some way. He didn't impart that information to me himself."

"Oh, he wouldn't. He's quite ashamed of it."

"Did you know any of this, Miss Pemberley?"

"Now that Mrs Twig has mentioned it, it does ring a bell."

"Right."

"I can't be expected to remember everything that's ever happened in this village, Mrs Churchill. A lot goes on here, as you well know."

"Indeed. How long ago did Mrs Glossop move to America?"

"Oh, it was about four years ago now," replied Mrs Twig.

"Golly. So the family rift and all this tit-for-tat business has been going on since then?"

"Oh yes. In fact, it started before then. It's one of the reasons Mrs Glossop moved to America."

"How did it all start?"

"Mrs Cobnut decided from the very outset that Farmer Glossop wasn't good enough for her sister. Whether he was or not, I can't form an opinion. But I do know that she wasn't very happy being married to him, and when she told Mrs Cobnut this she began saying 'I told you so' over and over again."

Churchill tutted. "There's nothing worse than someone who does all that 'I told you so' business. How terribly annoying. Mrs Glossop presumably fled to America to escape both her husband and her sister."

"Yes, and her parents. They weren't very nice either."

"Oh dear. That isn't a terribly happy tale. Are the parents still alive?"

"No."

"And everything you've just told us, Mrs Twig, are you sure it's all true?"

"Yes, of course it is! Why wouldn't it be?"

"No particular reason. It's just that we have a lot of people telling us all sorts of different things, and they might not always necessarily be true."

"Well the Cobnut-Glossop feud is true. You can ask Farmer Glossop yourselves."

"We'll certainly have a chat with him about it."

"I think he cut the brake cables on her bicycle as part of this tit-for-tat situation they had going on, but unfortunately it went a little too far. He probably didn't realise she would die as a result."

"Perhaps not."

"Although I do have another theory. As you know, Mrs Cobnut and I had an uneasy relationship before her death because I owed her money, but there was another conversation we had that sticks in my mind. Not long before she died, she mentioned to me that she was in fear of... Oh, what was that?" Mrs Twig spun around and glanced at the trees behind her. "I heard a noise!" she hissed. "A snapping twig. Did you hear it too?"

Churchill nodded. "I did indeed, Mrs Twig." She peered closely at the trees, looking for any sign of movement.

"I think someone was listening in," said Mrs Twig with a shudder.

"It's probably just Ramsay the goat," replied Churchill, itching to hear what Mrs Twig had been about to say. "Now, what were you going to tell us?"

Mrs Twig glanced around again. "No, not here. Someone might be listening."

Churchill felt a snap of impatience. "I'm sure it's nothing, Mrs Twig. An animal at the very most. You can whisper what you were going to say if you like."

"No." She shook her head. "I shall have to tell you another time. It's too risky."

"But no one will hear if you whisper!"

"I'll speak to you again soon, Mrs Churchill." And with that, the frightened lady hurried on her way.

"Oh, how annoying, Pembers! Mrs Twig was about to tell us something."

"But how do we know if we can believe what she's telling us?"

Churchill sighed. "I suppose we don't. Let's explore the woods and find out who was eavesdropping."

Chapter 34

AFTER AN EXHAUSTIVE SEARCH OF THE WOODS, CHURCHILL and Pemberley had found neither the eavesdropper nor the goat.

"How completely unsatisfactory, Pembers," grumbled Churchill as she sank into her chair back at the office. "We still can't get hold of Ramsay and we have no idea whether to believe the latest yarn Mrs Twig has spun us. She certainly lied about Mr Storks, that's for sure. She denied all knowledge of him!"

"That's probably because she's embarrassed. Few people would care to admit that they've been handing money over to a crook."

"True. The Glossop story sounds feasible, though, doesn't it? I only wish we'd known about the feud sooner. Had I known about the family background I would have questioned him about it."

"There would have been little point in doing so, Mrs Churchill," said Pemberley. "He would only have thought you suspected him and clammed up."

"I suppose you may be right there."

"Farmer Glossop and Mrs Cobnut obviously hated each other very deeply."

"They must have done. The thing about tit-for-tat situations is that they always escalate, don't they? Someone does an initial tit, which usually isn't too bad, then someone does a tat, which is slightly worse than the tit but still not too bad. Then the next tit is usually worse than the previous tit and tat, then the tat that follows that one is worse again, and so it descends into a terrible spiral. And unless someone puts a stop to it, there can only be one outcome."

"Someone dies?"

"Sadly, yes."

"I wonder if cutting the brake cables was a tit or a tat."

"I was wondering the same thing. However, we needn't consider it at great length because we all know the outcome now. There will be no more tits or tats in this instance."

"It's all very sad."

"The pair just needed to have their heads knocked together and be made to shake hands. It should never have descended so far. I'm surprised no one tried to stop them."

"I'll make us some tea," said Pemberley. "I would offer you a slice of prune cake, Mrs Churchill, but I'm beginning to think you don't like it."

"Not like it? What makes you say that?"

"I keep finding pieces of it discarded about the place."

"Nonsense, Pembers. Pieces of it just happened to fall off plates here and there. It happens with all the cakes we eat."

"I've never noticed it before. When it's something from the bakery I rarely see a single crumb on the plate. It's practically been licked clean."

"I never lick plates. How uncouth!"

"I really thought you'd like it, Mrs Churchill, and I so enjoyed baking it." Pemberley's lower lip trembled a little.

"Cut me the largest slice of prune cake yet and I'll eat every bite, Pembers."

"You're just saying that to make me feel better."

"What piffle! Come along now, give me a great big slice of that cake."

"Are you sure?"

"Yes!"

To Churchill's relief, Pemberley smiled and lifted the cake tin lid. "All right, then. The largest slice yet, you say?"

"Absolutely!" Churchill forced a wide grin and prepared herself to tackle it.

A scurry of quick, light footsteps on the stairs was followed by the door flinging open and a boy swiftly depositing a brown paper package on Churchill's desk.

"Delivery!" he shouted before disappearing again, escaping the admonishment Churchill had been about to unleash for his poor manners.

Churchill shook her head in despair before turning her attention to the package. "There's a stamp here bearing the name Timmins and Hurberry. It must be the new copy of Monsieur Legrand's memoir. What swift delivery, and I should hope so too, given the pretty penny we had to pay for it."

"Mrs Higginbath will be pleased," replied Pemberley.

Churchill pulled off the parcel paper and admired the smart new book. "It almost seems a shame to give this to her, doesn't it? I don't suppose it would do any harm if I held on to it for a few days."

"That's all very well, so long as you don't get any of this on it," said Pemberley, placing a thick, heavy slice of prune cake on Churchill's desk.

"Thank you, Pembers," she said as brightly as possible.

A recollection flitted into her mind of being forced to swallow bitter medicine by her nanny. "This book seems to be an updated edition," she said. "It's even got some colour plates in it. How annoying that we'll have to give Mrs Higginbath a superior copy, Pembers."

"It's not for her; she won't even read it. Just think of all the patrons of the library who will glean great enjoyment from this nice updated book."

"Patrons of a library for which I don't even own a reading ticket! Life can be terribly cruel sometimes. I like these colour plates, though. Books should have more pictures in them, shouldn't they? We don't all want to read endless pages of writing."

"Unless it's *Clandestine Encounter*," responded Pemberley.

"That's the one I didn't get to finish. How odd that the Murderer of Marseille was turned into a play. Who would want to sit through that? Look, Monsieur Legrand has even included a picture of the playbill and a photograph of the cast. What an enormously big head that man must have."

"In his defence, he doesn't behave like a man with an enormously big head."

"I suppose I've met more boastful people than him in my time. He's smug, though, isn't he? And a little too sure of himself."

"I thought you admired him, Mrs Churchill."

"I admire his achievements, to a point. But I don't like the way he pops up when one is least expecting it and makes comments about sawdust on one's shoes and that sort of thing. I haven't warmed to that at all. Wouldn't it be wonderful if we could solve this case before he does? The first thing we need to do tomorrow morning is visit Mrs Twig."

"To find out what she was going to tell us before that twig snapped in the woods?"

"Absolutely. The twig that put a stop to Mrs Twig. She twigged something was afoot when she heard the twig. Or should that be, Mrs Twig twigged—"

"I get the joke, Mrs Churchill."

Chapter 35

"Monsieur Legrand has chosen some rather flattering photographs of himself for this book," commented Churchill as she continued to leaf through his memoir the following morning. "Having met the man in person, I can vouch for the fact that he's far less prepossessing in real life."

"He does have an excellent mind, though," added Pemberley.

"So we're told. I never thought I would find myself agreeing with that librarian fiend Mrs Higginbath, but I admit to having given a subtle nod when she mentioned that we never hear about the cases he was unable to solve or the cases where he has wrongly accused someone."

"Maybe because there aren't any such cases."

"Maybe. But I happen to be a little sceptical about these things, just like Mrs Higginbath."

"Golly. Monsieur Legrand must really be rubbing you up the wrong way if you've started sharing the opinions of Mrs Higginbath."

"Only one opinion, Pembers. Just the one. And who

knows, perhaps Mrs Higginbath and I will be proven wrong."

"There's a general bluster on the high street," commented Pemberley, peering out of the window next to her desk.

"What does a general bluster look like?"

"It's hard to describe. There are people getting together in groups, pointing, looking about themselves and then suddenly taking off again. I'd say there was a lack of the usual day-to-day weariness, and in its place a sense of urgency and excitability about proceedings."

"Well I never." Churchill walked over to the window and surveyed the high street. "I think you might be right, Pembers. It seems as though something's afoot. Shall we go down there and investigate?"

The two ladies and their dog went out onto the high street.

"There's been a terrible murder," said Mr Simpkin the baker. He stood outside his establishment, hands in his pockets and shaking his head in dismay.

"Goodness me!" exclaimed Churchill, her heart racing. "Whom? Where?"

Her question was soon answered when a hysterical, red-haired lady came hurtling toward them. "Mrs Churchill, Miss Pemberley! Oh, it's too terrible. Mrs Twig is dead!"

"What? No!"

"They think someone bopped her on the head."

"Where? How?"

"She was walking along Hyacinth Lane this morning in broad daylight. She always walked that way to the shops. *Every day*. Then someone crept up behind her and bopped her on the head!"

"What with?"

"No one knows yet."

"How do we know the culprit crept up behind her?"

"Because she'd just passed the old oak tree with a trunk as wide as a cart horse. It's the only hidey place on that little lane. It must have been where the person had been hiding. And no one nearby heard a sound. If Mrs Twig had seen her assailant she'd have cried out or screamed or something, but there was nothing. The poor lady must have been taken completely by surprise."

"Well, that's truly dreadful."

"Maybe someone thought she'd murdered Mrs Cobnut," suggested Mrs Thonnings. "Perhaps they did it as an act of revenge."

"If so, someone must have known for sure that she was the culprit."

"Or perhaps they just suspected it."

"That would be a bit of a vague reason to murder her. I suspect she knew something about the murderer. She was probably just about to speak out before she was silenced. Golly, how awful!"

"And poor Mr Twig," said Pemberley. "Another widower in the village within the space of a week."

"Yes, it's terrible. He's rather an emotionless man, and I can't say that I warmed to him enormously, but I do feel terribly sorry for him now that his wife is deceased. Dreadful, I say. Mappin and the renowned detective really do have their work cut out for them now."

"There's a big crowd all trying to sneak a peek at Hyacinth Lane at the moment," said Mrs Thonnings. "Morbid, it is."

"A suspicious death in the village always brings out a crowd. People don't have anything better to do, do they? Come along, Pembers. Let's take a look at the crime scene for ourselves."

. . .

The two ladies and their dog walked toward Hyacinth Lane, which led from the high street to the duck pond. There was nothing to see other than a crowd of people standing on tiptoes and craning their necks to view the spot where the murder had taken place, a task made all the more difficult as Oswald scurried between their legs. One enterprising man was doing a roaring trade in toffee nearby.

"It's awful, isn't it, Pembers? I wonder what Mrs Twig knew. The trouble with her was that you never knew whether the words coming out of her mouth were fact or fiction."

"Which begs the question as to why she was murdered. If no one was ever sure whether she was telling the truth about something, people weren't likely to have believed what she was going to say anyway."

"I suppose we're just making an assumption with regard to the possible motive. I wonder what it was that she knew. Who was she seen speaking to in the days leading up to her death?"

"Us."

"Oh, good grief, Pembers, you're right! And she was about to tell us something, wasn't she, before the twig snapped?"

"Perhaps the eavesdropper who snapped the twig is the culprit," suggested Pemberley.

"Oh golly, what a thought."

"He was lurking in the woods, listening in to our conversation, and when he grew concerned that she was about to spill the beans he made a move to stop her."

"Maybe he realised the twig snap would be enough to temporarily silence her."

"Or maybe we're lucky the twig snapped because it gave him away before he bopped all three of us on the head."

"Oh, goodness, Pembers! Surely that can't be true." Churchill felt an icy shiver run down her spine. "I refuse to believe that. It's too unnerving for words."

"I wonder why she was murdered," said Pemberley. "Did she know something about the murder of Mrs Cobnut? Was it connected to the money she owed? Perhaps Mr Storks had something to do with it."

"I can't say I relish the idea of speaking to Mr Storks about it."

"No. Perhaps we should leave that up to Inspector Mappin. We could tell the inspector about Mrs Twig gambling on Mr Storks's greyhounds and leave him to pursue that line of investigation himself."

"Good idea. But did she know something about Mrs Cobnut's murder, I wonder?" mused Churchill.

"I think she must have done. Either that or she was responsible for it herself. But then we haven't found anyone who liked Mrs Cobnut an awful lot, have we? It would have to have been someone who was desperately upset that she'd been murdered if that were the case. I can only think of Mr Cobnut, her husband. Perhaps he somehow learned that Mrs Twig had carried out the murder."

"Or suspected she had."

"Ah yes, that's a good point. It could have just been a suspicion, couldn't it? He either knew or suspected she had cut the brake cables on his wife's bicycle, then lay in wait for her behind the oak tree and carried out the dreadful deed."

"But if he knew or suspected that Mrs Twig had done it, why not just let Inspector Mappin and Monsieur

Legrand know? That way she would have received proper justice."

"Good point."

"And given that she was in debt to Mr and Mrs Cobnut, it would have been even harder to recover the money she owed if he murdered her," said Churchill.

"I suppose he could have claimed it from Mr Twig, if he was trying to claim it back at all."

"Perhaps Mr Cobnut suspected that Mrs Twig had murdered his wife and also intended to murder him. Perhaps he simply got there first."

"Which still begs the question of why he didn't just leave the matter to the police. He doesn't strike me as someone who would leap out from behind a tree and bop someone on the head."

"No, that's true."

"I'm not convinced it was Mr Cobnut," said Pemberley. "And I don't think Mrs Twig murdered Mrs Cobnut. My feeling is that Mrs Twig knew something about the culprit and was killed to maintain her silence."

"Or she had become embroiled in a high level of criminality with Mr Storks and was murdered for that reason. Maybe there was a high-powered illegal betting syndicate somewhere and there had been a falling-out over money. How complicated this all is. It's rather interesting how the two murders differ in style, isn't it? The first was a rather detached, calculated murder, while the second was rather brutal. The murderer attacked Mrs Twig with his own hands, which is quite different from cutting brake cables in the middle of the night and leaving things to chance. It's as if the two murders were committed by two different people."

"You don't think the same culprit was behind them both?" asked Pemberley.

"Maybe he was. I suppose the attack on Mrs Cobnut was well planned – almost an experiment, if you like – to see if she could be got rid of. The murder of Mrs Twig, on the other hand, appears to have been an act of desperation more than anything. It was carried out in broad daylight at a time when the culprit knew she would be out and about, running her usual errands. It was a frantic move to be rid of her, as if it were a race against time."

"Which it was if she intended to open her mouth and reveal something he wished to remain secret."

"Very interesting indeed. So are we now looking for one murderer or two?"

"We can't possibly know that yet."

"I'd like to know what Monsieur Legrand's great detective brain will make of it all," said Churchill. "I'd pay a small fortune to find out how his mind processes incidents of this kind."

"I'd say it's undoubtedly all in his head. If he made notes other people might find them. He wouldn't want to write anything down in case it gave away his thought process."

"I think you're right there, Pembers."

"Perhaps Mr Twig murdered his wife."

"Golly, do you think so?"

"He may have found out about all the lies and debts and murdered her in a rage."

"But why wait behind the oak tree for her?"

"He wanted it to look as though someone else had done it."

"Oh, that's a very clever thought! But hold on, Mr Twig was presumably in Dorchester doing his very important job at the time."

"I suppose he would have been," replied Pemberley. "But that's still an assumption."

"Indeed. I imagine it would be fairly easy to find an alibi for him. If he wasn't at work that day it would look very suspicious indeed. I think there must be others who are more likely to be behind this than Mr Twig."

"Farmer Glossop, perhaps."

"Do you think so, Pembers?"

"That's who Mrs Twig was telling us about just before the twig snapped."

"You're right. So she was!"

Chapter 36

CHURCHILL, PEMBERLEY AND OSWALD LEFT THE BUSTLE OF Hyacinth Lane and made their way toward Farmer Glossop's farm just outside the village on the road to South Bungerly.

"What are we going to ask him, exactly?" queried Pemberley.

"Let's start by confirming what Mrs Twig told us. After all, she had a funny habit of concocting stories."

"And then?"

"I think we need to observe him closely while we talk. We'll do what Monsieur Legrand does: concentrate more on what he doesn't say than on what he does."

"He may think I'm not listening properly if I do that. He'll see it in my face."

"I doubt he'll notice at all, Pembers. Most people don't even consider the other party during a conversation; they merely talk at them under the blind belief that everything they say is important and interesting. Some people wouldn't even notice if you walked off while they were talking at you. Mrs Figgins at the Richmond-upon-Thames

Ladies' Lawn Tennis Club was like that. I once stepped out onto the clubhouse verandah as a test while she was talking at me inside the building. She didn't notice for three whole minutes."

Churchill and Pemberley reached the tumbledown farmhouse, which had a rusting plough outside it. They made their way down a muddy path, while Oswald skipped off to make friends with some geese.

"I can't see a knocker," commented Churchill, surveying the weathered door, "or a ringer."

She hammered on the door and waited.

"The geese love Oswald," commented Pemberley fondly as she observed her dog playing with the farm birds.

Churchill knocked a few more times and grew impatient when no one answered. "Where is the man?" she asked. "Perhaps he's out in the fields tending to his crops."

"Maybe he went into hiding after he murdered Mrs Twig," suggested Pemberley.

"Golly, I hope not."

"It might explain why he's not answering."

"You won't get no answer there," came a voice from behind them.

The two ladies spun around to see a stout lady in a canvas shirt and saggy trousers standing behind them. She held a chicken under one arm and her face was as brown and wrinkled as a piece of dried fruit.

"Oh?"

"We don't live in that part o' the house no more. That bit's empty."

"Oh. We're looking for Farmer Glossop. Is he about?"

The woman pointed at a neighbouring field. "Fixin' the fence," she replied before shuffling away.

. . .

"I didn't realise the late Mrs Cobnut was your sister-in-law, Farmer Glossop."

"Only in name."

The broad, red-whiskered man thwacked a fence post with his sledgehammer and Churchill winced at the noise.

"Isn't that usually the arrangement?"

"What?" He slammed his hammer into the post again.

"I said, 'Isn't that usually the arrangement?'"

"Eh?" He brought the hammer down on the fencepost once more.

After some gesticulating and polite requesting, Churchill managed to persuade the farmer to pause his work for a moment. He paused and stared at her, his eyes steely beneath his heavy brow. Churchill imagined him wearing a horned Viking helmet for a moment, then tried to remove the image from her mind.

"She may 'ave been me sister-in-law," he growled, "but there weren't no affection between us."

"That's not uncommon with in-law relationships. After all, one can't choose one's in-laws, can one?"

"You're tellin' me."

"What caused the fallout, exactly?"

"I married 'er sister."

"And that was the moment it all went wrong, was it?"

"Yep. It all went wrong from there."

"And when was this?"

"'Bout fifteen year ago."

"When did you become estranged from your wife, if you don't mind me asking?"

"When I married 'er."

"Immediately?"

"It were gradual, but it all started back then."

"I see. And when did Mrs Glossop move to America?"

"Four year ago."

"Quite recently, then."

"Blamed me for it, she did."

"Your wife blamed you for her move to America?"

"She did as well."

"I'm a little confused. Your wife blamed you for it?"

"Yep, and Cobnut."

"I see. So if I've understood this correctly, and please let me know if I'm wrong at all, Mrs Cobnut was never quite happy about you marrying her sister, and when your wife moved to America Mrs Cobnut blamed you for it."

"Yep. Who told you Mrs Cobnut weren't never 'appy with me marrying 'er sister?"

"Oh, no one. I merely felt as though you had inferred it."

"Well, she weren't."

"I see."

"But I didn't know it were common knowledge that she weren't."

"Ah, right. Did your wife ever explain the reason for Mrs Cobnut's discontentment?"

"Mrs Cobnut didn't like me face. That's what Cressida told me."

"Cressida is Mrs Glossop, is she?"

He nodded.

"So Mrs Cobnut didn't like your face and therefore she didn't like you?"

He nodded again. "Truth be told, I didn't like 'er face neither."

"When one discovers that someone dislikes one, I find that one tends to reciprocate with dislike."

"Summat like that."

"I understand that the animosity between you led to various tit-for-tat activities, such as sheep trampling turnips and fences being painted orange. Is that right?"

"She started it."

"I see. And when your horse, Jasper, was spooked and ran away with the vegetable cart, had Mrs Cobnut intentionally caused the upset?"

"Yep. That was the sort o' thing she done all the time. But I didn't do nothin' to her bicycle if that's what you're suggestin'."

"I was suggesting nothing of the sort."

"Because some people's suggestin' it, yer see."

"Well, that's just some people. Has Inspector Mappin spoken to you yet?"

"Oh yeah, 'e's been round. With that detective fella from Sweden."

"Switzerland."

"Wherever that is. I don't want 'em comin' round here no more suggestin' I had summat to do with her bicycle."

They've been speaking to a lot of people, Farmer Glossop. Have you heard the sad news about Mrs Twig?"

"Who's that?"

"A lady in the village who was murdered this morning."

The farmer raised an eyebrow. "Another one? Strewth! World's gone barkin' mad. Talkin' o' barkin', ain't that your dog over there?" He peered over at the farmhouse.

"Yes. He's playing with your geese."

"'E'd better not kill 'em."

"He won't."

"I'll shoot 'im if 'e worries 'em."

"There's really no need. He's quite safe with geese."

"Or Magda'll get there first." He pointed in the direction of the stout lady in the canvas shirt. "She'd shoot a dog first, then ask questions of it later."

Pemberley gave Churchill a worried glance, at which point Churchill felt the need to hurry things along a little.

"Were you in the village yesterday, Farmer Glossop?" she asked.

"Yeah. I fetched some seeds off Scurridge down the allotments."

"Ah yes, the chap who had his veg eaten by Ramsay the goat. Interestingly enough, we spoke to him yesterday, too."

"Did you now? I reckon Magda's gone in ter get the shotgun." He squinted in the direction of the farmhouse again.

"No!" exclaimed Pemberley.

"She don't trust 'im. Never believes a dog owner when they says they're harmless, she don't."

Pemberley took off in Oswald's direction as fast as her legs could carry her. Farmer Glossop chuckled, which angered Churchill.

"I shall bid you a good day, Farmer Glossop."

He gave an amused nod. "You gonna run too?"

"Certainly not!"

Chapter 37

"WHAT A HORRIBLE MAN!" FUMED PEMBERLEY AS SHE marched away from the farm with Oswald safely in her arms.

Churchill felt Magda's eyes boring into their backs as they went.

"He has to be the murderer," continued Pemberley. "So cruel and heartless, and he pretended not to know who Mrs Twig was. Plus he admitted to being down at the allotments yesterday!"

"Yes, he volunteered that information quite readily," replied Churchill. "A little too readily, perhaps. And what's most interesting is that Mrs Twig appears to have told us the truth about him."

"It *has* to be him!" exclaimed Pemberley. "We must tell Inspector Mappin at once."

"He'll only make a fuss about there not being enough evidence and whatnot if we do. And so he should, as we can't be certain yet that Farmer Glossop murdered Mrs Cobnut or Mrs Twig."

"The attack on Mrs Cobnut's bicycle was part of the

tit-for-tat arrangement. Then he overheard Mrs Twig telling us about him and decided she also had to go. You saw the way he hammered at that fencepost, Mrs Churchill. Bopping someone on the head would be as easy as pie for him!"

"You're right, Pembers."

"Oh, how I hate him!"

"Calm down, Pembers. We need cool heads."

"Whatever for?"

"For cracking this case once and for all. If we're to solve it, we must remain calm and put our thinking caps on."

"There's no need. It was Farmer Glossop, I'm telling you! Inspector Mappin may not listen, but Monsieur Legrand will. Why don't we tell him?"

"If he's half as good as everyone says he is he'll have worked it all out for himself by now."

"Good. I'm looking forward to seeing handcuffs being slapped around that horrible farmer's wrists."

"Farmer Glossop may be too obvious a suspect, Pembers. Let's at least give this a little more thought before raising our suspicions. Farmer Glossop looks to be the clearest culprit, but something doesn't feel right about it."

"It feels right to me."

The crowd in Hyacinth Lane had thinned a little by the time the ladies returned to the village, but the high street was still busier than usual, with people chatting animatedly.

"Just the ladies we were looking for!" chimed a familiar voice as Churchill and Pemberley passed the tea rooms. They turned to see Inspector Mappin and Monsieur Legrand.

"Good morning, Inspector. Another busy day, eh?"

"You could say that." He readied himself with his notebook and pencil. "You were seen talking to Mrs Twig at the allotments yesterday afternoon. Can you explain yourselves?"

"Who saw us?"

"Each witness statement is confidential, Mrs Churchill. I'd like to hear your version of events in your own words."

"Well, I can only speak in my own words, can't I? What silly nonsense."

Churchill and Pemberley spent several minutes explaining their conversation with Mrs Twig to Inspector Mappin.

"And we think the murderer is Farmer Glossop," added Pemberley when they had finished.

"*You* think he is, Miss Pemberley," corrected Churchill.

"But you agree with me, don't you, Mrs Churchill?"

"I agree that he must be considered a suspect, but there are others, too. I wonder, Inspector, if you have looked into Mrs Twig's association with Mr Storks at all?"

"Storks? That good-for-nothing, low-life criminal?"

"Yes, him."

"I don't see what Mrs Twig would have had to do with him."

"I'll tell you, Inspector. We have reason to believe she was gambling on the greyhounds."

"But that's illegal!"

"You don't need to tell me that. Miss Pemberley and I observed Mr Storks visiting Mrs Twig's home on two occasions, and we believe he was collecting money for his little bookmaking operation."

"Oh, so he's doing that again, is he?" Inspector Mappin shook his head. "He's always up to something."

"Don't you have men keeping an eye on him?"

"We don't have enough men for that, Mrs Churchill. If we lived in a big town like Dorchester or Blandford Forum it would be rather easier, but times are tough in rural constabularies. I'm lucky if I can borrow a few men from Dorchester during an emergency."

"I see. Well, it appears he has his betting operation up and running again, as you suggest. Miss Pemberley and I observed him visiting various houses around the village."

"Was that on the same day you crashed into him?"

"Oh, you heard about that, did you? Yes, that was the same day."

"So you were observing him up until the point that you accidentally squashed him?"

"Yes. Thank you for the reminder, Inspector."

"You want to be more careful, Mrs Churchill."

"I realise that. I certainly have no wish to go near the man again, but I thought it might be worth informing you of his association with the unfortunate Mrs Twig."

"Thank you, Mrs Churchill. We'll look into it."

"I do hope you're not still considering myself or Miss Pemberley as suspects, just because we happened to speak to Mrs Twig yesterday afternoon."

"I'm keeping an open mind," replied the inspector, folding his notebook closed. "Isn't that right, Legrand?"

"Ah yes," responded the detective, his eyes fixed firmly on Churchill. "One very open mind."

Chapter 38

"What a sad development," said Churchill once the two ladies had returned to their office, "and quite frightening to think that people who cut bicycle brake cables and bop people on the head are still freely walking around this village. It makes one rather nervous to step outside the door!" She surveyed the incident board and sighed. "I suppose we should rearrange things on here. The murder of Mrs Twig will require some reorganisation." Churchill began to move pins, pictures and pieces of string around.

"Poor Mrs Twig," said Pemberley sadly. "She may have told a few tall tales but she wasn't a bad person."

"Not at all."

"Not like that awful Farmer Glossop!"

"Let's move his picture into a prominent position," said Churchill. "Goodness, he really does have something of a Viking warrior about him, doesn't he?" She gave a shudder. "Quite frightening, really."

Once the board had been rearranged, Churchill sat at her desk to ponder the case while Pemberley made some tea.

"There's only one slice of prune cake left," she said.

"You have it, Pembers."

"No, no, I'm saving it for you. You did so well with that enormous slice I gave you yesterday. And there was me worrying that you didn't like it!"

"I'll have it later if you don't mind. This latest murder has affected my appetite a little."

"Ah yes, I know what you mean. It's difficult to eat when someone's just been murdered."

"A great many thoughts are running through my mind." Churchill picked up Monsieur Legrand's memoir and absent-mindedly leafed through it. Then she turned to the incident board and peered at it for a while. "A great many crumbs have been scattered, Pembers, and now we must decide which are worth picking up and nibbling on."

"Are you referring to the pieces of prune cake we keep finding?"

"Something like that, but not really, no. I was speaking metaphorically."

"Oh, it's terribly confusing when people do that."

"It wasn't my intention to confuse. I just need to put my thoughts in order to ensure that I'm nibbling on the right crumbs. What do you know of theatrical agents, Pembers?"

"Nothing at all."

"I thought you'd have encountered at least one during the excursions you took with your lady of international travel."

"Sadly, no."

"That's a surprise. Did you ever stay at a hotel on Lake Garda?"

"Oh yes, I did indeed."

"Can you remember the name of it?"

"La Rocca Hotel, I think."

"I'll start with that one. I need to speak to the directory enquiries operator, so I'll have to come over and sit at your desk to use your telephone."

"Theatrical agents and Italian hotels, Mrs Churchill? What on earth is going on in your mind?"

"I'm just trying to decide which crumbs warrant a further nibble, Pembers."

Chapter 39

CHURCHILL SPENT AN INDUSTRIOUS FEW HOURS AT Pemberley's desk conducting her research. Many telephone calls were made and copious notes were scribbled down on pages of foolscap paper.

"Aren't you hungry yet, Mrs Churchill?" asked Pemberley.

"Yes, but I'm trying to ignore it." Her stomach gave a loud rumble. "I don't want to interrupt myself at any cost. Oh, darn it, Pembers. Someone's come to visit us!" She listened to the heavy footsteps on the stairs. "We should have locked the door."

"Those footsteps sound rather serious and purposeful," commented Pemberley. "They sound awfully like someone's about to have a strong word with us about something."

There were three sharp raps on the door.

"As does that purposeful knock."

"Oh dear." Churchill cleared her throat and took a deep breath. "Come in!" she said as cheerfully as possible, hoping the lightness in her voice would improve the mood of whoever was at the door, meaning business.

In strode a squat, dark-suited man wearing a trilby hat. Churchill forced a smile onto her face.

"How nice to see you again, Mr Storks! Quite recovered from our little collision, I hope?"

"Quite recovered," he snapped. He removed his trilby, smoothed down his oiled hair and scrutinised her with his dark eyes.

More footsteps followed, and into the office stepped a large man in a dark suit with a dark expression to match. His thin lips were firmly pressed together, as if he were unaccustomed to speaking a great deal. When Churchill noticed the size of his fists, she deduced that he conducted most of his communications with his hands.

Churchill fixed a carefree grin onto her face, walked over to her desk and invited the men to sit. Pemberley brought over a chair for Mr Storks's companion, giving him a nervous sidelong glance.

Mr Storks sat, but his companion remained standing in the centre of the room.

Oswald tentatively greeted them both.

"Nice dog," said Mr Storks in a rather perfunctory manner. He picked Oswald up, set him on his lap and stroked him.

"We were just about to make tea. Would you like some tea?"

"No thank you."

"What about your friend?" Churchill glanced at his impassive companion.

"He doesn't want any either."

In less intimidating circumstances Churchill might have made a quip about Mr Storks making the decision for his friend, but on this occasion she decided to get straight to the point.

"How can we help you, Mr Storks?"

"I had a visit from the police." He spoke as if this were the first time it had ever happened.

"Oh?"

"Just over an hour ago. Inspector Mappin and some foreign gentleman."

"That would have been Monsieur Legrand, I imagine."

"They asked me a series of questions about Mrs Twig."

"Oh?"

"There was a suggestion that I had been seen visiting her home."

"Was there?"

"There's no need to pretend that you know nothing about this, Mrs Churchill. I can read people like a book."

"Can you indeed?"

"I saw you and..." he turned and looked at Pemberley, "...your sidekick here... I saw the pair of you on your bicycles near Mrs Twig's house."

"You may well have done. We often bicycle that way, don't we, Miss Pemberley?"

Her assistant gave a wary nod.

"And later that same morning you flattened me."

"I don't think 'flattened' is quite the word, Mr Storks." She glanced at his companion and surmised that he would be far more capable of flattening than she was.

"I suspected it at the time, and now I feel suite sure of it." He gave Oswald an extra strong pat, which the dog seemed to enjoy. "The pair of you were following me."

"Following you? No, I don't think so. But it's only a small village, and I do remember encountering you once or twice that morning."

"I wasn't born yesterday, Mrs Churchill. I know you

were following me. And now you've gone and reported me to the police."

"Ah, now we really didn't do that."

"No? Then why did I receive a visit from Inspector Hapless then?"

"Inspector Hapless!" Churchill laughed. "Oh, that's funny!" She quickly quashed her smile when she saw that Bobby Storks wasn't smiling in return. "Oh, erm, well I suppose I may have mentioned something to Inspector Hapless about having seen you visiting Mrs Twig. But that was only because, well… there was some fairly general discussion about whom she had been seeing in the days leading up to her death. These things are very important when someone's been murdered, you see. I should add that she saw lots of people in the days leading up to her death; myself and Miss Pemberley included. I'm quite sure Inspector Mappin was merely carrying out some routine enquiries."

"And I'm quite sure that he wasn't. He specifically visited me to ask about Mrs Twig."

"I see. Well, I suppose your name was mentioned—"

"I'm not worried about Inspector Hapless," said Mr Storks. "And that bigwig Chief Inspector Llewellyn-Dalrymple over at Dorchester doesn't bother me either. In fact, we've played cards together a few times."

"Have you indeed? How lovely."

"It's that foreign detective I don't like, Mrs Churchill. I don't like the way he looks at people."

"Maybe that's just the way they look at people in Switzerland."

He shook his head. "It's not that. There's something about his unblinking stare. Have you ever noticed it?"

"I have, actually."

"He has the ability to stare into your very soul. Have you noticed that, too?"

"He certainly scrutinises people—"

"That's the perfect word. I like that. *Scrutinises.*"

"Good. Yes, he definitely scrutinises. But this business about staring into one's soul. I don't think that's possible, is it?"

"Not for most people, but he manages it somehow."

"I suppose that's why he's such a famous detective. He's got the edge on the rest of us if he can stare into people's souls."

"I don't like him at all. Do you?"

"I haven't really formed an opinion on whether I like or dislike the man. There's no doubt he has an intensity about him, which is a little disconcerting at times."

"It's unnerving."

"You think so? You don't strike me as the sort of man who would be unnerved, Mr Storks."

"I'm not very often. That's why I don't like his face."

"Is it the moustache, perhaps?"

"It's all of him."

"Well, perhaps one only needs to worry about him if one has done something one shouldn't have done."

He gave a slight nod. "Are you suggesting that's why he unnerves me, Mrs Churchill?"

"Not at all. I'm merely suggesting that if one lives by the rule book, as it were, there should be nothing for one to worry about, even if he does have a scrutinising stare."

"I rip up the rule book, Mrs Churchill."

"Do you indeed? Well, good for you, Mr Storks. Some say that rules are there to be broken."

"I don't think this is about people sticking to the rules; it's about him. He adopts that stare purely to intimidate people."

"I suppose he does, yes."

"I know a lot of people who do that, and I don't like seeing it in a man who happens to be accompanying the police. What's he doing with Hapless, anyway?"

"Inspector Hapless needs a little help, I suppose. Even more so now that he has two murders to investigate."

"Well, the sooner my name's in the clear, the better."

"I'm sure it soon will be, Mr Storks. With that expert detective about the culprit will be caught in no time and you'll have nothing to worry about."

"He can't be that wonderful a detective if the murderer has managed to get away with killing twice now."

"A fair point, Mr Storks, but this happens to be a tricky case."

He puffed out his lips and looked around the room, noticing the incident board. "You two old ladies keep yourselves busy in here, don't you?"

"This is a detective agency, Mr Storks, so we do have a few cases to be working on."

"I'm glad to see my picture isn't up on that board."

"Why would it be?"

"You tell me, Mrs Churchill."

"It would only be on the board if we suspected you were up to no good, Mr Storks."

"Ah, but I *am* up to no good. You know that."

"Yes, well… not murder, though."

"Exactly." He pointed at her and smiled. "Not murder. So it would help if people would stop mentioning my name in association with Mrs Twig."

"Yes, indeed."

"Do we understand each other, Mrs Churchill?"

"Oh, absolutely." She smiled again, but her knees were quivering under the desk.

Mr Storks decanted Oswald from his lap and got up

from his seat. "Thank you for your time, Mrs Churchill. I hope the understanding we've come to today will endure long after I've departed."

"It certainly will."

"Even if Hapless and his foreign friend ask you any further questions?"

"Absolutely."

"Good." He put on his trilby hat and left the room.

"Nice meeting you," Churchill called out after his wordless companion as he left the office.

Chapter 40

"OH, POOR OSWALD!" LAMENTED PEMBERLEY. "TO THINK that he had to be held by that horrible man!"

"I don't think he was too bothered by it," replied Churchill, observing how the little dog's tongue was lolling happily from his mouth. "He quite enjoyed his cuddles with Mr Storks, it seems. Now, I've almost finished here, and then I think I'll be ready to make an official announcement."

"Do you really think so, Mrs Churchill?"

"Yes, Pembers. All the people I've spoken to on the telephone today have been extremely helpful. All I need to do now is get my thoughts in order, and then—"

A series of excitable footsteps thundered up the stairs.

"Oh, what now?" she lamented. "Can't I ever get any work done in peace?"

The office door flung open and Mrs Thonnings almost fell into the room.

"It's the big reveal!" she said, all of a fluster. "Monsieur Legrand is calling everyone together!"

"What?" exclaimed Churchill, her mouth hanging open.

"He's solved the murders!" continued Mrs Thonnings. "He's calling everyone down to the town hall. Come along! Surely you want to hear what he has to say?"

"But how can he?"

"How can he what, Mrs Churchill?"

"How can he have it all worked out?"

"He's a detective of international renown; this is what he does. You should know that, Mrs Churchill, seeing as you've read his memoir. In fact, I see a shiny new copy lying on your desk there. You went and bought a copy!"

"I haven't read it yet, but I've been looking at the pictures."

"That's what I prefer to do with big, long books."

Churchill gathered her papers together. "Well, I suppose we'd better go and hear what he has to say for himself."

"You must be feeling rather disappointed that he's solved the murders before you, Mrs Churchill," said Mrs Thonnings.

"Disappointed? Not at all," she replied through clenched teeth. "This is what he's internationally renowned for, as you say."

"Come on, then!" enthused the haberdasher with a little clap of her hands. "'I can't wait to hear what he's come up with!"

"It'll certainly be interesting," muttered Churchill.

Chapter 41

"Do you know what I've always wondered, Pembers?" said Churchill as they followed Mrs Thonnings along the high street. "Why does a village like Compton Poppleford have a town hall? It's not even a town, it's a village."

Pemberley was carrying Oswald in her arms. "I think there were high hopes of it becoming a town once, but some bigwigs in Dorchester decided the village wasn't important enough. It dealt a terrible blow to civic pride."

"I can imagine."

As they drew closer to the attractive stone building, they saw Monsieur Legrand standing outside the portico. He politely doffed his hat to everyone who entered the building. In his hand was a length of rope and attached to the length of rope was a goat.

"I don't believe it!" hissed Churchill. "He's found Ramsay!"

The one-horned goat was lazily chewing its cud, seemingly unperturbed that it had been captured at last.

"Congratulations on apprehending Mr Pyeman's goat,

Monsieur Legrand," said Churchill. "You've clearly had a productive day."

"Thank you, Mrs Churchill." He gave her a wide smile. "And how is my favourite little dog today?" He gave Oswald a tickle under the chin. "We shall have a nice play together once my work is done this afternoon."

"Will the goat be helping you?" asked Churchill.

"Oh no, I shall tether him to a lamppost and return him to his owner once we're all finished up here. Do go inside, ladies, and I shall see you shortly."

"Smug," whispered Churchill to Pemberley as they stepped inside the town hall. "Did you see how smug he was, Pembers? Shamelessly so."

Heavy velvet curtains hung over the long windows. A variety of shields and plaques celebrating various civic achievements adorned the walls, and at the far end of the room was a small stage. Rows of chairs had been arranged in front of it, and approximately two dozen people had already taken their seats.

"Good grief!" muttered Churchill. "He really is planning to put on a performance, isn't he?"

A line of chairs had been arranged on the stage, three of which were occupied by Inspector Mappin and two police constables.

Churchill and Pemberley took their seats next to Mrs Thonnings and glanced around them.

"Good, Farmer Glossop's here," said Pemberley.

"I think everyone's here," replied Churchill. "Even poor Mr Twig."

"And Mr Cobnut," said Pemberley. "He's sitting in the row behind Mr Twig."

"Most of the Compton Poppleford Ladies' Bicycling Club members are over there," said Churchill.

"And the South Bungerly ones are over there," added Pemberley. "Including Miss Garthorn and her sister."

"Miss Plimsoll is here," said Pemberley, "but she's not sitting with Mr Cobnut. I wonder if they've had a tiff."

"And there's Mrs Higginbath over there," said Churchill. "She always turns up to these things, doesn't she? Even though she never has anything to do with them."

Brisk footsteps through the main door announced the arrival of Monsieur Legrand. He was accompanied by the mayor; a small, wizened man weighed down by the gold chain around his neck. They made their way onto the stage with news reporter Smithy Miggins and a lanky photographer following close behind.

"Quite a lot of fuss, wouldn't you say, Pembers?" whispered Churchill. "It'll be quite embarrassing if he gets it all wrong!" She gave a nervous laugh.

"It's terribly annoying that you were so close to solving it all, Mrs Churchill," said Pemberley, "and now your chance has gone."

"Perhaps I should bow to the superior detective," she acknowledged, "but let's see what he has to say for himself first."

Monsieur Legrand now stood on the stage. He took off his hat, rested it on one of the chairs and stepped forward to greet his audience. General chatter subsided into silence, and the detective gave a wide smile before clearing his throat.

"Thank you all for coming here at such short notice," he said. "I am indebted to the Mayor of Compton Poppleford for allowing us to use his town hall."

"He should have sold tickets and made a few bob," whispered Churchill to Pemberley. "They could have laid on a few refreshments, don't you think?"

"Shush, I'm trying to listen."

Monsieur Legrand walked over to the left side of the stage, fixed his eye on a distant point above everyone's heads and assumed a sombre expression. "Ten days ago," he began in a strongly accented, stentorian voice, "a much-loved lady in this village, Mrs Mildred Cobnut, climbed onto her bicycle to begin her morning ride. As you all know, she lived on the top of Grindledown Hill, and it was her custom to travel down this hill to the village every morning. However, on this fateful day she was not to make it."

He paused to allow the solemnity of his words to sink in, pacing slowly over to the other side of the stage in the meantime.

"Mrs Cobnut liked to bicycle fast downhill," he continued, "and she had to rely on her brakes to negotiate many bends in the road. As she approached the first bend on the hill she will have applied the brakes, just as she did on every other journey in that lane. But on this occasion..." He gave a snap of his fingers. "Nothing. *Rien!*"

He gave the audience an unblinking stare.

Churchill sighed. "He's enjoying this a little too much, Pembers," she whispered.

Off the detective paced again, detailing the accident in Sloping Field and how Mrs Cobnut had been found by one of Farmer Drumhead's men.

"Why did the brakes not work?" he asked the audience.

"Someone cut the cables," someone shouted out.

"With snippers," added another.

Monsieur Legrand scowled, clearly displeased by the interruption. He lifted his chin and addressed a window to his left. "We know that someone had cut the brake cables on Mrs Cobnut's bicycle the previous night. Someone carried out an act of vandalism that would have fatal consequences. This person," he raised a finger, "knew that Mrs Cobnut kept her bicycle in the shed, so, during the hours of darkness, they broke the shed window and positioned an upturned urn underneath it so they could climb in through the window and vandalise her bicycle. Did they realise the severity of their actions?"

"Yes!" someone shouted out.

"I'm quite sure they did," he continued, giving the heckler a sharp glance. "They must have known Mrs Cobnut bicycled down Grindledown Hill every morning, and they must have known that the removal of any braking mechanism would have had disastrous consequences. This person had plotted a murder!

"So who wished Mrs Cobnut harm? Our esteemed Inspector Mappin identified a number of people in Compton Poppleford who had locked swords with Mrs Cobnut over the weeks, months and even years before her death. But which one of them decided to murder her?

"My great sympathies lie with Mr Cobnut, who found himself widowed so suddenly. There has been much speculation over the nature of his relationship with the housekeeper, Miss Plimsoll, but they have both assured me there is nothing untoward about it. Miss Plimsoll was dismissed from her work for the Cobnuts only a week before Mrs Cobnut's death. Could she have cut the brake cables in revenge?"

"No!" said Miss Plimsoll, jumping to her feet. "I've had to defend myself against such accusations a good many times now, and I think it's quite clear that I never would have done such a thing!"

"Thank you, Miss Plimsoll." The detective motioned for her to sit down.

"What about Mrs Twig?" someone called out. "She was murdered too!"

"All in good time," Monsieur Legrand said reassuringly. "Now, let me move on to the most important matter."

Chapter 42

"There is a lady here," said Monsieur Legrand, wagging his finger, "who was once a good friend of Mrs Cobnut's. But she has carried out a terrible deception!"

Gasps from the audience followed this announcement, and the renowned detective hooked his thumbs into the pockets of his neat waistcoat before proceeding.

"A terrible deception indeed! Just yesterday I made a long-distance telephone call to the owner of a hotel on the shores of Lake Garda."

"Didn't you also do that, Mrs Churchill?" whispered Pemberley.

"Yes, I did. Let's hear what he has to say."

"It was a Mr Esposito!" announced Monsieur Legrand, "and this Mr Esposito confirmed to me that a lady matching Miss Garthorn's description had recently stayed with him."

A muttering began and faces turned to look at Miss Garthorn.

"That's correct," she confirmed. "I stayed in Mr Esposito's fine hotel, the Villa Cipriani, though I don't see what that has to do with anything."

"Did you telephone that one, Mrs Churchill?" whispered Pemberley again.

"Yes, I did. I got the name of it from the manager of the La Rocca Hotel."

Monsieur Legrand began to pace the stage again. "I ask you all to consider the words 'a lady matching Miss Garthorn's description'. In most cases when we hear that phrase, we can make the assumption that the description applies to one person and to one person alone. But not on this occasion!"

He spun around to face the audience and pointed a finger at Miss Garthorn.

"Non! In this instance there is not one but *two* people who match Miss Garthorn's description!"

Fervent muttering from those gathered built into a crescendo at this point.

"Quiet!" the mayor called out.

"This…" Monsieur Legrand raised an eyebrow and wagged his finger, making the most of the moment. "This can only mean… *one thing*!"

Silence fell across the room and Churchill held her breath.

"It means that it would have been perfectly easy for Miss Garthorn's sister, Mrs Heston, to pass herself off as Miss Garthorn in Italy while Miss Garthorn remained in Compton Poppleford under the pretence of being Mrs Heston!"

"And miss out on an opportunity for a lovely Italian holiday?" Miss Garthorn piped up. "I don't think so."

"Perhaps you were planning a holiday of your own later in the year, Miss Garthorn," said the detective, "to celebrate the demise of your great rival!"

"Are you saying that Miss Garthorn pretended to be her sister in order to murder Mrs Cobnut?" asked Mrs Higginbath.

"Yes!" said the detective. "Why would Mrs Heston murder Mrs Cobnut? There is no motive, simple as that. But when it came to Miss Garthorn, well, she had lots of reasons to murder Mrs Cobnut."

"Such as?" asked Miss Garthorn, visibly baffled.

"How shocking!" said Mrs Thonnings, shaking her head. "It's quite unbelievable."

"It is indeed," replied Churchill.

"While the lady we assumed to be Miss Garthorn was on the shores of Lake Garda, the lady we assumed to be Mrs Heston was here in the village waiting to carry out her despicable act of criminality," said Monsieur Legrand. "She broke into the Cobnuts' shed at night and cut the brake cables on Mrs Cobnut's bicycle!"

"How utterly deplorable!" exclaimed Mrs Harris.

Inspector Mappin got up from his seat and retrieved his handcuffs from his pocket. He squinted at the twin sisters.

"Which one am I arresting?" he asked Monsieur Legrand.

"Miss Garthorn."

"Which one is Miss Garthorn?" asked the inspector.

Mr Cobnut leapt to his feet. "Arrest both of them, Inspector! One has murdered my wife and the other has colluded with her sister to do so!"

Inspector Mappin nodded. "I see. Constable Dawkins, I need you over here."

A range of scorn-filled adjectives were shouted out by the audience, and various lively discussions ensued. Inspector Mappin and Constable Dawkins climbed off the stage as they prepared to apprehend the twin sisters.

"I've had enough of this farce, Pembers," said Churchill. 'It's exactly what I thought it would be."

"Really?"

"I've given that man enough time to speak. It's time for me to step in."

Churchill got to her feet. "Ahem!" she announced.

There was too much noise for anyone to notice her.

"I said, *ahem*!" Churchill shouted. The people sitting in front of her jumped, and the noise gradually subsided.

"Do you have something to say, Mrs Churchill?" asked the mayor.

"No, I just thought I'd stand up and clear my throat."

"Oh, I see."

"I was being sarcastic, Mr Mayor. May I speak for a moment?"

"Will it take long? I think we're almost finished here."

"I want to hear what Mrs Churchill has to say," Mrs Thonnings piped up.

"Me too!" called out Miss Garthorn, who was now handcuffed to Inspector Mappin. "This Swiss gentleman has it all wrong. My sister and I would never dream of harming Mrs Cobnut!"

"But it's Monsieur Legrand," said the mayor. "Europe's most famous detective."

"So he says," responded Churchill, "but we only have his word for it."

Chapter 43

"Is that all you wished to say, Mrs Churchill?" asked the mayor.

"No it is not! Far from it!" She squeezed her way along the row of chairs and began to make her way toward the stage.

"I don't think we have time for anything else, Mrs Churchill," said the mayor. "The culprits have been arrested and everybody's becoming rather restless."

"Will there be refreshments?" someone called out.

"I wish there were," replied Churchill, climbing the steps to the stage. "I'm rather peckish myself. I could devour a whole bag of currant buns right now. But refreshments will have to wait, I'm afraid. There's some important work to do first."

As Churchill joined Monsieur Legrand on stage, he regarded her with his arms neatly folded. The smug smile had left his face for the first time that afternoon.

"What do you mean we only have his word for it, Mrs Churchill?" called out Mrs Harris.

"I mean exactly what I say."

"I have solved the crime, Mrs Churchill," said Monsieur Legrand. "What more is there to say?"

"You haven't explained who murdered Mrs Twig."

"Those two!" He pointed at Miss Garthorn and Mrs Heston. "And they probably would have worked their way through the entire Compton Poppleford Ladies' Bicycling Club if I hadn't put a stop to it!"

Churchill attempted to dismiss the astonished gasps. "That's not true," she said. "Miss Garthorn and Mrs Heston are innocent."

"Thank you, Mrs Churchill!" Miss Garthorn called out.

"What? But Monsieur Legrand said—" a member of the audience chipped in.

"I know what he said," Churchill replied. "Now, please listen to what I have to say. I shall make this as succinct as possible. Monsieur Legrand mentioned the word 'deception' earlier. Let me tell you now that no one has carried out a greater deception than he has."

"What do you mean?" Inspector Mappin called out.

"Do please let me explain. This man standing before you is not Monsieur Legrand. He is an imposter."

"Impossible!" someone shouted.

The voices in the hall rose to a loud murmur again.

"Quiet!" shouted the mayor. "Let's hear what Mrs Churchill has to say. Are you sure what you're saying is right, Mrs Churchill? How do you know the man is an imposter?"

"My suspicions were tickled into existence by this book," she stated, pulling out her copy of Monsieur Legrand's memoir from her handbag.

"Is that the new copy you bought to replace the one you soiled?" Mrs Higginbath shouted. "If so, it belongs in the library!"

"Yes, yes. I'll be more than happy to hand it over to you as soon as I'm finished here. Anyway, this edition contains some interesting colour plates, including a playbill for a play called *The Murderer of Marseille*, alongside a photograph of the cast. Intrigued, I placed a telephone call to Monsieur Legrand's publisher, Timmins and Hurberry, and the nice lady I spoke to there was able to confirm that the renowned detective Monsieur Legrand is currently enjoying a pleasant retirement in a little village just outside Geneva. He's writing a book there, but it isn't the second volume of his memoirs. It's a book about alpine plants, which he has apparently enjoyed growing and studying in recent years."

"It can't be true!" responded Inspector Mappin.

"The lady at Timmins and Hurberry was extremely helpful," continued Churchill. "She confirmed to me that Monsieur Legrand hasn't left the sweet shores of Switzerland for some time."

"Pah! Switzerland doesn't have any shores!" scorned Farmer Glossop.

"Other than lake shores," added Mrs Harris.

"Borders," said Churchill, correcting herself. "Call it what you like. Either way, he has been confined to his home country for some time. I further investigated this by calling the post office in the village where he now lives, and the lady there confirmed it."

"Then who is *he*?" asked someone, pointing at the pretend Monsieur Legrand. The imposter had taken a step closer to the back of the stage.

"*He*," replied Churchill, "is an actor who goes by the name of Mr Tommy Malone. After making a number of telephone calls to theatrical agents, I was able to find one who could tell me a little more about him. Mr Malone has enjoyed a successful career and received a great deal of praise for his role as Doctor Dolittle at the Ambassador Theatre in Margate. Apparently, he prided himself on doing a good deal of research for the role and was well suited to it, having cultivated an excellent rapport with animals."

Churchill met Pemberley's eye, knowing her assistant would be recalling the man's surprising skill with Oswald.

"But the most notable praise for Mr Malone was bestowed for portrayal of Monsieur Legrand in *The Murderer of Marseille*," continued Churchill. "The pictures in the detective's memoir show Mr Malone receiving top billing on the playbill, and he appears in the photograph of the cast. The play did so well after it opened at the Corinthian Theatre in Liverpool that it toured the country, ending up with a run in London's West End. Critics stated that Mr Malone's performance was almost indistinguishable from the behaviour of the great detective himself."

She glanced at Mr Malone and saw that one side of his mouth was lifted in a flattered half-smile.

"There's only one way to prove all this," said Inspector Mappin, "and that is to make a long-distance telephone call to Monsieur Legrand himself."

"Please do, Inspector," said Churchill. "I have a telephone number for him here." She retrieved the slip of paper from her handbag. "Monsieur Legrand doesn't have a telephone himself, as he prefers not to be bothered too much these days. However, this is a telephone number for the lady who runs the post office, which I believe is a short walk from his home. I spoke with her this morning and her English is reasonably good. She confirmed that Monsieur Legrand will be expecting a call from you this afternoon, Inspector Mappin."

"I shall look forward to speaking to the great man himself," replied the inspector, glaring at Mr Malone.

"Why's he pretending to be the detective, then?" asked Mrs Thonnings.

"A good question," replied Churchill. "Perhaps he enjoys being seen as such a revered character. I'm sure this is the case. However, there happens to be a more sinister side to Mr Malone's character. Let me briefly discuss the other suspects in the sad saga of Mrs Cobnut's murder. Farmer Glossop was—"

"It wasn't me!" the red-whiskered farmer called out. "It was those twins!"

"Farmer Glossop was Mrs Cobnut's brother-in-law, and the two did not get along well," continued Churchill. "The trouble began when he married her sister. She never approved of the match and, in true Mrs Cobnut form, she made her feelings known."

"She was a beast!" shouted Farmer Glossop.

"It's safe to say that Farmer Glossop and Mrs Cobnut were never friends, and when Mrs Glossop moved to America the animosity intensified into a rather childish tit-for-tat situation."

"Childish?" exclaimed Farmer Glossop. "There was nothing childish about it. And anyway, she started it!"

"I shan't go into the details of orange fences and turnip-trampling sheep for now."

"But what about poor Jasper the horse?" someone called out. "She frightened him half to death!"

"Jasper was spooked," said Churchill, "there's no doubt about that. But he quickly recovered. It doesn't lessen what Mrs Cobnut did, but I think it's fair to say that they were just as bad as each other."

"As bad as each other? That's not fair!" Farmer Glossop argued.

"May I ask if you ever involved yourself in the feud

between your wife and Farmer Glossop, Mr Cobnut?" Churchill asked.

Mr Cobnut shook his head. "I stayed well away from it."

"Very wise," said Churchill. "Now, the question is, did the tit-for-tat escalate into something rather more sinister? Painting someone's fence orange in the dead of night is one thing, but is cutting the brake cables on someone's bicycle the obvious next step? Both could be dismissed as mere pranks. Perhaps the person who cut the brake cables never intended for Mrs Cobnut to lose her life. But I also like to think that if it were little more than a terrible mistake, the culprit would have confessed the misdeed to the authorities."

"I think it's the same sort of thing," said Mrs Harris. "I bet he painted her fence, then thought it would be a wheeze to cut the brake cables. He probably thought she'd just end up in a hedge with nothing more than a few cuts and bruises."

"But I didn't cut her brake cables!" protested Farmer Glossop.

"And now on to something of a more sensitive nature," said Churchill. "I have no choice but to allude to the gossip surrounding Mr Cobnut's relationship with his house-keeper, Miss Plimsoll."

"That's just idle gossip!" Inspector Mappin shouted out.

"I was also tempted to think that," replied Churchill, "until I witnessed the pair of them emerging from the overgrown path by the allotments."

"Not the overgrown path!" someone called out. "Only people having illicit affairs use the overgrown path!"

There was a general shaking of heads and tutting.

"Which is what I feared at the time," said Churchill.

"It's not true!" Miss Plimsoll called out. "You must have been mistaken, Mrs Churchill!"

"Do you think Mrs Cobnut dismissed you because of the affair, Miss Plimsoll?" asked Churchill.

"No, it was because I hadn't polished the silver properly."

"She's right," agreed Mr Cobnut. "It was all about the silver."

"Now, Mrs Twig was an interesting character," continued Churchill. "She was a member of the Compton Poppleford Ladies' Bicycling Club, and had borrowed money from its founder, Mrs Cobnut. Mrs Twig had great difficulty repaying this money, which led to some conflict between the two women. It reminds me of an old adage I've always stuck by: "Neither a lender nor a borrower be." Anyway, no one chose to issue such a warning to these two ladies, and they probably wouldn't have listened anyway. So before long, Mrs Twig was in debt to Mrs Cobnut.

"But what did Mrs Twig do with the money she had borrowed? Appearances suggested she had no need for it. She shared a nice home with her husband, who had a very important job in Dorchester, and there were no dependants to support."

"And we all know how expensive they can be," said Mrs Harris.

"Exactly. For a time, Mrs Twig invented the existence of a wayward son, whom she claimed was spending all of her money. This story was repeated to at least one other member of the Compton Poppleford Ladies' Bicycling Club, but it came as a surprise to Mr Twig, who told me they didn't have a son."

Mr Twig shook his head sadly.

"And then there was the story of her husband's drunkenness."

"What?!" exclaimed Mr Twig.

"I'm afraid your wife told Miss Pemberley and me that you had a drinking problem, which meant all your income went on alcohol. She told us she'd had to borrow money from Mrs Cobnut to get by."

"She said that about me?"

"I'm afraid so, Mr Twig. But you'll be pleased to hear that when we discussed your alleged drinking problem with someone else, that person disputed the story."

"You discussed rumours that I had a drinking problem with someone else? And I was none the wiser?"

"It was merely a line of enquiry we had to pursue. The sad truth about Mrs Twig's debts was that she was gambling her money on the greyhounds."

"Not a chance!" exclaimed Mr Twig.

Churchill felt great sympathy for the man, who had clearly endured more than enough for one day.

"I'm afraid so," she said solemnly. "Mr Storks, an illegal bookmaker, regularly called on her to take her bets. He probably deposited winnings with her, too, but as we all know, gamblers usually lose more than they win."

Mr Storks rose to his feet. "I didn't take the bets myself. I merely passed the money to a friend because Mrs Twig didn't like going down to the greyhound track. It's not a place for ladies. I'd just like to make it clear that there has been no wrongdoing on my part."

"How awful," said Mr Twig, holding his head in his hands. "My poor, dear wife! Even though she told every-body I was a drinker, I still forgive her. I had no idea she was spending all that money on the greyhounds. No idea at all! She liked greyhounds, come to think of it. She liked all dogs, in fact, but I wouldn't allow her to have one. I told her they made a mess of the house. It's the hair, you see.

All that hair they have on them. I don't like hairy animals. Oh, if only I'd let her have a dog…"

"This wasn't about owning a pet dog, Mr Twig," said Churchill. "It was an addiction to gambling."

"But how did she get into it?"

"That might have had something to do with me," said Mrs Thonnings. "I told her I'd once had a cheeky little flutter on the dogs. Only once, mind you. I'd been rather lucky and won a few bob, but I've always been sensible about such things. I know that once you've had a win you should stop right away. You should never be tempted to gamble it away again. The same is true if you've had a loss; you shouldn't gamble more in an attempt to win it back. Anyway, it's rather a sticky situation whatever you do, so it's better not to do it in the first place. I wish I'd explained all that to Mrs Twig at the time, then she might not have been tempted to try it herself. Oh, I feel so terrible about it now!"

"You weren't to know that you'd invited her into a life fuelled by addiction," said Churchill. "You can't be responsible for the behaviour of others, Mrs Thonnings. Some people are able to resist these temptations completely or to only indulge in them lightly. Others fall for them rather heavily."

"I do struggle to resist temptation at times," said Mrs Thonnings. "Terrible really, isn't it? But I had no idea this chain of events would occur, and to think that poor Mrs Twig is now dead!"

"So that's it, then?" someone asked. "Mrs Twig borrowed money from Mrs Cobnut to gamble on the greyhounds, then murdered Mrs Cobnut because she couldn't repay it?"

"It certainly gave her a motive," said Churchill. "May I

ask, Mr Cobnut, whether you continued to pursue Mrs Twig for the money she owed after your wife's death?"

"I didn't get a chance to think about it, if the truth be told. I was aware that some money had been loaned to Mrs Twig, and I probably would have followed the matter up with her when the opportunity arose. But after my wife's death... I, well, I just didn't have a chance to think about it. I had no communication with Mrs Twig at all after Mildred died. It simply wasn't a priority."

"But there's a possibility, isn't there, that you would have asked for the money to be repaid?"

"Oh yes, I would have asked for it eventually, without a doubt. She borrowed the cash from Mildred and then failed to repay it."

"So you see, everyone, this couldn't have been a reason for Mrs Twig to murder Mrs Cobnut. Getting rid of Mrs Cobnut wouldn't have removed the problem of her having to repay the debt. With Mr Cobnut alive and well there would still have been demands for payment."

"Are you saying that Mrs Twig didn't murder Mrs Cobnut?" asked Mrs Higginbath.

"Or was Mrs Twig also planning to murder Mr Cobnut?" asked Mrs Harris.

"Who murdered Mrs Twig?" asked Mrs Thonnings.

"Who murdered Mrs Cobnut?" asked Farmer Glossop.

Chapter 44

"All your questions will be answered in just a moment," said Churchill. "Now, shortly before Mrs Cobnut's death, she and her husband spent a few days holidaying in the Peak District. I made a number of telephone calls, one of which was to the manager of the Peak View Hotel. He confirmed that Mr and Mrs Cobnut had stayed there, and he was able to offer some interesting observations about their visit. One such observation was that they made friends with another couple and enjoyed walks together. He also told me that the party enjoyed a few drinks together after dinner, and that the two gentlemen regularly stayed up chatting into the night, long after their wives had gone to bed."

"And?" someone called out.

"The two gentleman, to be clear, were Mr Cobnut and Mr Malone."

"They met in the Peak District?"

"Yes."

"Where is the Peak District?"

"Look it up on a map when we've finished here. Now, I

have no idea how the two gentlemen began hatching their macabre plan; perhaps they will explain it to us in due course. But, smitten with his housekeeper, Mr Cobnut must have expressed an awful intention to be rid of his wife at some point. After this, I can only imagine that a large sum of money must have been offered to Mr Malone to visit Compton Poppleford, pose as the great detective Monsieur Legrand and influence the police investigation. After all, would a lowly village police inspector question the opinion of such a respected man?"

"Excuse me!" Inspector Mappin piped up.

"It's true," replied Mrs Thonnings. "You believed him."

"So did everyone else!" retorted Mappin.

"A large sum of money would have appealed to Mr Malone," said Churchill. "According to his agent, his acting work was beginning to dry up. Mr Malone had begun his descent into a has-been.

"So it is with sadness," she continued, "that I must state that Mr Cobnut crept into the shed where his wife's bicycle was stored and cut the brake cables. Who knows what he did with the cutters? They're probably hidden somewhere nearby."

"But someone broke into the shed!" exclaimed Miss Plimsoll, rising to her feet. "They upturned the urn and all the petunias fell out. Barny loved his petunias! And they smashed the window. Someone broke in, Mrs Churchill. Barny would never have caused such damage to his own shed!"

"I can only imagine that he caused the damage because he wanted it to appear as though someone had broken in, Miss Plimsoll," said Churchill. "And it worked, because Inspector Mappin seemed persuaded by it, especially with the pretend Monsieur Legrand at his side encouraging him to investigate elsewhere."

"And what about Mrs Twig?" someone asked. "Did Cobnut murder her, too?"

"Miss Pemberley and I last spoke to Mrs Twig near the woods next to the allotments. She was about to tell us something but we were interrupted by the snap of a twig. Someone appeared to be listening in to our conversation, and it was enough to stop Mrs Twig in her tracks."

"Twig and twig," said someone.

There was a chuckle, followed by a reprimand from someone for laughing at such a serious moment.

"Mrs Twig told us she would explain everything another time, but sadly we didn't find another opportunity to speak to her before she was so cruelly murdered. I don't know what Mrs Twig was about to tell us, but perhaps it was something that would have incriminated Mr Cobnut. I suggest that *he* was the person listening into our conversation that afternoon and it was *he* who snapped that twig underfoot. Poor Mrs Twig was murdered to buy her silence. Inspector Mappin, I suspect you'll need to do a little more investigating to establish Mr Cobnut's whereabouts this morning."

Inspector Mappin nodded.

"Or perhaps we shouldn't rule out Miss Plimsoll?" said Churchill. "Whichever of them it was, they realised Mrs Twig knew more than she had previously let on. And if she'd been about to tell all about the Cobnuts' marriage it would have been difficult for Mr Cobnut to escape scrutiny. Mr Malone's plan to convince us all that someone else was guilty would have started to look rather shaky."

"It wasn't me!" exclaimed a tearful Miss Plimsoll, rising to her feet. "I didn't hurt her. When Barny told me he would arrange the matter, I assumed he was just talking about a divorce. And after Mildred died, I believed him when he told me the culprit must have been one of the many people who hated his wife. I never thought for an instant that my dear Barny could be capable of murder. He went out this morning and when he came back, he told me he'd been to visit his solicitor. He said he was terribly worried that if anyone found out he'd been to see a solicitor they'd think he was seeking advice because he had something to hide. He asked me to say he'd been at home all morning if anyone asked. Now I understand why he asked me that. He'd killed Mrs Twig!" She burst into tears and dropped her head onto the shoulder of the lady sitting next to her.

"How interesting. Thank you, Miss Plimsoll," said Churchill. "It seems Mr Cobnut has already tried to set up an alibi for his whereabouts at the time Mrs Twig was murdered. Why are the twins still handcuffed, Inspector? Go and clap them on Mr Cobnut, please!"

"Right you are," replied the inspector, hurriedly freeing Miss Garthorn. "Dawson! Go and handcuff that dreadful actor!"

"Dreadful?" retorted Mr Malone with no trace of a Swiss accent. "If I was so dreadful, how did I convince you I was the great man himself? I convinced all of you. Haha! You were fooled, all of you!"

Churchill marched over to him. "We can finally get rid of that silly moustache!" She pulled at the end of it, but it wouldn't budge.

Mr Malone gave a huge yowl and recoiled. "It's real!" he protested. "I grew it so I could reprise my role at any given time!"

Churchill shook her head in dismay as Constable Dawkins handcuffed Mr Malone's wrists.

Meanwhile, Mr Cobnut was attempting to head through the door before he could be handcuffed himself.

"Stop him!" yelled Inspector Mappin, who was still stuck between two rows of chairs. In one swift movement, the large, red-haired Farmer Glossop leapt into action. He flung himself at Mr Cobnut's legs in a deft rugby tackle, bringing the man crashing to the ground. Then Farmer Glossop sat on him and chuckled as Mr Cobnut's legs flailed helplessly.

Chapter 45

CHURCHILL AND PEMBERLEY STEPPED OUT ONTO THE HIGH street and joined the onlookers as they watched Mr Cobnut and Monsieur Legrand being frogmarched down to the police station.

"Thank you, Mrs Churchill," said Miss Garthorn. "My sister and I were nearly done for back there. To think that we could have been wrongly arrested and even stood trial! What a dreadful pair of men they are, and what an awful scheme. Poor Mrs Cobnut suffering at the hands of that scoundrel." She dabbed at her eyes with her shirt sleeve.

"I cannot believe the lengths an out-of-work actor would go to," added Mrs Heston. "It's shocking."

"The book, please, Mrs Churchill," said Mrs Higginbath, holding out her hand.

Churchill pulled Monsieur Legrand's memoir from her handbag and handed it to the librarian. "I never did finish the thing; it was rather a dry read. The pictures were helpful, though."

"Congratulations on solving the crime, Mrs Churchill. And perhaps I even helped in some way."

"*Helped*, Mrs Higginbath? How so?"

"I told you these expert detectives aren't always what they're cracked up to be. Perhaps I helped you see through him."

"I'll decide whether you were any help or not when I'm permitted a reading ticket for the library."

Mrs Higginbath strode off with her nose in the air.

Churchill felt a nudge at her side.

"Here," whispered Mrs Thonnings as she pulled a worn paperback from her handbag. "*Clandestine Encounter.*"

Churchill held her own handbag open so Mrs Thonnings could swiftly deposit it inside.

"You'll finally get to finish it now."

Churchill snapped her handbag shut. "Thank you! I didn't think you'd be allowed to borrow any more books after the ticking-off you received."

"I'm not. I received a three-month ban, but Mrs Harris has been borrowing books on my behalf." Mrs Thonnings tapped the side of her nose and gave a wink. "Not a word."

"Absolutely not."

"Well done, Mrs Churchill!" said Mr Pyeman. "You got him!"

"It wasn't me, it was Monsieur Legrand. Or rather, that actor chap, Malone."

"I weren't talking about the goat. I meant the murderer!"

"Ah yes, him. Nasty man. Now then, Ramsay's just over here, Mr Pyeman." Churchill turned toward a nearby lamppost with a length of rope looped around it. "At least, he *was* here. Mr Malone said he'd tether him to a lamppost, but…"

"The scallywag's gone an' chewed righ' through it!"

exclaimed Mr Pyeman, scratching his forehead. "Where's he got to now?"

They glanced up and down the high street.

"There!" said Pemberley. "He's just outside the hair-dresser's!"

"Right!" replied Churchill. She was just about to take off after the goat when Mr Pyeman grabbed her arm. "He'll run, Mrs Churchill, then you won't never catch up with him. What you need's a bitta food. You got anythin' on you?"

"No, nothing." Churchill's stomach gave a rumble and she was suddenly reminded that she hadn't eaten a crumb since elevenses. "But I have an idea!"

Churchill dashed off in the opposite direction toward her office. She returned a few minutes later, red-faced and puffed out, with a cake tin in her hands.

"Really, Mrs Churchill?" asked Pemberley. "Even Oswald won't eat it."

"It's worth a try. Now, where's that blasted goat?"

"He's moved up toward the bank."

"Here you are, Mr Pyeman," said Churchill, handing him the cake tin. "He knows you, so I'd say you have a better chance of catching him than I do."

"What's in here, then?" he asked.

"Prune cake."

"Prunes?"

"Just go, Mr Pyeman, before he takes off again."

Churchill, Pemberley and Mrs Thonnings watched as Mr Pyeman, accompanied by Oswald, walked toward Ramsay, stopping about ten yards short of him. He placed the tin on the cobbled ground and removed the lid. Then he gave a low whistle and stepped back a few paces.

Ramsay watched him, then cautiously began walking toward the tin. Oswald ran back to Pemberley, and the street fell silent as the goat approached the tin, sniffed it and swiftly began to devour its contents.

"He likes it!" exclaimed Pemberley triumphantly. "He likes my prune cake!" She picked Oswald up and gave him a hug.

"Well done, Pembers," said Churchill.

So distracted was the goat by the cake that Mr Pyeman was able to step forward and grab him by the horn. Churchill stepped over to the lamppost, untethered the rope and took it over to where Mr Pyeman was standing. The goat didn't even flinch as the rope was tied around his neck.

Churchill glanced down at the cake tin and saw that Ramsay had licked it clean of every crumb.

"Thank you, Mrs Churchill," said Mr Pyeman.

"I didn't really do anything."

"You fetched this here cake."

"Which my trusty assistant, Miss Pemberley, kindly made. She's the one who deserves your thanks."

Pemberley beamed. "The cake has been quite a success after all, hasn't it? I still have several tins of prunes in the cupboard. I could bake another one this evening."

"So soon?" asked Churchill.

"Yes, why not?"

"I was thinking that it might be nice to vary things a little. A different flavour, maybe… How about a bit of walnut cake instead?"

"I suppose I could try a walnut cake."

"Lovely."

"But I can't promise it'll be as good as the prune cake."

"I'm perfectly willing to give it a try."

The End

Doris Pemberley's Recipe for Prune Cake

There have been a number of requests for this recipe ever since my prune cake successfully captured Ramsay the goat. It's my pleasure to share it here.

Miss D Pemberley

- 8oz flour
- 4 eggs (preferably from Farmer Jagford's hens)
- 1 tin of dark treacle
- 8oz butter
- 2 tins of prunes, mashed
- Chestnut puree (made from 1lb of chestnuts)
- 3 spoonfuls of Special Spice (I bought mine in India fifteen years ago, but you can make your own)
- Salt and pepper to taste

Mix everything together in a bowl then spoon the mixture into a baking tin. I bake it on Gas Mark 3 for two-and-a-half hours because my oven only does Gas Mark 3. You may need to adjust your oven accordingly.

Leave to cool in tin (out of the reach of dogs).

Thank you

~

Thank you for reading *Wheels of Peril*, I really hope you enjoyed it!

Would you like to know when I release new books? Here are some ways to stay updated:

- Join my mailing list and receive the short story *A Troublesome Case*: emilyorgan.com/a-troublesome-case
- Like my Facebook page: facebook.com/emilyorganwriter
- Follow me on Goodreads: goodreads.com/emily_organ
- Follow me on BookBub: bookbub.com/authors/emily-organ
- View my other books here: emilyorgan.com

Thank you

And if you have a moment, I would be very grateful if you would leave a quick review of *Wheels of Peril* online. Honest reviews of my books help other readers discover them too!

Get a free short mystery

～

Want more of Churchill & Pemberley? Get a copy of my free short mystery *A Troublesome Case* and sit down to enjoy a thirty minute read.

Churchill and Pemberley are on the train home from a shopping trip when they're caught up with a theft from a suitcase. Inspector Mappin accuses them of stealing the valuables, but in an unusual twist of fate the elderly sleuths are forced to come to his aid!

Visit my website to claim your FREE copy:
  emilyorgan.com/a-troublesome-case
  Or scan this code:

Get a free short mystery

The Poisoned Peer

A Churchill & Pemberley Mystery Book 6

The 99-year-old Earl of Middlemop has had his future cruelly snatched away from him. Who could have poisoned the richest man in Wessex? The answer lies within the walls of Gripedown Hall where family secrets and bitter rivalries prevail.

Senior sleuths Churchill and Pemberley investigate on the behest of their friend Tryphena Ridley-Balls. However, another friend needs their help too. Mrs Thonnings's haberdashery shop is the target of a poison pen letter campaign. Her weak elastic has caused a stretch of sartorial mishaps, but are the claims true?

Just as they're close to the answers, an embarrassing slip-up results in Churchill and Pemberley's dismissal. With their reputations sagging, can the two old ladies snap into action and bounce back?

Find out more at: emilyorgan.com/poisoned-peer

The Augusta Peel Series

Meet Augusta Peel, an amateur sleuth with a mysterious past.

She's a middle-aged book repairer who chaperones young ladies and minds other people's pets in her spare time. But there's more to Augusta than meets the eye.

Detective Inspector Fisher of Scotland Yard was well acquainted with Augusta during the war. In 1920s London, no one wishes to discuss those times but he decides Augusta can be relied upon when a tricky murder case comes his way.

Death in Soho is a 1920s cozy mystery set in London in 1921. Featuring actual and fictional locations, the story takes place in colourful Soho and bookish Bloomsbury. A read for fans of page-turning, light mysteries with historical detail!

Find out more here: emilyorgan.com/augusta-peel

The Penny Green Series

Also by Emily Organ. Escape to 1880s London! A page-turning historical mystery series.

As one of the first female reporters on 1880s Fleet Street, plucky Penny Green has her work cut out. Whether it's investigating the mysterious death of a friend or reporting on a serial killer in the slums, Penny must rely on her wits and determination to discover the truth.

Fortunately she can rely on the help of Inspector James Blakely of Scotland Yard, but will their relationship remain professional?

Find out more here: emilyorgan.com/penny-green-victorian-mystery-series

Made in the USA
Las Vegas, NV
16 August 2022

53391508R00177